the Survivors

S the Survivors

ALEXANDER DAVIDSON

SCOPE BOOKS

First published in Great Britain in 1990 by:
Scope Books Ltd
62 Murray Road
Horndean
Waterlooville
Hants PO8 9JL

Phototypeset by Barbara James, Rowlands Castle, Hants
Printed in England by Clays Ltd., St. Ives plc

Jacket illustration by Val Biro

British Library Cataloguing in Publication Data

Davidson, Alexander, 1959 -
  The survivors.
  I. Title
  823'.914 [F]

  ISBN 0-906619-26-2

For my friend

When the poor have cried, Caesar hath wept:
Ambition should be made of sterner stuff.

[Shakespeare: *Julius Caesar III.ii.*]

Chapter 1

It was twilight now in Rome, and Maria turned thankfully from the dusty streets that were already appearing to blur before her jaded eyes. She touched her shoulder-length blonde hair, relieved to find it untangled. Fingering the handle of her parents' back door, she turned the key in the lock, took a deep breath, and tiptoed inside. She was dressed childishly in blue jeans and a white cheesecloth top. With her small sharp face and lithe compact body, she was like a little monkey.

Suddenly a child again, she no longer felt like the hardened pickpocket and street thief she was. Nonetheless, the white carrier bag she clutched which contained a wealth of wallets and purses told its own tale. Tourists were her prime target, and she fleeced them as only a streetwise Italian could.

Maria was merely eighteen years old, yet she felt as withered and raddled as the middle-aged painted whores she encountered on the streets. For as long as she had remembered her life had been void of luxury, geared only towards survival. And yet, like others of her kind, she envied the easy life that was lived by most victims of her crime.

As her thoughts wandered, she forgot to tread silently. There was a scuffling on the stairs and her mother appeared, slightly breathless, in the hall. Anne Soccolini was in her thirties, and wrinkles lined her angular features. Wisps of blonde hair peeped from under her scarlet headscarf. 'Veni, veni.' She beckoned the girl into the enormous kitchen. The atmosphere inside was warm and comfortable. The walls were panelled in dark wood and the decor was spotless. Anne did her housework conscientiously, with a little extra help from Maria in the evenings. The delicious aroma of pizza baking in the oven wafted through the room, making Maria's mouth water. Pizza was sold on the streets all day, but it couldn't compare to Mama's home cooking. She handed over her carrier bag.

Anne smiled. Money had that effect on her. With a practised alacrity, she upturned the carrier bag on the table. Wallets and purses, variously sized, spilled on the table, a confetti of leather with its delicious animal aroma. Anne sighed happily. She deftly unzipped and unclipped, removing the banknotes nonchalantly, then stacking them in a neat precious pile under her small bosom. She reminded Maria of a bitch panting over pups, and it annoyed her. Who was it, after all, who had risked life and limb to steal it all?

'How much is here?' said Anne curtly.

Maria shrugged. 'Why don't you count it? I've not had time to.'

Anne narrowed her eyes. 'You are slipping Maria. I can see for myself you have virtually nothing here. Your Papa won't be going on his usual binge tonight I see.'

Maria screwed up her face. 'What a waster he is. Earning not a quarter of what I do, and spending it all on booze.'

Anne flushed. 'He's going through a bad phase.'

The front door banged. The two women glanced stealthily at each other, jolted into conspiracy by the familiar signal.

'Time for the family get-together,' said Maria sarcastically.

'That's enough, young lady,' snapped her mother. 'I may have married a devil, but I need not have spawned a witch.'

Maria grinned. She gathered the wallets and purses in her arms, thrusting them back into the carrier bag and shoving it under the table.

With the banknotes, she took craftier measures, flipping up her skirt and stuffing them unceremoniously down her knickers. She dropped back her skirt, complacent in the knowledge that nothing showed. Nor did a vestige of guilt appear on her face. Of course, Papa would still be suspicious, not surprisingly in view of the fact that his daughter had inherited her sly traits from him.

Striding into the room, Paulo Soccolini glared at the two women. His handsome red features quivered. A chunky man he was, shorter than both the women. Although his grey flannel trousers, grey jacket, blue shirt open at the collar and red handkerchief in breast pocket were smart, there was a stiffness in his gait and a blaze in his chestnut eyes that made him appear superhuman in strength and power.

He sniffed. 'Get the pizza out of the oven,' he snapped. 'I could eat a stallion.'

'Wait a few moments, unless you want it underdone,' said Anne shortly. 'Why don't you relax with the newspaper while Maria and I lay the table?'

Paulo grinned and shook his head. He was a snarling hunter who had found its prey, and who wouldn't let it go. He fixed his eyes suddenly on Maria's, and they blazed with contempt, enhanced by her refusal to flinch.

'What's my little jewel brought home?' he sneered.

Maria lowered her eyes. 'It's been a rough day, Papa.'

Paulo stretched out a hand. 'If you hold anything back, I will beat you to a pulp.'

Maria shrugged. She was as calm as the peasant women at their market stalls in the early morning. 'I have given my takings to Mama,' she lied.

'Leave off, Paulo,'' said Anne. She tried to sound contemptuous but there was a tremor in her voice. 'How am I to feed you, to pay the rent, and all the bills, without any money? When is it you last gave me a sou?'

Paulo spat in her face. Unflinching, she wiped the gob from her cheek with a handkerchief.

'I've told you what it's like in stockbroking,' he said. 'There's zilch yet, but big money's on the horizon. Until then, the bills will just have to wait. And I'm taking a hefty whack of any money that comes into this house. Got it!'

Anne quivered. 'You're a drunken violent fool, Paulo! You don't deserve a family. I'm keeping any money I've got.'

Paulo smiled quite genially. 'Surprise, surprise, I will have to beat it out of you. I'm beginning to think you're always wanting that!' His roving eyes fixed on the splintered wooden broom under the sink. He had used it many times before on her. She only had to set eyes on it to tremble like a prisoner facing the death sentence.

'No!' gasped Anne. 'You'll injure me bad. If you can't restrain yourself, hit me with your hand.'

Paulo shook his head as he strode over and picked up the broom. 'I might hurt myself,' he said. 'And it wouldn't be hard enough on you. I'd like to kill you.' She screamed, as with the broom under his arm, he gripped her shoulders until they felt on the verge of cracking. He forced her onto the table where she struggled briefly, her legs flailing crazily as she screamed, but then he smacked her mouth, and she lay limp and silent.

Paulo paused, momentarily releasing her. Anne closed her eyes tightly, cringing from the expected blow. Her husband chortled. He had the impudent bitch where she was most useful, which was on her back! He raised the broom and paused, aiming to hit her where it would hurt yet not show. He knew that she would be too ashamed to talk afterwards although he had his doubts about Maria in this respect. The girl was getting too brazen by half, and he'd be dealing with her shortly.

At this moment he was working on her mother. He beat Anne's thighs, then her stomach, while she screamed in agony, tearing her hair and banging the back of her head hard on the table as if desperate to crack her own skull. Maria averted her eyes, sick at the sight. She had come to an arrangement with her mother that monies would be kept from Paulo wherever possible, even if it meant beatings for both of them. Each of the two women was independently saving cash, so one day they could together escape from the clutches of this lunatic, maybe even out of the country.

Paulo suddenly turned. A sixth sense had alerted him of an escape attempt on his daughter's part. As she started to run, he sprang like a panther. He landed on Maria's back and brought her crashing down onto the floor, 'You sneaky little cow,' he said gleefully as he sat astride her.

Maria suppressed a sob. 'What do you want of me, Dad? Not getting enough of it?'

He slapped her cheeks six times until they blazed. 'I don't lower myself to your level, you street whore,' he said. 'Now get up.' He stood up himself, but she lay immobile, her breath coming in pants. He leaned down and shook her shoulders. Reluctantly and painfully, Maria rose to her feet.

'Now stand still.' He slavered as he unbuttoned her cheesecloth top and removed it. She shuddered but didn't dare to resist as his chilly fingers slipped inside her taut white bra, probing, she knew, for hidden money. He was a canny bastard. There was no deceiving him, or receiving fair play from him either!

As he unbuttoned her jeans, she wriggled and he smacked her bottom. 'OK, I'll give you the money Dad,' she cried out.

'Sshh,' he hissed as ferociously as an alley cat confronting a rival. She shuddered visibly and long as he slipped his hands down her jeans, feeling longer and harder than he needed to for naturally his fingers had closed on the bank notes almost immediately.

Almost gurgling with pleasure, he pulled her jeans and knickers right down and the banknotes spilled out in an avalanche. He gathered them up and stood flicking through them, counting, like a child with an abacus. He then pocketed the crisp notes.

Maria meanwhile hastily dressed, and took a seat at the table, pulling out another chair for her mother and helping the shaken woman on to it.

Paulo leered at them both. 'You two couldn't pull the wool over the eyes of an idiot. Don't try it on with me again, or I won't be so lenient.'

He turned away, and was gone almost as he spoke. He slammed the front door so hard that the flat shook as if from an earthquake. The two women looked at each other, and smiled wryly. The tears in their eyes derived out of an intense sympathy with each other. This confrontation with Paulo had been simply the latest of many.

'One night I'm going to get him,' said Anne.

'What? Stab him in his sleep?' asked Maria.

'Worse than that!' grinned Anne. 'I'll take a pair of scissors and cut off his wedding tackle.'

Maria grinned with delight at the thought. Was not revenge sweet? 'You'll need to tie him up first,' she remarked. 'I'll help you there. But right now let me check your body. If he's broken any bones, I'll kill him.'

Anne stood up, cringing at the pain. Maria unzipped her cream blouse from behind, jerking it up over her head.

Her mother's walnut brown skin was blotched with swelling bruises. Maria ran her fingers over ribs and her small firm breasts as deftly and lightly as a champion pianist playing a quick dance theme. 'You'll live, Mama,' she declared.

10

'Let's hope he doesn't,' grumbled Anne, lowering her brown skirt and stockings while Maria knelt to inspect her thighs. She tut-tutted at the bruising but again pronounced her mother uninjured in any serious sense.

Anne laughed. 'You know my body better than a daughter should.'

'This is no time to get embarrassed, Mama,' said Maria sharply. She turned away, leaving her mother to get dressed again. She took from the cupboard a sketchpad and charcoal. Sketching was her favourite relaxation. She would have loved to become an artist and to paint the thieves, whores and hustlers, the sordid street life she knew so well, rather than continue to experience it at first hand.

She sat at the end of the kitchen table, head bent over her pad, sketching away, lost in her own world. Anne was excluded and cheerfully accepting this, set about preparing the meal. The pizzas were a little overdone, but hot, crisp and appetising for the pair of them. Maria who had in the past eaten scraps out of dustbins rather than starve now took the view that any home cooked meal was marvellous and didn't complain.

The two women guzzled their food like dogs with bones, washing it all down with rough Chianti that seared Maria's throat. Oh, how Maria loved it. What she craved most all the time was sweet alcoholic oblivion followed by a stupefied sleep. Anne, who cared little for drink herself, was quite happy with this, knowing that drunkenness did not turn her daughter violent. It was only in Paulo that she dreaded it. How he had deteriorated from the handsome and charming brute she had married!

Anne's troubles had started in childhood. She had been brought up in England. Unfortunately, her parents had died while she was in her infancy, and so she had been packed off to a convent boarding school by a strict uncle and aunt who had begrudgingly assumed responsibility for her upbringing.

Paulo Soccolini had captivated the teenage Anne, offering romance and excitement to a girl who had known only loneliness and routine. While in London 'on business' as he'd put it, he had picked her up at a party. She had almost instantly desired his stalwart, hirsute body. She had been charmed by his fruity Italian accent, his energy, and above all, his recklessness. He had pressed her to marry him when she was only eighteen and in the bloom of youth, just out of school.

Anne had assented immediately. Her uncle and aunt had been holidaying in India at the time. He had insisted they were wedded in Sicily, where he had been brought up.

Anne, falling as much in love with the beautiful and backward south of Italy as she already had with Paulo, was not to return to England. There was nothing for her there.

It was only at this point that Paulo had told her the true nature of his business. Narcotics. Contraband. Car-stealing. Mugging. Petty crime. He had been in the habit of operating for paymasters whose terms he would not specify, but of whom he spoke in awe.

Anne found herself sinking into an alien and backward culture. The glamour of her Sicilian husband evaporated as he showed himself in his true colours, a lazy, temperamental crook.

Just as she was thinking of abandoning him and returning to sweet England, she found she was pregnant. When Maria was born Paulo, disgusted that the baby had not turned out to be a boy, turned his back on his home and took to the bottle.

Anne, working all day keeping house and selling leather goods to tourists, while her husband was out idling and spending their money, would always find time to instruct Maria as she grew up.

Despairing of the local school, Anne passed on to the child all she knew about literature, mathematics and science. Maria grew up virtually bilingual, speaking English to her mother, as well as often to her mother's friends, and tourists, but Italian to her father and at school. She became versed in Keats and Shakespeare, Anne's favourite poets. Most importantly for her, she developed a talent for sketching and painting which was also encouraged at school.

One day, Anne dreamed that the girl would marry an English gentleman and have a decent cultured life, such as she felt had been denied her. Maria had grown up with her father's stubborn aggressiveness, but with her mother's romanticism. In Anne's opinion, greatness lay ahead of her. Maria would inherit the earth, and all that it had to offer.

As soon as Maria had finished eating, Anne put Paulo's uneaten pizza on her plate. Maria finished it in almost no time, then turned back to her sketchpad.

Anne peered over her. 'Where you get your energy from, I'll never know. What are you drawing?'

Maria giggled. 'You're gonna love it, Mama, but hold off for the moment and as soon as I have finished, I'll reveal all.'

Twilight had turned to darkness and the kitchen had become a harbinger of shadows and unfathomable corners, which didn't bother Maria who was by circumstances a creature of the night. Anne, however, switched on the electric light before she cleared the dishes off the table. As she washed them up in the sink, Maria sketched frantically, like a woman composing a masterpiece at death's door.

She didn't notice her mother creeping over. Anne was a stealthy mover when she wanted to be, if she was not quite so streetwise as her daughter. She leaned over Maria's shoulder, frowning at the sketch. Suddenly a grin cracked her careworn features.

She was blocking the light like an enormous bird, when Maria glanced up. 'Like it?'

Anne flushed. 'It's your Papa. And so lifelike, I can't believe it. But aren't you wicked to poke fun at him like that.'

Maria pouted. 'It's all right for you to criticise him, even to tear him to pieces. But if I as much as say a word, you snap at me. Well he stripped me like a prison officer tonight and I'm getting my own back.'

She stabbed the sketch with her forefinger. 'Recognise his cow's eyes? See here his cauliflower ears? The snout he calls a mouth? Well I'll show you what I think of that ugly mug.' She started to her feet and tugged her mother's sleeve. 'Come with me, don't be frightened.'

Holding the drawing by its corners, Maria led Anne from the kitchen upstairs to the spare bedroom, which Paulo was currently in the process of converting into a sort of recreation room. She turned to a worse-for-wear darts board hanging on the wall and pinned her drawing on it. Standing back, she surveyed the result with a smug satisfaction. Paulo seemed to leer down at them in a diabolical caricature. His fleshy face was puckered, his lips swollen, his nose wrinkled and his eyes contemptuous. Maria heard Anne gasping behind her and swivelled to catch her eyes. Her mother opened her mouth and shut it again like a goldfish. Maria turned her back to her again and grinned faintly. She was going to enjoy this, even if Anne wasn't. Her manoeuvres didn't mean she didn't love her father deep down, but rather vindicated her disgust with the way he man-handled them both, the lack of time he spent with them, his drinking away all his money, and much of hers to boot.

'This is fantasy, Mama,' she said as she picked up the darts. 'If we did this for real we'd land ourselves in the shit.' She threw a first dart at the nose and it hit the target with a satisfying thud. Maria chuckled. 'Imagine it's him, Mama,' she said. 'Watch me again.' This time her darts hit each eye in turn. She turned to Anne. 'Your turn if you like.'

Anne reddened, but her hand closed on the darts her daughter proffered her in a grip of iron. She took a deep breath then threw a dart with all the vigour she could muster at the mouth. It was bang on target, lodging in one of the oversized teeth that Maria had penned to represent in unison a crazed smile.

'Good shot, Mama. Again!' exhorted Maria. Inspired, Anne aimed for his cheeks. The shot proved as deadly accurate as her last.

'At the rate we're going, there won't be much of his face left,' laughed Maria.

Again and again they threw darts. His faced seemed to fade beneath the damage they were inflicting, as flesh rots on a corpse.

Maria darted out to the kitchen. She returned with a bottle of tomato ketchup. Dipping her finger in it and scraping it around she removed a dollop of sticky red which she daubed round the nostrils and mouth. It looked exactly like blood.

Anne giggled. 'We've made mincemeat of him. Poor dead Paulo!'

'You can go back to loving him now if you like,' said Maria.

'Don't you believe it,' said Anne. Sweat pricked her brow, a reminder to Maria how warm it was in this tiny room. 'We have willed him harm and real harm will surely befall him as a result of it.'

Maria shrugged. 'Stockbroking in Rome has corrupted him. Papa's easily influenced by criminal elements, so you're always telling me.'

'I know,' sighed Anne. 'I should never have allowed him to drag us out here to Rome. But what work was there for him in the depressed south of Italy? Not that we're not considerably worse off here. Especially you my darling. We've been living off your earnings for the last six months. Without you, we wouldn't survive . . . '

Maria nodded. 'Speaking of which, I'm working tonight.'

Anne hung her head, and Maria felt contempt for her. If Anne had been able to handle her husband more firmly, the daughter's financial contribution mightn't have been so necessary.

Maria ran upstairs. In her bedroom, she relaxed. She thought of this place as her stage dressing room. Scattered around were clothes and make-up. She slipped on her frilly blouse, climbed into a black leather skirt, and selected a comfortable but stylish pair of black boots.

Sitting at her dressing table, she applied rouge and eyeshadow. Her features were transformed, the last traces of youthful innocence being painted out. She now looked hard and coquettish, no longer the innocent virgin. She smiled as if the transformation was likewise within her personality, but to her true self this adopted persona was as false as Judas. Despite her talent for playacting and her streetwise business acumen, inside her she nurtured an aching heart.

As she left the room, she glanced at an oval framed portrait of her father on the chest of drawers. A wish to smash it suddenly pounded through her head, then evaporated. She'd had her symbolic revenge. Her father was her flesh and blood. She owed him some allegiance even now.

Any sentimental thoughts that she might have allowed to intrude in her consciousness at home rapidly passed as the cold wind hit her and she was surrounded by the blackness of the night tempered by the lights of the city glittering like fiery sapphires.

She had trained herself to seek out prey. She was a shark who could smell her victims a mile off. They were usually wealthy foreigners who couldn't see further than the ends of their pricks. Every night she dressed a little differently, to reduce the risk of being recognised by one of her previous dupes.

She recognised her first punter that evening, as soon as she had spotted the businessman in a grey Savile Row suit who was hovering on the curb, his eye out for a pick-up. He looked as if he had a greedy unsuspicious temperament, and what was most important, money to burn. His eyes glimmered behind gold-rimmed spectacles to meet her cool gaze.

She sauntered towards him, conveying interest and disdain together. She knew she turned men on all the more for refusing to flaunt herself. She thus reminded them of their daughters, a neat trick in her line of business that rarely failed to pull them.

He grinned once she was within speaking distance. 'Fancy a good time tonight?' he said in a casual New York accent.

She shrugged. 'I'm choosy. And I don't come cheap.'

The man came closer, and she deliberately brushed against him. He was quite plump and randy, breathing hard. He rummaged for his wallet. 'My hotel's only a few minutes away . . . '

About to reply, Maria spotted a silent onlooker. She avoided looking at him directly. A suave slim gentleman in a dark suit, he was lounging at an outside table of a café, eyeing her over the top of his *International Herald Tribune*. She felt uncomfortable. Her sixth sense warned her away from him, away from this area tonight. She jerked her head at the onlooker, and her pick-up glanced back too.

'You see that fucker,' she said. 'Who is he?'

The man had averted his eyes now, and was holding his newspaper higher. 'How should I know?' said the pick-up.

She shrugged. 'He was watching us and I don't like it. However never mind about that. To business. My charge is 400 dollars.' She paused, watching his reaction. His face, however, remained bland. 'For that I'll stay an hour or I'll stay the night. It's up to you. I'll take a deposit now, and we'll go to your hotel. If you are like most of my clients you will want to go first and I'll follow, arriving a few minutes later.'

He nodded. 'I'll give you 100 dollars now. The rest in the hotel.'

'200 dollars,' insisted Maria. He acquiesced, counting out bills which Maria made a great show of checking before she thrust them into her handbag.

'I'm at the Excelsior on the Via Veneto,' he said.

She nodded. 'No need to give me your name. I'll be in the foyer five minutes after you get there, so have the other 200 dollars ready for me. Call me Princess.'

He winked. 'If you're good to me, you'll have another 400 dollars the morning after, Princess.'

She smiled. 'You can take that as a certainty.'

She watched him walk away into the darkness. She then turned and walked smartly in the opposite direction. Although she'd worked this confidence trick many times, she could not resist chuckling. There was one born every minute. She would put a little more distance between herself and the Via Veneto before she found the next mug.

When she heard running footsteps, she stopped dead. Her heart was pumping like a piston. Who was this? Not her latest dupe, surely? For a wild moment she contemplated making a run for it, then decided not to. Her pursuer might then give chase. It was safer to confront him. She turned, and the man who'd been sitting over a newspaper in the café came puffing up beside her. She started, but was more dismayed than surprised. He was alluring enough, being tall and handsome. Hardly the type who needed a whore!

She raised her eyebrows. 'Che c'è?'

'My apologies for startling you,' he said. What a smoothie he was with his beautiful Roman accent. 'May I request the pleasure of your company tonight?'

Maria scrutinised him. There was a hard streak in his eyes that scared the shit out of her. She'd give him the brush-off, she decided. 'What do you think I am?' she said. 'Buona Sera, Signor.'

'Un attimo.' He lunged into his pocket, removing a wad of notes which he thrust into her hand. She glanced down at the sum offered. It significantly surpassed any fee she would have quoted him. Fools and their money are soon parted, she told herself cheerfully, and thrust aside her doubts. 'All right,' she said. 'Mind you, only for an hour.'

'That is all I want.' He linked his arm in hers. 'Let's beat it to my hotel, eh?'

Maria frowned. 'Isn't it better I follow you?'

He laughed. 'I don't think so. I wouldn't want you to get lost. Besides I'm not scared of being seen with you. Who would know you were a whore?'

The hotel was seedier than she expected, a very basic boarding house near the Stazione Termine, full of students and backpackers. It was just the sort of place where you would find bugs in the bed and Maria recoiled from it.

He smiled, as if reading her thoughts. 'It's not as bad as it looks,' he said. 'And I have a lovely room.'

Maria suppressed a shudder as she accompanied him. Usually she could take the punter's money and run, without having to go through the rigmarole of having sex. But on the rare occasions she had to actually go through with it, she preferred to perform in the luxury of a five star hotel where there were plenty of staff about. Plenty of telephones. In this hovel she would have to keep her wits about her. She wouldn't be so safe.

His room was dingy, cramped and airless. A large old fashioned double bed occupied most of the available space. Maria coughed. 'Open a window, please,' she said.

'Sorry my love,' he said. 'We wouldn't be private.'

Maria lay on the bed as he rummaged beneath it. She grimaced as he handed her handcuffs, whipcord, a black mask, a gag and a riding crop. So he was one of those!

'For your use. But gently, please,' he explained with a gallant smile as he deftly removed his clothes.

She knew how to handle him, and actually preferred domination to straight sex. It was cleaner, and less energetic. This fucker wouldn't be able to make it with a woman if he tried, she told herself, snapping the steel handcuffs conclusively on his wrists, which made him shiver with delight. Tying his ankles firmly to the bed posts, she gagged him so firmly that he gurgled.

She put on the slit-eyed mask, then taunted his flesh with the riding crop. He shuddered and groaned. Impatient to hurry proceedings, she masturbated him hard. It was all over quickly, a messy, sordid little business in her opinion. He smiled in apparent ecstasy.

For a wild moment she thought of robbing him, leaving him trussed up like a chicken, but there was a look in his eyes that warned her off. If she left the hotel alone, maybe she'd be stopped.

She uncuffed him. And now, perhaps she could go? But no! He smiled disarmingly. 'Your turn.'

She giggled. 'You must be fucking joking.'

'You shut up and do what I tell you if you want to keep your money,' he snapped. Maria lowered her eyes. She felt the blood rushing to her head. She smelled danger. The door was nearby. All she had to do was run for it. But he was dipping again into his pocket, producing more notes. 'I'll be gentle, and quick,' he said.

She took the money and laughed. He was almost pleading. How stupid she was to feel frightened of him! 'You'd fucking better stick to that,' she said as she undressed.

She allowed him to handcuff her and tie her ankles to his bed. He left the gag off and poked her in the ribs with the riding crop. She had a sudden sick feeling of fear. This time, had it come too late?

He laughed as if reading her thoughts. 'Isn't being a thief enough, without being a whore too? Are you not ashamed of yourself, Maria Soccolini?'

She started.

'You see I know your name,' he continued. 'I know all about you. I know all about your family. Perhaps I know the most about your father, far more I would imagine than you do. He's betrayed his friends and now he is paying the price.'

He untied her ankles and removed her handcuffs, helping her off the bed. He left her to dress quickly. 'Don't even think of running away,' he said, opening his jacket briefly and showing her the automatic inside.

He led her out firmly, as he had brought her in. A red Alfa Romeo with driver was waiting for them. Maria was ushered into the back seat, her handsome escort keeping his hand hard over her eyes so she could see nothing of the route as the car sped away into the night.

After what seemed an age, they had apparently arrived. Although it was cool, Maria was sweating profusely. Her escort helped her out of the car. He and the driver, a thin moustachioed Roman with hard grey eyes, escorted her across a huge lawn, gleaming like black velvet in the night.

They mounted some steps at the entrance to a magnificent house. Light shone between gaps in the curtains behind the bay windows. Maria shivered in the night air.

The driver unlocked the massive front door and she was led into a large reception room with a polished parquet floor. Before her was an antique grand piano beneath a dark oil painting of a hunting scene.

Nearby, a dark form was slumped with ghastly finality in an armchair. She recognised her father immediately, and dismay gripped her like a cancer. He lay like a waxwork, glassy eyed and helpless. A white cloth was wrapped around his neck. Knowing, but not daring to admit to herself the cause of his paleness, she screamed.

A heavy set man emerged from the shadows behind. His face was wrinkled and hard, his iron grey hair smoothed back. She glanced into his faded grey eyes and he smiled. 'Buona sera, Maria Soccolini.'

'What have you done to my father?' she asked.

'You can forget him now,' said the man, 'except when you pray for the dead!'

She stepped forward and fingered his body. Although inert, it seemed not entirely at peace. His seemed too strong and vivacious a presence to have been snuffed out like a candle.

She jerked the white cloth from his neck, feeling somehow it was there for her to do that. The red marks on his neck where he had been strangled were quite horrible. She screamed again, glaring around her. Her eyes took in several sombre oil portraits hanging on the walls. She faced her host squarely 'Why?' she whispered.

He shrugged. 'We employed him in our stockbroking firm. He tried to do the dirty on us. He got what he deserved, so don't pity him. If you don't do what we say, you will suffer the same fate. You'll be working for us one day. We have been watching you, and have the measure of your abilities.' He nodded at the driver. 'Isn't that so, Georgio Thomassino.'

Georgio nodded with a sly grin.

'We know how well your mother has educated you over the years, despite the poverty of your formal schooling. It is most useful that you speak English as well as Italian. We will be sending you back to school to get some formal education in England where exam certificates and the school you went to count for something. We have your future mapped out.'

'Who are you?' asked Maria.

'My name is Roberto Calafato. You may as well start getting used to me now,' he said.

Maria bowed. What choice did she have?

Paulo's body, as she might have expected, was disposed of immediately, by means which were kept from her. He became just another unexplained disappearance, a statistic. Maria wondered who had actually killed him. She would keep her ear to the ground and might one day find out. Then she wouldn't be making the mistake of informing the police. If she had learnt only one hard lesson on the streets, it was that she had to fight fire with fire.

Chapter 2

'Regulations in the City of London have been tightened up, but it's still a cinch to make a killing there. Particularly in stockbroking,' remarked Padre Lorenzo chirpily. He stroked a plump chin. He was red faced and fat like many of his fellow Franciscans.

Roberto Calafato grinned. 'That's just as well. Let's get on with it. I need a huge haul, enough to set me up for life.'

The two men were ensconced in armchairs in the whitewashed privacy of Lorenzo's cell bedroom – identical to the rest in this ancient monastery off the Via Appia Antica. Here the Franciscan Fathers had the undemanding duties of guarding the catacombs, and guiding tourists around them.

Lorenzo smiled. 'Be patient, Roberto. You will be deep in it soon enough, then you'll be longing for a breather. Your first job will be in a Paris stockbroker that is likely to be closed down shortly. You will get a feel for the business there. So when you move to London, you will be ready for the big scam!'

'You are smart,' said Roberto. 'I have the utmost confidence in placing my future in your hands. But why are you of all people hiding away in this monastery?'

'The middle-aged Franciscan raised his eyebrows. 'I never thought I would hear you asking that, Roberto. You are as full of tricks as a monkey yourself. Don't you recognise the sense in keeping a low profile?' He yawned and stood up. 'Come, let's stretch our legs.'

Lorenzo slipped his brown cassock over his grey suit, while Roberto put on his coat. The two men sauntered out, down a winding stone staircase to the scrubbed hallway. Outside, both blinked in the sunshine as they started strolling across the courtyard. En passant, Roberto glanced up at the magnificent white portals of the famous Chiesa. He followed Lorenzo into the dark vestibule of the catacombs, starting point for guided tours 40 feet deep into the bowels of the earth.

It was only ten o'clock in the morning and no visitors were yet waiting for a tour. If this had been a weekend, the vestibule would already have been crowded. Today there would be no rush until lunchtime. From his vantage point behind the ticket desk, the Padre Guardiano gave them a brief nod, a mountain of a man with a balding

balding pate and red sweating face. Leading Roberto down a long steep flight of steps into the catacombs, Lorenzo winked like a naughty schoolboy. 'The Padre Guardiano doesn't trust me an inch.'

Roberto allowed himself a twisted grin. 'I'm not surprised!'

'Not that it's a problem,' continued Lorenzo. 'It's my wealthy backers who keep this convent going. The Padre Guardiano simply can't afford to get rid of me.'

Underground, Roberto marvelled for the umpteenth time at the sheer complexity of the tunnel network. It was as if a gigantic spider had spun a fabulously organised web out of dark red tufa brick. Fairy lights strung along the low crumbling ceilings defined the comfortable tourist paths, but here and there dark tunnels led off the beaten track. 'They go on for miles,' Lorenzo explained, 'connecting with other catacombs. The fathers have been lazy about blocking up entrances, and almost every week we have to send a search party down to find tourists who have strayed.'

Roberto laughed. 'I'll know better than to do that.' As he followed Lorenzo down the umpteenth lit corridor, typically too narrow to permit walking abreast, Roberto ran his fingers along the tablets hung on the walls. The marble was moist with condensation. He glanced at the bust of the Roman Emperor Constantine. Its inscription carved in bold Roman lettering gave him the exhilarating illusion that he had stepped back thousands of years in time.

Huge horizontal gaps yawned like toothless mouths in many of the walls. These were the loculi, where the ancient Christians had buried their dead.

The path suddenly became rougher as Lorenzo, pressing hidden light switches, ushered Roberto down a dark tunnel so narrow that its walls seemed almost to close in on them, the red rock scraping their arms and hair. In a cavern where they stopped for brief respite, picturesque icicles hung from the lofty ceiling.

'We are a hundred feet underground,' said Lorenzo. He smiled to see Roberto taking great gulps. 'Don't worry, the air is good.'

Walking briskly down a further long tunnel which broadened into an archway, they ducked into another cavern. Before them, barely discernible from the rock, loomed an old oak door.

'This is our underground chapel,' announced Lorenzo proudly. 'And you are talking to its official keeper.'

He removed a rusty key from his belt and unlocked the door, pulling it open with a grating that set Roberto's teeth on edge. Inside the floor was covered with rushmats and the whole small window-less chamber was cleanly swept. Lorenzo reached for a switch, and suddenly it was flooded with light. For the first time, Roberto noticed the simple altar at the far end of the chapel, with a telephone resting upon it.

Thrusting aside the altar table, Lorenzo dropped to his hands and knees, scraping the hard red earth to find a faintly defined trap door.

His fingers closed on an inset iron ring and he heaved the trapdoor open to reveal a cellar. Lorenzo reached under and pulled a hidden switch. Light came on and he lowered himself onto a downhanging ladder. His shuffling beneath echoed in the chapel like the noise of ghosts. He re-emerged rapidly, dragging after him a smart black and chrome suitcase. After closing the trapdoor and replacing the altar table, he opened the case on the floor.

He took out a bundle of papers and started rifling through it. His eyes sparkled. The clandestine nature of this operation seemed to bring the holy man to life. Soon he glanced up, giving Roberto the ghost of a wink.

'These forged documents are for you,' he said briskly. 'Keep them safe, in more than one hiding place. You will find here passports, ID papers, testimonials, the works. And another set for Maria. Here, too, are a couple of address books. One with useful names, which you must keep hidden. One with dummy names, to carry about with you as a decoy.

'You may have noticed the documents under the names of Dario Abella and Laura Jones. Those are the names you and Maria will be assuming,' he continued. He indicated a sheaf of notes. 'Mug up on your backgrounds, so you'll never be tripped up. Dario Abella, you will be pleased to learn, is from an aristocratic Roman family with connections in the highest circles.' He grinned. 'By the time you two have mastered the details, you really won't be feeling yourselves.'

Roberto shook his head. 'If we're rumbled . . . '

'You won't be,' snapped Lorenzo. 'Aren't you aware that the Stock Exchange has leaden feet? You must surely realise that the UK regulatory authorities are corrupt. This will work in your favour, of course. The richer you appear, the more hesitant will be the bureaucrats about attacking you. Bullies are always cowards. They will concentrate on poorer victims who can't afford the best legal help.' Lorenzo laughed, clapping his companion on the shoulders. 'What a long way you have come, Roberto, for a poor boy of Calabria, an uneducated peasant! A stockbroker and international financier. My word!

'Never forget, though, you're answerable to me. If I see you making a slip because you've been too proud to ask for my help or take my advice, I will come down on you like a ton of bricks.'

The telephone rang. Roberto started; such a mundane interruption seemed eerie in this isolated underground chapel. Almost sacrilegious.

'It must be the Padre Guardiano,' said Lorenzo, picking up the receiver. Speaking briefly, he then turned to Roberto. 'Georgio Thomassino is waiting in the reception to see you. We had better go back up.'

'He's always turning up like a bad penny,' grumbled Roberto.

22

Following Lorenzo out, he was bowed in thought. 'How detectable are these documents?' he asked.

'Hardly distinguishable from the genuine article, so long as you don't use them to pass through country of origin.' said Lorenzo. 'I have bought your passports from a corrupt clerk in the passport office for a few thousand dollars apiece. I've made them look well used with a bogus rubber stamp.' He smiled. 'Did you know, there are some ten million false passports being used throughout the world? Well now there are two more. Government agencies and spies aren't the only ones who can use new identities.

'The secret of getting away with it is never to use forgeries. Unless they are expertly manufactured, they will not have the watermarks, the intricately engraved designs, and the colour blends of the originals. When you need to change identity again, make sure you obtain all your documents through me.'

They were emerging now onto the familiar tourist tracks, where Roberto, to his relief, would have known his own way back up. Also the going was more comfortable.

In the old days, I would have given you ghosted passports. You could have taken on dead people's,' continued Lorenzo.

'That's dangerous.' said Roberto.

'The risk in taking on a dead man's identity is that another imposter may be assuming the same name, before or after you have.

'You must go about the business carefully. Firstly, gravestones, public records or obituaries should be searched for someone who was born about when you were but had died in infancy. It helps if his profile is similar in other ways too. You will need to obtain a certified birth certificate then other documents such as a driving licence, ID card, and credit cards. You should apply for a passport by post.'

'You're opening my eyes to crime, Lorenzo,' grunted Roberto.

Lorenzo grinned. 'It takes two. Let's face it, Roberto, you were born a scoundrel. You would crack your own grandmother's skull to get a few hundred dollars under her mattress. Well, I'm like that too! A go-getter. We're birds of a feather.'

'I'm certainly glad you're on my side,' said Roberto. 'And I would hate to meet you on a dark night.'

Tourists were already crowding out the vestibule, waiting in groups for the next guided tour. Others were strolling in the courtyard where the air was fresh, and the sunshine dazzling. Leaning against the colonnade smoking a pipe was Georgio Thomassino, the tall thin Roman with a moustache who customarily put fear into the hearts of his enemies. Like Roberto he worked for Lorenzo, figuring with equal prominence in the Padre's future plans.

Leaving Lorenzo in the vestibule, Roberto approached him. Georgio's eyes lit up to see his fellow criminal. But Roberto wasn't smiling. 'Don't tell me. Maria is in trouble?' he ventured. Georgio pulled on his pipe, blowing circles of smoke into the air. 'You must be telepathic. She is proving a handful, that girl. I took her, as you requested, to the English boarding school we arranged for her. She has only been there a month and they already want to expel her.'

'She must have done something,' said Roberto.

'Quite so. She has been dealing drugs,' said Georgio drily.

Roberto sniggered. 'She's got all her life to do that! She had better curtail it now. We'll bail her out of trouble – or we'll have to send her to another school.'

Georgio shrugged. 'Why the hell have we sent her to school at all? Let's put her out to work for us immediately.'

'She'll be more use if she has the airs and graces of a lady,' reasoned Roberto. 'But it could be she's not capable of it. Maria's got her chance. If she blows it, I wouldn't like to be in her shoes. Meanwhile, we had better see the headmistress.'

'I've booked flights to Gatwick this afternoon,' said Georgio. 'While we're in England, we'd better send for Maria's mother too – Anne's threatening to overdose if she can't see her daughter.'

'What a good riddance that would be,' said Roberto. 'But it might finally unhinge Maria, on top of her father's death. No, we'll arrange for Anne to visit her.'

At this point, Padre Lorenzo sidled up to them. He looked the part of an ageing and innocent Father, at peace with the world, nodding and smiling at the tourists he passed, gathering the folds of his cassock up with dignity. How deceptive appearances could be, thought Roberto.

After they had talked, Lorenzo touched Roberto's forearm. 'Don't waste too much time on Maria and Anne,' he advised. 'Nobody is indispensable.'

'Don't I know it,' said Roberto.

'One further piece of advice that I have saved until the last minute in the hope that you will remember it. Never cross a border carrying more than one passport at the same time. Officials will have a fit and inspect them closely, doubtless discovering which one is not genuine and what mischief you are up to.'

Georgio had already turned back to his car, and Roberto joined him immediately for the drive to the airport, leaving Lorenzo to explain his sudden departure to the Padre Guardiano.

After spending the night in a luxury London hotel, Roberto and Georgio set out in a hired Bentley for Maria's boarding school. Roberto caught his breath upon seeing it for the first time. It was a beautiful mock Tudor building nestling amidst fifty acres of Berkshire countryside. The school was struggling to attract pupils after a recent unwelcome fee increase. Maria had been accepted for sixth form entry at the age of eighteen despite her foul language and her chequered past.

'I'm delighted you could make it,' cooed Lydia Vernon-Jones, the headmistress. In her long brown tweed skirt and sensible flat shoes she made Roberto and Georgio fidgety. They felt not just uncouth, but unworthy in her presence – as of course they were. But there wasn't much time for such thoughts as Miss Vernon-Jones swept them into her study.

What a scholarly little chamber it was! The walls were concealed by huge bookcases from floor to ceiling, all full of leatherbound classics.

Waving her visitors into chairs, the headmistress sat at her desk before them. Sunlight streamed onto the brown leather blotting pad on her tidy desk. She leafed through some notes as she spoke, in a low key, officious tone to the two men now seated before her. She was like a mother hen over her brood coping with intrusion from the world.

'Maria has been caught red handed, dealing out marijuana, like another girl might sweets. The girls say she's taken large sums of money off them for it, which Maria denies.'

'Unlike most of your girls, Maria has had an underprivileged background,' said Roberto. 'Put all this down to teething troubles. It won't happen again. I will make sure of that.'

'If she is caught with drugs, she's out, whatever her background,' said the headmistress. 'Maria is not fitting in here easily in any case, although of course it's early days. Her classwork is careless, and she plays truant at every opportunity. Nor does she make any effort to mix socially with the other girls. She doesn't seem to understand the basic principles of give and take. And yet for some reason I can't fathom, they all look up to her. But perhaps I'm unburdening *our* problems now.'

'Not at all,' said Roberto. 'I want to help any way I can.'

A knock came on the door, and Maria burst in. She stopped breathless before the headmistress's desk, turning to face Roberto. Her blonde hair was dishevelled and her white blouse flapped loose over her navy blue pleated skirt. Her yellow and black striped tie was pulled loose, with her top button open.

'Hello, Roberto,' she said.

Roberto nodded to her and looked back at Miss Vernon-Jones. 'May I take her away for a couple of days and sort her out?'

Agreeing to this after giving Maria a pep-talk, the headmistress ushered the three of them out into the courtyard towards the Bentley. Girls peered at them from all corners as Georgio drove them away.

He took them to a comfortable hotel in nearby Henley where they booked into three adjoining rooms. The two men stayed initially in Maria's room, in case she should get depressed and try to leave, but she undressed there quite brazenly in front of them. Her body was brown and wiry, tough from the years of fending for herself that she'd known. She climbed deftly into bed where she lay on her back, snug under the blankets, peeping out at them.

Roberto and Georgio laughed involuntarily and Maria smiled.

'You little fool,' said Roberto. 'If you must deal in pot, offer it to my friends, not at school. You were bound to get caught.'

Maria giggled. 'They have not got enough evidence to expel me. I only took cash, and that's all well hidden. They don't know my supplier. All the girls smoke the stuff, Roberto.'

'If you are caught again, getting expelled will be the least of it,' said Roberto. 'Need I remind you of your father's fate?'

Helpless rage flashed for a split second across Maria's features, the effect of which was not lost on Georgio and Roberto. Suddenly, she was calm again. 'How is Mama?'

'You will see her shortly and can judge for yourself,' said Roberto cryptically.

'Don't tell her about this drugs incident,' said Maria.

'Agreed,' said Roberto. 'On condition that you smile at her, and tell her you are happy at school. We will work together to make her happy, eh?'

On the morning they had taken her back to school, Roberto conferred with the headmistress inside her study while Georgio waited outside with Maria.

Roberto then took the girl out onto the lawn. It was breaktime, and the other girls were running about, skipping and playing other sweet games in the sun. They looked innocent and English, delectable young virgins that would soon be ripe for the plucking.

'Miss Vernon-Jones is going to give you a last chance,' he said. Maria lowered her eyes. 'If you get in trouble again, you will have me to contend with,' he added.

A few minutes later he, Georgio and Maria went up to the dormitory. It was unpeopled, as always in the daytime. The beds were well spaced and neatly made up with pink covers. In accordance with the rules, there was nothing in the way of clothes or possessions on the floor.

Anne Soccolini was ushered in by the smiling headmistress. Maria, who had been told only five minutes earlier, sprang forward to hug her. Anne was crying. The lines on her face had deepened over the previous few weeks and she was quivering with love and anxiety as she held her tough, grown up daughter close, stroking her hair.

There was surprisingly little for anyone to say. Mother and daughter seemed to want little more than to embrace one another. After quarter of an hour, Maria saw her visitors out, trying to cling to her mother as she said goodbye, but Anne pushed her back quite sharply before she climbed into the back seat of the Bentley with the two men. She didn't look back at her daughter as Georgio drove away, although Maria was waving frantically.

'She is getting the education she never had,' said Roberto. 'In the nick of time too. Maria is no longer a child.'

'It's what I always dreamed for her. But what price will she have to pay you?' asked Anne.

Roberto laughed. 'We will look after her, don't you worry.'

Georgio drove through the Berkshire countryside with exemplary steadiness. So smooth was the ride that they might have been in a liner, gliding over the calmest of oceans.

'If you are providing a good future for Maria, I'm happy, Signor Calafato,' said Anne.

'We won't be abandoning you, either,' said Roberto. 'You will be taking a live-in job as a cleaner in a monastery next week. The famous catacombs of Rome will benefit from your diligence. My advice to you is work hard, turn a blind eye to anything that doesn't concern you, and keep your mouth shut.'

Anne smiled thinly. 'I know which side my bread is buttered on. It would have been better for Paulo if he had too!'

Roberto returned to Rome briefly to pay his last respects to Padre Lorenzo before embarking upon the course of deception for which he'd been so well prepared.

'All set for Paris,' grinned Lorenzo as they clinked glasses in a discreet restaurant near the Vatican.'

'I'll be in touch with you probably every week,' said Roberto. He knew that fear showed on his face, and that it wasn't lost on Lorenzo.

'Damn this slow service,' grumbled the holy father, 'I'm hungry.'

'Relax, Lorenzo. The night is yet young.' said Roberto.

The food arrived and the two men tucked in. Lorenzo devoured half a roast duck, then wiped his dripping jowls with a napkin.

'You will be looking after Johnnie Butler's Parisian stockbroking firm. He's a big time con man you know, and has already done a spell in jail for securities fraud. Butler was born in Canada and trained as a lawyer which has been useful to him. Never trust him an inch. But don't cross him, either.'

Lorenzo glanced around the restaurant. The candlelit tables were peopled with merry groups in smart evening dress. There were no obvious eavesdroppers.

'When Johnnie Butler makes an enemy of anybody, he's dead!' he hissed. 'I don't mean he's just shot or knifed, although that has happened. I'm talking about the so called accidental deaths that never get reported, all over Spain and Gibraltar, for instance. The police know to turn a blind eye to them. People are hit by cars, and bodies are left strewn in the streets, heads and limbs rolling into the gutter.

'Can't we have him watched?' said Roberto.

Lorenzo shook his head. 'We are supposed to be working with him, not against him. I'm just giving you a friendly warning to take care. For instance, when you later resettle in London, you may want to poach some of the Paris brokers, but you mustn't give Johnnie any hint of that now or he will carve you up.'

Roberto passed on the warning to Georgio as the two men flew to Paris. His companion silenced him with a wave of the arm. 'I already know of Butler's reputation. Thankfully, we won't be seeing much of him. He's busy running from country to country to dodge the authorities.'

At eight o'clock the following morning they arrived at their new offices overlooking l'Arc de Triomphe. Johnnie Butler opened the door to them in person. An easy-going chap in his early fifties, he looked handsome and slim with his black fuzzy hair, twinkling brown eyes and a bronzed complexion. 'Bonjour,' he beamed as he ushered them in.

To their surprise, two brokers were already at work in the dealing room, speaking on the telephone. The one nearest the door, who had a Prussian style crewcut, was lounging back in his chair, his feet extended on the desk. Putting his client on hold, he nodded benignly at Roberto and Georgio. 'You two are taking over, I'm told. That's great. We need new blood in the management here,' he said in a fresh American accent.

'This is Mike, our star broker,' said Johnnie Butler, slapping him on the back. 'I want a million dollars from you today, son.'

Mike jerked his thumb at his colleague who was selling shares down the telephone, using a still harsher American accent. The man's horn-rimmed glasses under thin brown sideswept hair and a broad forehead gave him a delicate, almost professorial air. 'Tim has got in two hundred grand in dollars already,' he said. 'It's the Arab market he's tapped. Those blessed Sheikhs are so rich that tens of thousands of dollars are just monopoly money to them.'

Tim was saying. 'Listen, Muhammad. We both wipe with the same hand, even if I am on the other side of the world from you. Now take the camel by the reins . . . . '

He was writing out the bargain slip even as he spoke. Another sale in the bag.

'Mind you, the Arabs often cancel,' remarked Mike.

'Are you two the entire broking team?' asked Roberto.

'Not quite, but we're the best,' said Mike.

Tim put down the telephone receiver. He was grinning broadly. 'I've just roped in forty grand,' he said. 'The business is out there but it's tough finding it sometimes. The kids we've had working here often just can't hack it, so they are out.'

Roberto looked at Georgio who shrugged. 'We are here to build a team.'

'Quite so,' said Roberto.

'You will have to poach staff,' said Butler.

'Hardly a piece of cake now,' drawled Tim. 'Now the Financial Services Act is up and running, all the crooked brokers are clinging to their positions. If they come here, they will risk being investigated.'

Johnnie Butler shook his head. 'Most stockbrokers are losing money right now. Our network is making it by the bucketful.' He turned to Roberto and Georgio. 'Our stockbroking firms are everywhere, Geneva, Marbella, Rotterdam, Amsterdam, Costa Rica. You name it . . . It will only be a matter of time before we are operating in the UK too. The police never raid our offices all at the same time.

'This little operation in Paris is the safest of them all. You see, our whereabouts are secret. Our telephone number is ex-directory, and never given out. The clients ring into our offices in Geneva. The boys there tell them we are all at a meeting, but that their broker will ring them back. Geneva then rings us, and we ring the client from here in Paris. He thinks his broker is ringing from Geneva, from the office to which he had made his original call.

'It is due to secret tactics like this that we survive. Brokers from top City firms are begging to join us all the time. We pay up to thirty per cent commission, unbeatable anywhere these days.

'The best source of new brokers is England Securities. They are the dodgiest stockbroking firm left in London. They have a few friends in high places and so have survived the Financial Services Act. We've had some of their brokers join us in the past.'

'That will be my first hunting ground,' said Roberto.

In the weeks that followed, brokers enticed by Roberto started trickling into the Paris offices. A contingent came from England Securities, and some from other London stockbroking firms, shifting like migrant birds.

Soon the dealing room was nicely full, with brokers still asking to join them. Roberto was figuring out how best to enthuse Georgio into managing the dealing in his absence. But the work, as it turned out, was done for him.

One morning, Georgio and Roberto were in the dealing room early as usual, and typically by ten many of the brokers had not yet turned up to work. They were becoming lazy.

Sitting with Tim and Mike, Roberto smoked a cigar. Tim and Mike were loader brokers, which meant they 'loaded' clients whom the other brokers had traded once. The remuneration was considerable, fifteen per cent for all monies brought in, with a further fifteen per cent accruing to the brokers who had 'opened up' the clients, with the result that all were implicated in the loading process.

'It's a fucking joke the way all these kids come into work late with hangovers,' yawned Mike. 'I drink them under the table in the clubs every night. I spend five thousand dollars a year on whisky on top of my other drinking. And yet I'm in at seven o'clock always so I can screw the Arabs with all the bum stocks that we push on 'em. In fact, I do so many bargains that I'm hiring a local French cow for about six dollars an hour to write out my bargain slips while I continue dealing. But Tim here goes one better.' He nodded at his colleague. 'Spill the beans Tim, you dodgy fucker.'

'Yeah,' Tim grinned, and his chest swelled with pride. 'When I get fed up with the toy stocks that we push, I tell clients I'm selling 'em Guinness or ICI, or some other blue chip that they know is good. They send in their cheques, but they get no certificates or anything, the daft cunts. They might as well be taking their savings out of the Building Society and throwing them into the Seine.'

Roberto grinned. 'Make the most of it while it lasts, lads.'

'While it lasts?' Mike was astounded, 'Johnnie Butler is a genius, man. He's in cahoots with most Stock Exchanges and is far too clever for the rest. We'll survive forever!'

Meanwhile, Georgio was pacing the room, with an irate look on his face. Johnnie Butler, with so many stockbroking firms under his control all over the world, was characteristically absent from the premises that morning. He, Georgio, would put his foot down with an outward show of toughness that wasn't in the wily Roberto's nature.

By 11.30 the brokers had all trickled into work. Most lived in rented flats in the best parts of Paris. They kept their suitcases packed for obvious reasons; some even brought them to work daily, just "in case". All had booked into their hotels under false names so they could, in the instance of a police raid, do a runner without notice, leaving no clues for snoopers.

Naturally these dodgy brokers all worked under stage names. On the advice of Johnnie Butler, each broker used several aliases, so if it suited him, he could have officially 'left the company', or even no longer exist.

These were extra precautionary measures in a fraud manoeuvre which also involved cheating the Inland Revenue.

The brokers' earnings were paid cash in hand. Tax did not exist as far as these characters were concerned. Most brokers spent as fast as they earned, picking up whores in Montmartre or in the nightclubs elsewhere in Paris, drinking hard, and flying home to the UK at the weekends where they met up with, and compared dodgy tricks with their friends who worked in the City, buying lavish presents for girlfriends who never knew how they made their living.

For many brokers, this was the job of a lifetime. They would turn up at work dressed in jeans and T-shirts, such casualness not mattering as they never set eyes on clients.

Brokers here would lie about the stocks they were selling with impunity to punters in countries by whose jurisdiction they were unaffected. As their self-confidence grew, their morals were further eroded.

'I get most of my recommendations right,' they would claim.

Many would arrange for escorts to accompany them at nights, and would act as middlemen in oil and drugs deals, sometimes between Arab clients. What fabulous fun they had! What fortunes they made!

As every broker had a second and third passport, leaving for pastures new was no problem. Butler had insisted they obtain these. He employed several high-priced law firms whose members felt they were ethical consultants, unwilling to help criminals or those skirting the grey areas of international law. But they worked for Johnnie's boys.

These expatriation specialists taught their "straight" clients to get over the mentality that regards a passport as a mystical document symbolising patriotism. Butler had stressed to them the down to earth reality that travel documents were merely pieces of paper, and that the decision to get a new passport was a rational one.

Following Butler's advice, the brokers made four or five top passport choices.

The criteria for selection were often whether the brokers spoke the language of the country and looked the part of the country's nationals. This would obviously mean less questioning at borders.

Before even starting the process, the brokers had made sure to have in their possession not just passports of their home countries, but also duplicate passports of their home countries. Some countries demanded that prior passports should be handed in before the new one was issued, which necessitated an expendable duplicate.

The brokers would not have known how to obtain duplicate passports if Butler had not told them. 'Inform your passport office that you are visiting South Africa, then a black African country which won't admit anyone who has a South African stamp in his passport. So before you leave you need two passports, one for South Africa, and the other for the black African country. Alternatively, use the method I use. Pretend your passport is lost, file a police report on the loss and you will be given a duplicate.'

Armed with extra passports, the brokers discovered how dual nationality could open up moneymaking opportunities for them, and how, as foreigners in various countries, they were always treated better than citizens.

Butler told those who were having problems getting extra passports (often because on a whim they wanted expensive ones for places like Jamaica, Mauritius or the Dominican Republic on the cheap) that they could in an emergency always escape to Berlin or Austria as refugees, without passports.

Brokers who had got passports early, as from Ireland (if they had established ancestry there), Israel, Paraguay, or the Philippines were hooked on the game of getting new passports and started collecting them. Beyond a certain point, it was the most expensive of useless hobbies they had ever practised.

Butler confided in them that a tidy sum could be made out of exploiting people's interest in acquiring a passport together with an accompanying title. He himself had set up a bogus Order of Malta, and was finding through advertisements in the *Herald Tribune* plenty of people who were prepared to contribute tens of thousands of dollars for the right to call themselves titles like: 'Sir' or 'Duke'.

Butler's Knight of Malta passports were accepted by some border officials whose instruction books showed that Order of Malta passports were to be regarded as legitimate. But other border officials would ask awkward questions.

Another useful piece of advice Butler gave his brokers was to establish a domicile for tax purposes. His brokers, who were of various nationalities, would avoid being taxed by their home country through a legal domicile (unless they held a US or Philippines passport). One US broker there was, like ninety per cent of Americans abroad, not declaring his earnings to the US Government, which was a felony.

Which legal domiciles did Butler suggest? Andorra, Campione, Guernsey, Bermuda, Cayman Islands, Monte Carlo . . . He was in fact passing on perfectly sound advice which has for decades been followed by the rich worldwide, but which was unknown to these brokers.

Benefiting from all this sophisticated guidance made the brokers arrogant. This, coupled with their huge earning possibilities, was perhaps why they couldn't be bothered to start work on time. However, by 11.45 that morning most were in, and the dealing room was buzzing. Suddenly, Georgio raised his hand. 'Everyone off the phones,' he boomed. Grumbling, for they had not yet grown used to his authority, they obeyed.

'This room is getting too slack,' shouted Georgio, banging his fist on his desk. 'You are all to be in by eight every day or earlier. For fuck's sake you're stockbrokers, not day labourers.

'Also I want to see you all really doing the biz, doing the numbers. These clients don't know their arses from their elbows, most of them. Really screw them for what you can. Get the suckers to mortgage their houses and sell their cars. Clean the miserable bastards out. If it proves hard work, persist. Remember it's your commissions you are working for. And it's you who will be having the last laugh.

'Promise 'em quick vast profits. It's all the fuckers care about. Come on, here's your chance to make the kind of money most people can only dream about.'

The brokers murmured amongst themselves as they hit the telephones again. The ensuing buzz was unprecedented. Never taking his eye off the brokers in his charge, Georgio winked at Roberto. 'Wait until you see today's takings,' he said. Even as he spoke, several dealers came over to his desk where they dropped fresh white bargain slips into the already loaded wire basket.

'100,000 dollars . . . 50,000 dollars . . . ' Georgio read off the top two, and rubbed his hands together. 'Just leave it to me, my friend.'

'You're a good man,' said Roberto.

That night, meeting Johnnie Butler at his flat for drinks, Roberto told him of Georgio's enthusiasm. Butler's eyes narrowed craftily. 'So you're leaving the donkey work to your colleague, eh? Well, that's clever. As you've got some time on your hands, perhaps you would like me to fix you up with a woman?'

Roberto shook his head. 'Thanks, but my child, Maria (so he introduced her), breaks up for school holidays shortly. In a few weeks, she is coming out here to join me! She's looking forward to seeing Paris. I will have my hands full looking after her.'

Butler shrugged. 'If you'd like me to help out, I will. I could teach her a trick or two.'

'I don't doubt it,' said Roberto. 'But you would be surprised what she already knows,'

'Get her working as a broker here, then. That will test her mettle.'

'What a brilliant idea!' said Roberto.

Chapter 3

As it turned out, Maria took to stockbroking like a duck to water. Despite having only just turned eighteen years old, or perhaps because of it, she was highly persuasive, even cut-throat on the telephone, taking the dealing room by storm. Many of her fellow brokers gave her the cold shoulder. They were jealous, and when they made their usual crude sexual advances towards her, she laughed in their faces.

Maria shared Roberto's flat in central Paris, half a mile as the crow flies from the office. Ruthless at work, she was restless in the evenings and at weekends. She couldn't just be idle, as most young ladies are on vacation. One Saturday, over lunch, she cheerfully told Roberto she had been stifled at school, which had been full of silly upper class English twits, most of whom she could walk all over in the unprotected outside world.

'Haven't they given you holiday work?' he demanded.

Maria shook her head: 'I'm through with education now.'

Roberto marvelled at how colloquial her turn of phrase had become. 'Let's hope you have passed your exams.'

She yawned. 'I'll know soon enough, so let's not speculate at this stage. Roberto, you'll never guess how randy I'm feeling.'

Roberto smiled frostily. 'I thought my attention was unwelcome.'

'Not tonight,' said Maria.

She led the way into their bedroom, allowing him to undress her, resisting only when he was rough. They were naked and alone, which Roberto had wanted for a long time.

Mmnn, Maria seemed to melt into his body. What a marvellous fuck she was! Slow, teasing and thorough. The array of emotions from delight to disgust shot across her face as they made love, like strobe lights of many colours. Above all her expression conveyed a painful desire to lose herself in the experience, a sentimentality that on this occasion had overcome her natural hardness and cynicism.

He was drained before she was, lying panting on the bed, like a dog that has just finished swimming upstream against a strong current. He felt old. Maria duly slowed her passion, settling snugly on his torso from which vantage point she started licking his thighs and stomach with her delicate pink tongue. Never had she been so kitten like, so loving to him, with her long blonde hair splayed over his chest like an extra wrap. How fabulous it was!

'I'm privileged,' he told her. 'You could take your pick of men. Johnnie Butler if you liked.'

She giggled. 'He's panting after me, I know. But I wouldn't have it off with him. He's far too much trouble.'

Roberto grinned. 'He's desperate. Divorced like me.'

'Speaking of which, how is your ex-wife? You have not mentioned Emily recently.'

A cloud came over Roberto's face. 'She could be married to a sultan for all I know. I have no idea which country she is in, let alone what she's up to!'

His thoughts dwelling on his former marriage, he flinched. What a farce it had all been, as it turned out!

In a moment of impulse, he had succumbed to pressure from Emily and her family in Tennessee and had married her. The girl had turned out to be a lazy slut, squandering his money and having affairs on the side. All she had ever been good for was sex. He had divorced her, and fled the United States, where they had been living, back to his native Italy. He had reimmersed himself in business there, not keeping in touch with Emily (by that stage back with her parents) or even to let her know where he was.

Sensing his discomfort about his marriage, Maria would tease him. 'How much longer will you stay on the run?' she would ask. Or: 'It's a wonder you think you can make it with any woman!'

On this occasion, she didn't press him. Gratefully, he stroked her hair. 'You're my protégé, Maria,' he said.

'What choice do I have?' she asked quietly.

'With your knowledge of the world, you should know better than to want total freedom. You must appreciate when you're well off.'

He pushed her aside, suddenly tired of her, and eased himself off the bed. 'I have a gift for you Maria.'

'Makes a change,' she said.

He smiled. 'Come with me.'

She padded after him into the living room.

Sitting upright and grandly in an armchair, mistress of the flat, she watched him pull back the Persian rug and raise a loose floorboard. A grin crept over her face. What a wily dog he was. She knew that she could never trust him, and yet to appease him she had to pretend that she had dropped her guard.

He pulled out a large rectangular wooden box wrapped in polythene. Removing the polythene and lid, he extracted a deep blue cloak with a fur lined collar and sleeves. This cloak had one extraordinary feature which made Maria gasp. Gloved fingers on porcelain arms emerged from the sleeves in front of the cloak in a chillingly lifelike manner. She reached out and fingered the black suede. Underneath at waist level, were slits in the cloak which, as Roberto demonstrated, were for putting one's real hands through.

'It's a pickpocket's cloak,' said Roberto. 'It's been made to fit you, so try it on.'

Maria slipped it over her naked body. Thus clad, she looked dignified and substantial, although she would need a white blouse to match the sleeves on her false arms. Her own hands roved free under the cloak. She reached out through one of the slits in the cloth and pinched Roberto's bottom.

'Watch it,' he staggered back. 'It fits you perfectly, I can see. Now take it off. Keep it for pickpocketing. It will enable you to double your takings, and better avoid being caught.'

Maria unbuttoned the cloak, stepping nimbly out of it. 'I thought I had outgrown my days as a street thief.'

He shrugged. 'It will do you no harm to keep your hand in. Just as a hobby really. It's obviously nothing like so lucrative as our kind of stockbroking.'

'Very well,' said Maria. 'Anything, so long as I don't need to go back to school.'

'I like to think of you as a schoolgirl,' said Roberto.

'That's just your dirty mind,' she said.

'Naughty schoolgirls get punishment,' he said. Needing no encouragement to implement this, he hugged her in his powerful arms. Lithe and wiry as she was, she had a lightness and frailty that made her easy to manoeuvre. Her bright smile vanished and animal fear flashed across her features as Roberto dragged her to the sofa, where he forced her over his knee. He contented himself initially with massaging her buttocks, and she wriggled frantically, expecting the worst.

It was a relief when he ended up spanking her. That was harmless after all. He slapped her buttocks, at first softly then hard, leaving fiery marks until she started to cry with the mounting stinging pain. Eventually he subsided because his own hand was too sore to continue.

Afterwards, he and Maria laughed about it, over a bottle of wine. It set a new phase in their relationship, an unspoken peace between them, coupled with an unspoken resentment on Maria's part. No longer was she a whore, and she wasn't going to be treated like one. But for the time being, she would bide her time.

Not that they saw much of one another these days. Georgio was running the dealing floor, so Roberto hardly needed to go into work at all.

He took to wandering around Paris. Too lazy to sightsee, he whiled away long hours in cafes, reading English and Italian daily newspapers.

Whenever he paid a surprise visit to the office, the dealing room was busy, with Georgio screaming for more deals, and Maria yelling down the telephone, her face red and hot, her hair flying, and her blouse open at the collar.

Some evenings, Maria dragged him off as an accomplice on pickpocketing excursions. She had taken these up enthusiastically, finding that, with the help of the cloak, she was making hundreds of dollars a night. The excursions often took place on the crowded metro. They would walk separately into the same carriage. In her cloak, with the false arms intact, she would sit next to a likely dupe while Roberto hovered to hand, ready to intervene should Maria land herself in trouble.

How stupid people were! How easily they could be pickpocketed. Out of the corner of his eye Roberto would watch Maria operating with a surgeon's precision on middle-aged American tourists in particular, but on anybody wealthy and not too observant. She had an eye for good victims. The whole process took only seconds. Her hand would sneak out from the folds of her cloak. She would snatch a purse from a handbag, a wallet from a pocket, under cover of her false arms. Victims would twitch, and occasionally glance round, but Maria always seemed loftily unaware of them, staring soberly in front of her with her arms folded. In the blue fur-lined cloak and white blouse she looked, if a little strangely dressed, presentable and respectable.

Maria would try to give Roberto a cut, although he had been just a spectator, but he invariably declined it. 'This is your own little do,' he said. 'Enjoy it while it lasts.'

'I want you with me every time,' she said.

'That's fine,' he said. 'Even though you don't need me.'

'Don't speak too soon,' she said.

Johnnie Butler, it transpired, had a still greater sense of foreboding. Roberto told him of these excursions in order to build Maria up in his eyes, but it had the opposite effect. Butler whistled softly. 'Aach that girl is so sharp she'll cut herself. She will risk a great future for a bit of pockpocketing fun. How stupid.'

Sure enough the time came when Maria went too far. Fortunately Roberto was with her on the occasion. They were sitting on a public bench near the Champs Elysées. Maria, unlike Roberto, had been working hard all day, and was exhausted. With Roberto on her left, her target sat on her right.

He was a young businessman contemplating the twilight, who looked easy meat. His blue eyes were half-closed, his dark blond hair ruffled in the breeze. Although at that moment hunched, he was tall and slender. Neatly dressed in a dark grey suit and blue tie, he exuded gentlemanliness. He showed no awareness of the young girl seated beside him. What a mistake it could be to become so lost in one's own thoughts, Roberto concluded, and had to make a conscious effort to stop himself from chuckling.

Maria's hands flickered over his suit, reaching for his wallet. Perhaps it was because she was tired, or operating in the cold outdoors, but there was an uncharacteristic heavyhandedness about her work. The victim turned as she removed his wallet. He squinted with an ugly venom as he weighed the situation up.

Hitting out hard and unexpectedly, he smacked Maria's false arms. He grunted as he felt the lack of give in them. Experimentally, he hit them again and again. The china cracked, and a chunk dropped onto the road, a clean break. Maria staggered to her feet, dropping his wallet, and tearing away. But her victim grabbed her waist, his arms coiling round her like a cobra. 'Help!' screamed Maria.

'Stop thief!' shouted the man. 'Police!' His English public school accent, ringing out for a few yards then lost in the wind, seemed painfully incongruous out here in Paris. A passer-by stopped and stared at a distance, like a spectator at the circus.

Roberto stood up casually, as if embarrassed and wanting to be gone. They had rehearsed this little game, for if he was to rescue her in an emergency, it was vital he didn't appear a confederate. She, despite her desperation, never looked at him, playing her role to perfection.

Joining his hands, Roberto thumped the man's skull with the force of a thousand rapids. He groaned and writhed, but didn't let Maria go. Roberto, however, was far from finished with the victim. His hands, large and strong, closed on the Englishman's neck, and he squeezed, grimacing under the strain. His victim gurgled, his grip on Maria slackening. Kneeing him in the testicles, she tore herself free of his clinging arms and bolted like a wild horse.

It was not until she was out of sight that Roberto released the choking man's neck. Facing him, he punched his nose. His victim clapped his hands to it. Blood dribbled through his fingers, and his head sagged. For good measure, Roberto then punched him in the mouth. His knuckles cracked against his teeth, leaving his lips punctured by them.

The assaulted man fell on the ground in front of the bench, on top of his own wallet. Roberto didn't wait around to pick it up or to finish him off. With a nimbleness commendable for a man in his fifties, he ran away in the opposite direction from Maria. The twilight swallowed him up almost immediately.

He was back in his flat an hour later, having reached it by a cunning and tortuous emergency route. He collapsed in an armchair, fit for nothing for some minutes.

An hour later he was irked. It wasn't as if he was anxious whether Maria had made a quick getaway. He knew she was hot stuff at pickpocketing. The girl had been a sneak thief since childhood, and if she couldn't look after herself on the streets at eighteen years old, when would she be able to? But he would have appreciated her company just then, and not just for sex. It was bloody lonely being a criminal, and he had grown inordinately, dangerously fond of her. He didn't dare analyse his feelings deeper than that, but could not help being aware that she was never for a moment out of his thoughts.

It wasn't until around ten o'clock that Maria burst in. Her thin face, streaked with dirt as it was, glowed from the night air. Her bedraggled hair clung to her neck and shoulders, damp from the drizzling outside that was threatening to develop into a rainstorm. Her eyes sparkled mischievously, as she pecked his cheek. 'Thanks Roberto,' she said carelessly.

'You little fool,' said Roberto, pouring her a large brandy.

'Even if you hadn't been there, I would have got away, don't you worry,' said Maria cheerfully.

'I would have given him some sob story about being penniless and homeless, then would have fucked him – at a price, of course!'

Maria wasn't ready for what happened the next morning. She went to the office as usual, and was hard at work on the telephone. By 9 o'clock, she had sold a staggering 50,000 dollars' worth of stock.

Exhilarated, she took a well-earned break. She darted out into the corridor, towards theLadies. En route she heard voices from the boadroom and tiptoed over. The door was not quite closed, and inside, with a start, she recognised the visitor.

Horror of horrors, her previous night's victim was sitting there in the flesh. For a ghastly moment, she wondered if Roberto had killed him, and he had come back to haunt her. His nose was red and bulbous, while his eye was puffy and weeping. A plaster covered most of his chin, and his neck was tightly wrapped in a bandage.

Shifting in his seat, he caught her eye. She drew back into the shadows, her heart beating. Mistake number two in the last twenty four hours – she hadn't bothered to conceal herself from him.

She tore out of the office block, and back to Roberto's flat. She would just not be at work today. Telephoning Roberto on his mobile, she confided to him what had happened. He told her he would take her out for lunch. She should wait there, and he would be by her side in good time.

When the doorbell rang she was quite pleased. She assumed it was Roberto, and she had tarted herself up quite nicely so he could take her somewhere decent to eat.

She opened the door and gasped. A ghastly surprise lay in store for her from over the threshold. Johnnie Butler stood there with a wicked grin on his face, his eyes gleaming with sexual energy. It was as if the devil incarnate had turned up in person.

She half closed the door, but one foot was already in the hall. It was too late to shut him out. She really ought to have been more careful. There was nothing for it but to engage in a battle of wits. Anything to keep this egotistical maniac at arm's length.

'What do you want?' she asked. His grin broadened. She sensed a sadistic streak in him and ground her teeth. If she lost her nerve now, she would doubtless lose all else.

'You have really fucked things up now, haven't you?' he said.

She smiled weakly. 'What do you mean?'

He strolled into the living room, glancing around as if to ascertain that they were alone and slumped onto the green sofa. 'You know exactly what I'm talking about. The man you pickpocketed last night, and whom your colleague – Roberto I assume – beat up – he saw you in our offices this morning. Do you know who he is?'

Maria shook her head.

'It's the stockbroker, John Falmouth, who is about to become chairman of England Securities in London.'

Maria nodded. Like all the brokers she worked with, she knew the name of England Securities. Many of her colleagues had actually worked there.

Johnnie thumped his fist on the arm of the sofa. 'We need his business. Fortunately, he is one of the greediest sods in stockbroking, and nothing stands between him and his money. If you had lost him for us, then you and I wouldn't be sitting here just talking, I can tell you.

'As it turns out, Falmouth is still keen for us to sell shares in The Merden Group, which of course he owns. We could make him enough money to retire on from it, and that's an offer he can't refuse!' He paused, looking her hard in the eyes. 'I had to tell John you were working for me. Why else should you be on the premises? I told him also that you were the best broker we had. In the circumstances, he's prepared not to pursue justice. You never got away with his wallet anyway.'

Maria smiled.

'If you do any more pickpocketing, I will personally make sure the police pick you up,' he continued. 'So pack it in now. You are young and you have a great future ahead of you if you will only stay out of trouble! Forget any plans to carry on with your education. Believe you me, it's a waste of time for you! Come and work for me permanently. Right now, you are earning some two thousand dollars a week from broking. Soon I will make you a loader. Then you'll be earning a hell of a lot more besides.'

Maria bit her lip. 'It's a great idea. But I must ask Roberto. As I am sure you already know, I'm not my own mistress.'

'Leave that to me,' said Johnnie loftily. He got up, and took her arm, bringing her to sit on the sofa beside him. She complied with thunder on her brow. Her thoughts were in a whirl. How was she most easily to rid herself of him, without his taking offence? She tried to get up, but he increased the pressure on her arm. With his free hand he started caressing her shoulders.

'Get off,' she shouted.

His grip tightened and an ugly expression showed on his face. Maria realised she was a challenge for him. She felt up against the force of an incredibly powerful will and shivered like a pigeon caught in a trap.

'I can eat street walkers like you for breakfast, Maria,' he said. 'Here I am offering you a fabulous future. But you have got to trust me. Put aside all this ridiculous stiff upper lip . . . '

His hand was sliding under her blouse and closing on her bra, then fumbling underneath, his fingers gently pinching her nipples, and she screamed again, twisting around, finding her feet, and kneeing him with a deadly accuracy in the groin.

It was a manoeuvre she had used before at awkward moments on the streets. She had turned it into an art. Johnnie lurched, groaning as he clutched his nether regions. He was incapacitated hardly for seconds however, and before she could escape he gripped her wrist so tightly that she felt he would crush the bone. He shook her as if she was a giant sized pepper pot.

Nausea rose in Maria's throat. She felt as if all her limbs were being wrenched from their sockets.

'You fucking bastard!' she shouted. If he wanted to play dirty so would she! There was no doubt she could at least give him a run for his money. She closed her eyes and fought as only a girl dragged up on the streets knew how. She kicked his shins, and levelled her knee with his groin, but before she could go for the kill, he karate-chopped her kneecap, making her howl with pain. She staggered back then suddenly leapt at him, taking him by surprise. She clawed his face savagely, rummaging for his eyes while he tried to head butt her, fumbling at her jeans, unbuttoning and unzipping them.

He jerked them down, his tongue lolling for her. He was all of a sweat, and lust made his body hard, alert and unrestrained. Maria shuddered at the sight of his bulging crotch. Suddenly Butler screamed. His neck was in agony, as if its flesh was smouldering under pressure of a red hot poker. She was biting it with her young hard teeth, drawing on an unnatural strength. She had drawn blood, and it was seeping into her mouth.

For a split second he relaxed his hold. Here was the chance Maria had been waiting for. She promptly slammed her outstretched palm under his chin. His teeth clacked together like cymbals. She jabbed him in the solar plexus. He groaned and bent double, his head thrust towards her navel. Maria was not one for passing up opportunities. She gripped his black frizzy hair, and pulled his head down frantically while her knee heaved up, smashing his nose.

Johnnie gurgled, almost *hors de combat*. Still he clung to her, as a shipwrecked man might a treacherous leaking raft. Maria wriggled and jived like a cabaret dancer, finally shaking him off, staggering back with her jeans around her ankles, and then pulling them back up so she was decent again. She wasn't going to be just anybody's fuck, except when she chose to be.

She, too, was groggy, and was only dimly aware of the door opening. Roberto came in quietly. Relief flooded Maria's heart, and she took her place by his side. Never had the cunning old bastard been so welcome, for if he was bad, Butler had proved himself worse.

Roberto handed her a comb, and she ran it through her tangled hair, shivering as he put a comforting arm around her shoulder.

Butler stumbled to his feet. Maria let slip a slightly hysterical laugh, and the two men glared at her. But she just couldn't help it, seeing Butler now, the millionaire criminal who had just bungled a simple rape. What a shambling wreck he looked. His hair had been wrenched into a shaggy mop. Red scratches lined his face, as if he had been cut across it with wire. His eyes blinked unsurely, and his nose was a bloody mess. On the floor were scattered bits of his front teeth.

'You had better get the fuck out of here,' snapped Roberto.

'I was just leaving anyway,' said Butler, and strode to the door with incredible dignity, given the circumstances.

Just before he reached the front door, he stopped and looked round. There was an evil glint in his eye that made Maria and Roberto start.

'Don't think I will forget this,' he said. 'Just wait, Maria, and you will wish you had never been born.'

'She shrugged, showing no fear, only contempt. He reminded her of her father, when he had been alive, in one of his more violent moods. Suddenly he was gone, slamming the front door so hard that Roberto started inspecting whether he had splintered the wood, as Maria pulled the bolts and chain in case he or a confrère should pay another visit, this time armed.

Then they sat down. Maria was strangely calm. She was thinking her way round the problem. It obviously wasn't possible to continue working for Johnnie Butler. She wouldn't mind getting away from Roberto either. She had a sudden yearning to be free.

As if reading her thoughts, Roberto flinched. 'We must leave Paris immediately,' he said. 'Don't ever go back into the office. Johnnie Butler is a powerful man, and he may give you one more chance to have sex with him on his terms, or he may kill you. You have incurred the wrath of a Titan there. Could you not have handled him more tactfully?'

Maria shook her head. 'He assaulted me, and I don't have to put up with that. I hope his damned nose is broken.'

'It looked to be,' grinned Roberto: 'Best stop working for him now. Just stay well hidden.'

'Point taken,' said Maria.

She had however made up her mind to demolish Butler, before he could get her, although, for safety's sake, she would be keeping her own counsel. That afternoon, after Roberto left, she telephoned the city police. With a dictionary at hand she delivered her anonymous message in a fierce, impassioned whisper: One of the most fraudulent businesses in the world is flourishing here in Paris. It's under the control of Johnnie Butler. B-U-T-L-E-R. You will easily catch them at it, conning clients world wide out of millions of francs a day for shares which sometimes don't even exist.'

'Oui. Oui.' The officer on the line listened avidly and Maria had to request him to ask his questions slowly as French was not her native tongue.

'Here is the office address, a well guarded secret,' she continued, and dictated it to him. After she had put down the receiver, she contemplated warning Georgio Thomassino against returning to the office, then dismissed the idea immediately. What favours did she owe that crook, even if she was supposed to be on his side?

She and Roberto departed early the following morning, driving out of Paris in his shiny blue Mercedes towards the north of France. Maybe they would return to Paris in a few days, maybe not. Meanwhile, they would have a break. Roberto wanted to inspect some chateaux for sale. A keen if somewhat dodgy property developer and dealer, he looked to buying, restoring some of these and turning a fast buck on them, as there was a mild property slump in the UK. Besides being a criminal, he was also something of an entrepreneur, as he would proudly tell Maria from time to time.

As they cruised along the uncrowded motorway, Roberto spiritedly hummed some Italian songs. Maria sang along with him if she knew the words, perking up tremendously when he introduced her favourite which they both proceeded to sing with gusto: 'O sole mio. Dopo la tempesta . . . '

As pleasant thoughts drifted into her mind Maria gleefully congratulated herself on how she had well and truly put a spoke in Johnnie Butler's wheel.

'Tell me,' said Roberto good-humouredly. 'Were you teasing Johnnie Butler, in the way I know you can do so well? Were you leading him on?'

Maria shook her head. 'No. I've told you before I don't fancy the bugger. All the initiative came from him. He first tried to soften me up with an offer of permanent employment, then he rabbited on about how I nearly fucked up his business deal with Falmouth. However, he didn't waste much time before he tried to jump me. Well all I can say is that he picked on the wrong girl . . . '

Roberto grinned broadly. 'He's a crazy bastard.'

Roberto was driving at a steady 90 mph, and they had not heeded the truck edging up behind them. All they were aware of was a flash of white and two glaring young male faces in the front seats before it hit the Mercedes. Not just once, but twice, three times, and Roberto lost control.

The Mercedes went spinning with Roberto manfully trying to steady it. The truck meanwhile disappeared as a police car drew up almost immediately.

Maria and Roberto, both shaken, got out of the car. 'They tried to kill us,' complained Maria. The police took down details and descriptions, then gave chase.

Roberto and Maria had not been able to give the police an accurate description of the driver but had pointed out that Johnnie Butler was probably responsible.

They returned to Paris in a hired car. They were shocked and frightened but not seriously hurt.

As Roberto was half expecting, the flat had been broken into. Drawers had been rifled through, furniture upturned and crockery smashed.

'No prizes for guessing whose work this is,' he said.

Maria laughed. 'I'd say we have outstayed our welcome in Paris.'

She relaxed in front of the TV while he bolted and chained the door. As he settled down with her for the evening, the telephone rang. It was Lorenzo for Roberto. His fruity Italian accent reassured as well as annoyed him. Where had this big mouth been when he and Maria had almost been killed?

Lorenzo had already heard about the accident.

'You're not hurt I hope,' he said. 'Nor the girl? Well that's good. If you are to make your millions you will be forced to risk your necks occasionally.'

'This morning, just before you were nearly run over, there was an unexpected police raid on Johnnie's office. Butler himself, and Georgio Thomassino were arrested. So were some of the brokers. Others escaped out of the window.'

'My God!' said Roberto.

'Rest assured Butler won't blab about you and Maria,' said Lorenzo. 'He, too, has his masters and if he betrays them he's a dead man, in or out of the nick. His mouth will stay as tightly shut as a nun's cunt!'

'He may even take the rap for others, and go down this time for a good long stretch, the sort of sentence he has nightmares about! Share frauds in many countries – European and other – have been traced back to him. He has wriggled free of justice ever since he served a two-year prison sentence in Quebec some ten years back. He's a master at pulling the wool over the authorities' eyes. No doubt his legal training has something to do with it. His one real hope here is that he's not been selling to French Nationals.

'As for your mate, Georgio, if he stands trial, he knows not to land the rest of us in it, if he values his life! Still, he will probably get off scot free – we will certainly find him the best lawyers.'

'Maria and I are getting the hell out of Paris,' said Roberto.

'Just what I was coming to,' said Lorenzo. 'I have made arrangements for you to stay at my favourite hotel in Monte Carlo for the next couple of weeks. Monaco is a marvellous place if you don't mind treading in dog shit that is six inches deep on the pavement wherever you go. You will have a double room, so seize the opportunity to sow your oats . . . '

When Roberto didn't respond, he chuckled. 'Perhaps, though I don't need to tell you that. During the first three days, you will be attending a business conference in the hotel. Look out there for a Parisian businessman by the name of Gerard La Marche, who is currently negotiating to buy a stockbroker firm in London. He will be there with his half-arsed brother and business partner, Daniel, and they will both be looking out for you. Daniel in particular likes to play in the casino, so you may run into them there. When dealing with them, use your new names of – Dario Abella and Laura Jones.

'As soon as you get to London, and that's not long off now, you will be providing financial backing for their new stockbroking firm, while they will be recommending and pushing shares in "your" companies.

'A blueprint of the proposed deal will be made available to yourself under the name of Dario Abella, upon production of your ID papers at the Monaco branch of the Banque Manago-Suisse, which you will find a mere hundred yards from your hotel.'

They continued talking for a few minutes, then Roberto put down the receiver. He glanced at Maria who was watching him bright-eyed. 'Our next destination is Monte Carlo,' he said.

She clapped her hands gleefully. 'How exciting!'

'Lorenzo insists we leave tonight. So start packing,' he said.

Maria disappeared into their bedroom. Roberto's suitcases, including one fitted with a secret compartment for bogus papers, were lined up neatly beside the door.

She rummaged in a chest of drawers, carefully removing her favourite oval framed portrait. As she knelt by her bedside she gazed at it. Her thoughts drifted back to her childhood. A dreamy look came into her eyes.

Next door, Roberto lit a cigar. He felt uneasy, merely because Maria was out of his sight. He didn't trust her an inch. After squirming in his seat for a few minutes, he got up and pushed his way into the bedroom. The light was not on and Maria was kneeling by the bed. To his annoyance she hadn't started packing. He strode swiftly over, and snatched the photograph she appeared mesmerised by from her grip.

She looked up at him, her eyes wide and childlike, her body trembling. 'It's of Papa,' she said. 'My only memento.'

Roberto in his own turn scrutinised the picture. It certainly flattered Paulo Soccolini, showing him in his prime of life. What a glamorous Sicilian he had been, with his burning eyes, his broad shoulders, his devil-may-care sneer. For a moment, Roberto could see him in Maria. But the girl had to be divested of any loyalties she nurtured towards her father. Otherwise, before he knew it, she would be plotting vengeance.

Maria meanwhile was watching him closely. 'Something I've always been meaning to ask you, Roberto. Who killed him?'

Roberto shook his head. 'Believe me, his killer is beyond the reach of vendettas. Put your father out of your mind for good.'

'I have done really,' said Maria, but her voice shook. Standing up, she took back the photo from him, hastily tucking it in her skirt. 'Now I'll pack.'

She busied herself pulling stray clothes out of drawers and flinging them into her suitcases. She started whistling, as Roberto construed it for his benefit. In a rare moment, he pitied her.

Chapter 4

Maria was excited as Roberto drove them southward bound out of Paris, en route for Nice and Monaco. The night was yet young, and an early evening sunset glowed mauve and orange on the horizon.

Maria slipped a cassette into the player. English pop music conveyed a merry beat as darkness swooped. Roberto accelerated to 110 mph, a speed which he maintained.

They stopped at a small two star hotel on the roadside, not far from Paris. 'It will do for tonight,' grunted Roberto as they entered their tiny plain bedroom. 'Of course it's not what we will have in Monte Carlo, or else it would be intolerable going there.'

They enjoyed a leisurely meal in the hotel restaurant. Both were pigs when it came to French food, even when it was not the best.

'You eat too much,' Maria rebuked him.

'So do you,' said Roberto.

'Ah, but I stay thin,' said Maria.

Roberto patted his ample stomach comfortably. 'I'm too old to diet.'

After they had adjourned to their bedroom, he rushed to open the false compartment in his suitcase. 'Fuck it,' he breathed. It was just as he had thought.

'What is it now?' said Maria. She'd just climbed into bed.

'I've left your new passport behind.'

'I didn't know I was having one,' she snapped.

'Well, you are. And a new name. I'll explain as we're driving back to Paris to collect the passport.'

'What tonight?'

He nodded. 'The sooner the better. So get out of bed again, you sluggard. All you have to do is sit in the car and keep me company.'

It was eleven o'clock, and the roads were almost clear, a joy to drive on. Roberto, although he had drunk much that evening, was cautious and so safe enough at the wheel.

Within five minutes it was as if their journey had not yet had respite. Both were night-birds and could have continued cheerfully for some hours.

'From now on, I am called Dario Abella, and you are called Laura Jones,' said Roberto as they cruised along a straight stretch of road. 'I will be giving you identity papers and passports under your new name.'

'That suits me.' Like her fellow brokers, Laura had used false names in Paris. She was not oblivious to the advantages of anonymity.

Soon they were on the outskirts of Paris. In the centre there was life despite the fact they were in the early hours of the morning. As they approached the flat, they noticed crowds gathered round the block. Warily Roberto parked the Mercedes at the end of the boulevard.

At first, he rubbed his eyes, assuming that what he saw was a trick of the darkness, then he realised it wasn't. White smoke was coiling from windows, doors and cracks in the structure of their flat. Flames were licking the sills. He started the car again and drove a little closer. They were shocked to see how flames had enveloped the living room, glittering and flickering, like a bonfire on Guy Fawkes night. The flames were already spreading through the block.

Dario was white. 'We just got away in time.'

'Let's beat it,' said Laura.

'I will get a duplicate of your new passport,' said Dario as he drove back to the hotel. 'This must be Johnnie Butler's work again, even though he is in custody now. Did you inform on him, Laura?'

'Don't be ridiculous Dario,' she protested. 'Why should I do that?'

Although he dropped the subject, he continued to suspect her.

From their hotel in the early hours of the morning Dario telephoned Lorenzo in Rome. Upon hearing about the fire, the Franciscan promised to send a different passport for Maria by courier to the hotel.

Next, Dario ran a shower. The water gushed hot into the clean white bathtub.

Dario stepped naked under the spray. The water pricked his skin like thousands of tiny needles. He closed his eyes, as he wet his entire body. It was hot and sensuous. 'Fantastic,' he murmured to himself. 'Laura,' he called out.

She came in from the adjacent bedroom, dressed in a flimsy nightgown.

Standing before him, she watched him nude and dripping with an imperturbable expression on her face. For this girl, nude men had once come a dime a dozen.

'What is it?'

'Soap me, please,' he said curtly.

She hesitated, a look of faint repugnance and resentment crossing her face.

'Go on, and I'll do it for you,' he said.

Stripping, she set to immediately, for the alternative seemed to be to incur his wrath. In this she was weak, but also conniving. His skin under her firm practised grip felt as soft as the proverbial new born baby's bottom, as malleable as putty. Her strong hands first massaged his shoulders and back, until he felt that the skin had been torn off his body, then replaced, while his muscles were relaxing like springs released from duty.

She washed him then as only Maria could, spreading lather with the palms of her hands all over his body, lingering in and thoroughly fingering all nooks and crannies, so he already had quite a massive hard-on, before she started giving concentrated treatment to his groin.

One hand gently pumped him while another scrubbed his stomach and thighs.

'That's enough,' he said brusquely, saving himself for the bedroom. 'Your turn now.'

He washed her quickly under the shower, then led her to the double bed. Lust overwhelmed him, and although he was aware that she was responding in a reluctant mechanical way, he really didn't care.

'You are the daughter I never had,' he said. 'Aaah.'

She was soft to his entry, stroking him, willing to please. 'You remind me of my father,' she said.

He started, and pulled away. Their lovemaking was momentarily spoilt for him. 'Your father cared not a jot for you as I understand it.'

'Do you?' she asked.

He sat up. 'Of course I do. You are going to make me very angry in a minute.'

But Laura was already falling asleep. Her breathing was laboured and her body was curled in a foetal position. She looked all her young years at that moment. Roberto, hardened as he was, had pangs of regret. Was he exploiting this girl's vulnerability? He dismissed the thought. She had, after all, been a streetwise wench before his boys had picked her up! Laura was answerable to him, as he was answerable to Lorenzo who reported in his own turn to higher masters. He didn't have much choice. None of them had much choice.

Dario awoke at dawn. He would usually have been fast asleep at this time, but there was a tension in the air that he sensed. He needed to know. Without ceasing his own heavy breathing, or shifting his body, he opened his eyes a crack. With a start he saw a shadowy figure sitting on the edge of the bed. Sure enough, it was Laura. What on earth was she up to? As his eyes became adjusted to the dim light of dawn, he saw her father's photograph in her hands. So engrossed was she in this secret viewing that she appeared to be engaged in a quasi-religious experience which Dario shied from interrupting.

That wasn't to say it didn't worry him. He rolled over, and went back to sleep. An hour later he awoke, and Laura was in bed beside him.

'Slept well?' he enquired.

'Like a log,' she said cheerfully.

Laura's new passport and identification papers arrived by courier during breakfast. Dario handed them to her.

'Never forget you are now Laura Jones and I'm Dario Abella. Even amongst ourselves,' he reminded her.

They recommenced their journey and before they knew it were passing the crowded hot beaches of the south of France. The beauty of the surroundings and the holiday-making atmosphere made them relax.

Once they had reached Monte Carlo, Dario drove more slowly. What a fabulously wealthy town it appeared. 'We should be safe from Johnnie Butler here,' he announced.

'I don't see it,' said Laura.

He nodded. 'I know Monaco well. There are more police officers per resident here than in any other country in the world. That is to protect all the rich residents from thieves and fraudsters. There is also plenty of electronic surveillance here.'

Dario left Laura momentarily in the car, and picked up Lorenzo's package from the Banque Manago-Suisse. Then he drove up outside the hotel entrance. Laura took his arm as they walked smartly inside to register.

This was just the sort of hotel that Dario liked, as Lorenzo would have known when he had booked him into it. It was a five star businessman's hotel, fast, American and tasteless. Minitel facilities were available, as subsidised by the government and available all over France. The Minitel could be used for shopping, banking, indeed almost anything.

Service was abrupt, for the hotel was hosting several conferences at the time and was jam packed with businessmen. Dario and Laura made a beeline for their bedroom. It was luxurious and modern, featuring the latest Trinitron stereo television on a stand. Dario picked up the remote control and flicked through the many channels in French, Italian, American, and from all over the world via the hotel's satellite.

'If you do anything the teeniest bit naughty here, in Monaco, the authorities will jail or expel you without notice or appeal,' he announced with a grin. 'No drug-dealing. No porn magazines. No shoplifting. I'll have to each make sure you toe the line.'

Laura wrinkled her nose. 'What a prison! Not so different from school. My enthusiasm for Monaco has dropped like a stone. Who the fuck would want to live here?'

Dario laughed. 'This is a tax haven for the very wealthy. Many of the middle-aged wealthy residents here are what is known as sovereign individuals or SIs. In staying here they are comfortably avoiding tax.

'Of course Monaco is far from being the cheapest of tax havens. It costs twice as much to live here as in Andorra for example. But the residents here adore the French Riviera, the gorgeous Mediterranean climate, the golf and tennis facilities. The women can pamper their bodies in the excellent health clubs here. The men can hire jets and helicopters, and keep yachts. You will find here in Monaco the largest Rolls and Cadillac dealers in Europe.

'The residents have mostly made their money. They can afford to relax and really live. You'd be astonished how many millionaires, lords and princesses are involved in charity work here. If we were staying here for a while, which unfortunately we are not, it would be easy enough to meet such people. But to fleece them? We would never get away with it. Not in this mini police state!'

'You've raised a challenge now,' said Laura. 'I want to have a go at it.'

Dario grinned. 'I'll tell you a secret. You don't have to be rich to live in Monaco. Even now it is possible to live here for around £20 a day. For that, you will have to live in a room on the top floor of a huge house, with a shared lavatory. And you will have to buy cheap food from the market in Beausoleil two blocks uphill where you can sit in a local cafe and watch the world go by in an ordinary French village. It's just outside Monaco yet worlds removed from it.'

Laura shook her head. 'I can do without slumming it. I'd prefer the swinger's lifestyle. Even if I have to steal to support it.'

After they had both showered, Dario took a bottle of Mumm's champagne from the private fridge and opened it, pouring Laura a glassful. 'Let's drink to the future,' he said. They downed the sweet nectar instantly. While Laura then sauntered onto the balcony overlooking the sea, Dario turned to the telephone on his bedside table, and organised an outside line.

He was put through to Laura's school and asked for the headmistress. After exchanging pleasantries with her, he popped the question. 'How did Maria do in her exams?'

'I'm afraid she failed,' said Lydia Vernon-Jones. 'She will have to resit. Either here or at a crammer. It is unfortunate, but she really didn't study hard enough. The girl only has herself to blame.'

'She is a lazy little cunt,' said Dario, then bit his lip.

The headmistress appeared not to notice his language, so obsessed was she with putting across her schoolmarm's point. 'Next time round she will have to start doing some work. That means she must listen to her teachers! Do her homework on time! We had better meet and have a long talk about it if you want her to continue here.'

'I'll let you know,' said Dario enigmatically as he put down the phone on her.

Laura came in from the balcony. Her fraught expression indicated she had overheard Dario's side of the conversation. 'If I have failed, I won't be crying my eyes out,' she said.

Dario laughed. 'I wouldn't expect you to. The fact is, you are a clever kid. But you have failed your exams, every one of them. Why you couldn't have applied some of your brains to schoolwork, I'll never know!'

'I had better things to do with my time. I was too grown up for school,' she said. 'But I'm amused. Do tell me what my sweet headmistress said. I'm dying to know.'

'Just that you should retake the exams, doing some work this time, and all that shit,' yawned Dario.

'Enough shit to fill a sewer!' grinned Laura. 'What a mooing stupid cow she is! You should have heard her addressing our form.'

Laura's mouth contorted into a leer, her voice into a carping falsetto mime. 'This year is the most important time of your lives, girls. On your exam results, your entire future depends. If you don't do well you will never recover from it. So study hard now. However, remember, you are here not just to pass exams, but also to educate yourselves and become cultured.'

Dario laughed again. What an entertaining little thing Laura was! Perhaps she was right. After all, what did education matter?

'They are blinkered in that school all right. It's about time the fucking headmistress learned a few things about the real world,' he assented. 'Nonetheless, she should have taught you airs and graces, and it doesn't seem she has even done that! I blame her, of course. The real evidence of what a farce it all is lies in the fact she would keep you so long as I kept paying fees, maybe donating to the school's scholarship foundation as well. You can always buy your way into polite society, Laura.'

Laura suddenly looked thoughtful. Was she about to show the effects of her education? 'That's not entirely true, Dario,' she said. 'Some of the girls at the school, the scholars, achieve outstanding examination results, and yet they are as poor as church mice. Academically, I'm simply not in their league, although in the real world I would run rings round them. Of course, I'd never wish to become a bookworm . . . '

He laughed. She sat down on the bed next to him. He caressed her shoulders. 'You are above it,' he said. I won't be making you return to school. Scholarship cuts no ice in the real world anyway, and I know you realise that. Let's zip out to the casino. You can gamble your sorrows away!'

'Well that's not advice they gave me at school,' she smiled. 'But if it's your money, why not?'

She put on a green velveteen suit, with a cream blouse and yellow cravat. Applying eyeshadow and pale lipstick before the mirror, she looked suddenly a sophisticated young businesswoman on a night out. Dario looked at her with approval. He knew that it was to please him she was steering clear of her beloved leather and boots. The last thing he wanted in Monte Carlo was for her to look like the street thief and whore that she actually was.

While Laura was running a shiner over his shoes, he put on a pink shirt with a red silk tie, and a smart grey suit. Then, taking his shoes from her, he opened Lorenzo's package that he had picked up from their trusted Swiss bank. There was a computer print out inside which he started to unfurl. After fifteen minutes' solid reading, he looked up at Laura and smiled. 'We've got a fun evening ahead of us. But I'm not going to spoil it for you.'

Laura, though, was tossing her head as they took the lift down: 'Whom are we supposed to be meeting?'

'A con man and his brother,' said Dario. 'Gerard La Marche is the con man, and I'm told he's a bullheaded fellow. His brother Daniel's supposedly as weak as water. Apparently they are stockbrokers and both easily bought, and furthermore they are primed to do business with us. A fax has informed them of our arrival. We'll be bumping into them in the casino, but first let's eat.'

Over dinner in the hotel restaurant, Laura was quiet and withdrawn.

'I hope you are going to perk up shortly,' said Dario.

'Well what's in store for me?' she demanded. 'I don't relish a couple of surprise bed companions.'

Dario grinned. 'I won't push you. Knowing you, you may not need me to anyway, you're such a little sexpot! But take your mind off your knickers for once. The La Marche brothers are our future business partners. We have got to get to know them. So give them a taste of your charm. Tonight counts most since first impressions are lasting, but there will be other chances. The La Marches are staying at our hotel. They are invited to the same business conference that we are going to. Lorenzo has arranged this so we can meet them properly.'

Laura shook her head. 'You go too far sometimes, Roberto. Whoops, Dario. There had better be a bloody fortune in all this.'

He grinned. 'I'm glad you're not forgetting my new identity. Well there is money in this. Do you think I would be doing it if there wasn't?'

'You might be making a mistake,' said Laura.

He grinned. 'You are a smart little bitch. That's why we wanted you in the first place. But without my help, where the hell do you think you would be? Don't think a little street urchin like you would have been able to afford the luxury of being honest. You would almost certainly be languishing in jail by now.'

Laura said nothing but ate quickly. They left the restaurant early, and strolled out of the hotel. The evening air was cool, and several Rolls Royces were parked just outside. Dario and Laura walked fast towards the famous casino, and Dario felt a tug in his own heart. He loved to gamble and he adored Monaco. But most of all, if he would but admit it, he loved the chance to show this young girl around, to impress her, and to use her. She was essential to his immediate business plans, as well as to the gratification of his lust. Indeed, he would go so far as to say he would find it hard to live without her at the moment, and this despite the fact that he wasn't a sentimental man.

Dario showed their false passports and each paid the fifty francs entry fee. Then they wandered into the famous casino, imbibing the ancient, slightly decadent atmosphere.

The tables were crowded although it was not yet half past nine. All this took Dario back to his own dissolute twenties. But the punters here were mostly not young. They were businessmen in their fifties studying the tables with intensity.

'Messieurs, faites vos jeux,' murmured a croupier. Dario and Laura, who'd been watching the game, sprang to life. Dario placed his counters on several individual numbers, whereas Laura at this stage was more cautious. It was in keeping with his temperament that Dario was going for the long shot. If it came off, great. If it didn't, well what was a 50,000 franc loss? The loss came, as the odds had dictated. Dario grimaced and wandered off to try his fortunes on the blackjack table instead.

Laura remained. In Dario's absence she felt a welcome release. She had always maintained that pleasure was in direct proportion to money spent, and she felt too old to deviate from this viewpoint now. She determined to enjoy herself. She asked for the maximum credit available to hotel guests, and received 100,000 francs in chips. She then started playing with reckless abandon, scattering counters where she would on the roulette table. A few wins drove her to a frenzy, and she suddenly started taking loss upon loss.

The other punters stared, their eyes wide with interest. What was so young and attractive a woman doing losing so much in a place like this? Could she conceivably be here on business of the kind they were all interested in and would pay handsomely for? Why had her forbidding looking gentleman companion left her side? Laura sensed their interest and chuckled inwardly. She hoped they were wetting themselves, the dirty old men!

Only one interested her, perhaps because he was younger – in his early thirties – perhaps because he was an obvious profligate and she liked bad men, perhaps because he was playing still more recklessly than she was, and with much more money.

He looked like an overgrown schoolboy, tipping her a lecherous wink in return for her icy stare. His brown hair was long, almost like a hippy's, and he had a disconcerting habit of constantly flicking it to one side as if not quite at ease with himself. His loose full lips opened and shut, revealing a gold front tooth.

Several killings had bolstered his confidence too much. Seventeen was his favourite number and it had served him well in the past.

Feeling it was time again for its appearance, he nervously and suddenly placed all his chips on the number. So sure was he that his only bet was en plein. The croupier spun the wheel. 'Huit, noir, pair et manque,' he intoned.

The gambler had lost all and felt annoyed that Laura's gaze had caused him to act so impetuously.

As the croupier raked all chips in with an expressionless face, his fellow gamblers murmured sympathetically. Soon, however, they lost interest, but Laura was still watching him.

As he strolled over, his brown eyes glinting, she barely stirred. The top button of his yellow shirt was undone under the loose bulbous knot of his purple tie and his sparkling silver jacket was open. His shirt tailed over his trousers.

'How much have you lost?' she said brazenly.

He laughed agreeably. 'Oh a few hundred thousand francs. Nothing to speak of. I'm Daniel La Marche by the way.' He spoke with a rich cosmopolitan accent. A hint of New York. A touch of London. Plenty of Paris.

'I thought as much. I'm Laura Jones. Dario Abella's travelling companion.'

'Well isn't that a coincidence,' he beamed. 'Actually I suspected that was who you were. It hasn't taken long for us to make contact, has it?'

She half turned, but Dario was in another room, not to be seen.

'You're a stockbroker, aren't you?' she said.

'For my sins,' said Daniel. 'It's a lucrative profession, and I'm good at it, yet I always seem to be penniless. At the moment I'm not in work. But from what I hear from your end, I soon will be.'

'We're all going to be rich,' said Laura.

Daniel grinned. 'I've heard that one before. But there's no one I'd rather be rich with than you.'

'Don't be silly,' said Laura. 'You've only known me two minutes.'

'Sometimes you can just tell,' said the young man cryptically.

Laura was silent. He had hit on something. For want of a better word, a certain electricity between them. Staying silent, she lapsed into reverie. Supposing, oh supposing she was not bound in allegiance to Dario, and his ghastly gang. Supposing she was free. She could be meeting Daniel here, like the princess at the ball, nothing preventing her from romance.

But what a ridiculous thought it was! One of the advantages of her tough life and experience on the streets was that she could be grimly realistic. She wasn't going to succumb to romantic fantasy at this stage in her life, when she needed all her wits about her.

'The four of us must get together Daniel,' she said. 'Where is your brother?'

'He will turn up like a bad penny before we're ready for him,' said Daniel. 'I need him though. He is always my cashier and banker, once I've run out of money.'

Laura giggled mirthlessly. 'Well it's not much good asking me to lend you any. I have just squandered all mine at the tables.'

He laughed. 'You look too young to be gambling here. I wouldn't be surprised if you were underage.'

'I, with all my sophistication,' she mocked. 'Really, Daniel. Anyway you flatter me. It does a lady good to make her feel younger than she is. But something about the way you said that makes me wonder whether you have got a fetish for young girls.'

Daniel laughed. 'Perhaps I have. Perhaps I've got a fetish for anything in a skirt. Of course, I specialise in relieving women of their inheritances. The number of fat rich old bags I have had in my bed would make a list as long as your arm!'

Another man strolled over, taking his place familiarly by Daniel's side. Daniel seemed to shrink in his presence. The newcomer's black hair was short and neat. His intense, well proportioned face was tanned and relaxed, without appearing overindulged. But there was a glimmer in his blue eyes that unnerved Laura. He was like a tiger, constantly watching for an opportunity to spring.

'Laura. Meet my brother Gerard,' said Daniel brightly.

Gerard shook hands with Laura in a formal manner, then cleared his throat. 'I think we have all had enough of the casino tonight,' he said crisply.

'Speak for yourself, Gerard,' cried Daniel.

Gerard grinned, and looked with scarcely disguised interest at Laura. 'You listen to me, Laura. Don't start lending money to that good-for-nothing brother of mine, or you will never see it again. Supporting his profligate habits falls on my shoulders.'

Laura giggled. 'He can't be that bad.'

'Oh but he is,' said Gerard.

'Speaking of which I've run out of credit tonight. So lend me some more money, Gerard,' said Daniel.

'I will. After our business meeting,' the shorter man said sharply.

Laura laughed. 'You two will be the death of me,' she said. 'Are we here on business or on pleasure? I really don't know. But wait here while I fetch Dario. Maybe he will have the answer!'

She bustled away. Dario was hard at work on the blackjack table, where in Laura's opinion he stood a better chance than at roulette. Such a pity it was to break his concentration but still, business was business. Likewise her amusement was her amusement! She sidled up behind him and tweaked his sides with her fingers. He gasped and swivelled roughly, disturbing his fellow players who frowned at this woman who clearly didn't know better than to interrupt a men's game.

'What is the matter, Maria?' he said.

'Laura,' she reproved him. 'Come and meet the La Marches.'

'Wait a minute.' He finished his round, then cashed in his remaining chips. 'It's just as well I've been losing, or I would tell you to disappear,' he said.

'This way,' she hissed.

She made the necessary introductions, and Gerard seemed particularly pleased to see Dario, smiling profusely and shaking his hand hard. 'It's a lovely night. Let's get the hell out of here and find somewhere a little more private, where we can talk business,' he said.

Daniel laughed. 'No hurry. Why is it my brother is always so impatient?'

'Oh, come on,' growled Gerard.

'Business must have priority,' said Dario.

'There is no reason why we shouldn't enjoy ourselves at the same time,' said Laura.

Showing great sense of purpose the group quit the casino as one. 'We'll be back in the casino later tonight, with luck,' said Laura as they emerged into the night air.

'I would be obliged if you would keep Daniel company then, Laura,' said Gerard sourly. 'He is like a child with a toy when it comes to gambling. Make sure he doesn't lose all his francs immediately.'

'See how Gerard talks about me as if I wasn't there, Laura,' said Daniel, walking on her other side. 'What an ill-mannered chap he is!'

'Let us turn our minds to business,' said Dario. 'Difficult as it is, given the lavish beauty of these surroundings.'

Gerard chortled. 'At this time of night, more deals are swung in Monaco than in any other capital,' he said.

'I think I see why,' said Laura, as they stopped to view the sea. It was a warm night, the atmosphere being stirred by only the faintest of breezes. They all came to rest on the pavement overlooking the harbour. Below them millionaires' sumptuous yachts were motionless yet well lit. The sound of drunken merriment issued from one of the holds, wafting across the waters.

'Suppose you put us in the picture, Gerard,' said Dario.

Gerard spoke dreamily. 'We are onto a winner, Dario! The stockbroker we are taking over is barely more than a shell. It's called Thompson & Thompson. Its business was once highly profitable. The firm used to boast 190,000 private clients. You will agree that is quite a feat in the London market. The English are not active investors like the Americans. Until the British Telecom privatisation and others, the average Englishman had avoided the stock market like the plague.

'Since then private clients have been flocking to invest like lemmings, and getting their fingers burnt. The stock market is an expensive game these days. The smaller the sum invested, the greater the proportionate commission charged, and of course the less the broker can be bothered.

'Now private client business is on the decline. Many stockbrokers have closed down, but Thompson & Thompson has struggled on in the hope of recouping its losses.

'Their Chairman, Norman Thompson, is having a nervous breakdown. His wife, Lisa, acting on his behalf, has put the business up for sale. The other partners want out, and are willing to sell cheap. If we don't buy, there are others who will.

'We are aiming to woo back private clients, and to win some institutional business too, on the international as well as UK markets. We will be making money by the bucketful . . . ' Gerard chuckled. 'Of course, all that we'll make will be danger money. Once Thompson & Thompson shows signs of sinking again, we will take to our heels.'

Dario nodded: 'I think we can see eye to eye. Laura and I are fortune seekers, too. We are answerable to powerful masters. If you cross us, they will simply grind you down like pepper . . .

'We can finance your take-over, and your new broking operation. In return you will be promoting shares in our network.

'Ours are promising young companies, in need of venture capital. Investment in them is speculative, I won't deny it. To avoid trouble, you will have to kow-tow to the London Stock Exchange, which is currently going European, so will probably turn a blind eye,' he continued. 'Keep a low profile while you push the shares quickly on your clients. Drum up short term interest, and place all the shares you can.'

'Let's discuss all this in more detail,' said Gerard excitedly. 'I know of a café near here where we can talk at leisure.'

He led the group along the coastline, and up a winding road to the outdoor café of a lavish hotel. They took an empty table, and a white coated waiter glided over. Lighting a candle, he took an order for cappucinos. Dario glanced around him. The café, despite being busy had a relaxed atmosphere. He pulled out a pack of cigarettes and offered them round before lighting up himself.

"They stay open here well into the night,' said Gerard. 'Now tell us more about your companies whose shares we will be selling, Dario.'

'Sure I'll tell you,' said Dario. 'But always remember, what they are really like shouldn't matter to you. We are all going to make a fortune on this deal, regardless of how the shares perform. That's not however to say we don't believe in the shares. You will be the only market maker in them. If you offload a good number, the prices will soar.

'The pivot company is Security Planning Inc., which will be operating from the West End of London, providing security products to major corporations. Clients include some of America's biggest players in banking and insurance. All the other companies are satellites of Security Planning Inc.

'Arguably the most promising satellite is Sampsons Inc., a Nevada based door manufacturer, currently promoting an industrial front door that has so far proved indestructible. Orders for this door are flooding in at the rate of hundreds a month and will soon be thousands!

'Better known still is Safe Locks Inc., who have designed an unbreakable lock. The directors are offering a million dollars to the first person who cracks it.

'Safe Locks is incorporated in Delaware, where there has been a stampede to buy shares. Their price has rocketed, hence the company's momentous expansion into the UK.

'Safe Deposits Inc., too, is dynamic. They make safe deposit boxes for businesses all over the States, and are now receiving bulk orders from Europe and the Far East. We are in a boom area here, and the company has its fingers on the pulse of it.

'The most spectacular in our chain is probably Alarm Systems Inc., who manufacture the loudest alarm system known to man. It literally deafens burglars, and they will run a mile even from the name. Soon we will be advertising this product on UK television and then I swear the punters will be camping outside Thompson & Thompson all night to buy the shares.

'So there you have it,' concluded Dario. 'While you are offering the shares, we will be providing all the financing you require.'

Gerard grinned. 'The poor bloody punters. They will be left holding the shares, I suppose.'

'Dario swallowed, but Gerard touched his arm. 'I understand. This is business. And you're on!'

Dario nodded. 'I'm glad you see that it is an offer you can't refuse,' he said pleasantly. 'I will be visiting Thompson & Thompson from time to time, not necessarily every day. As I am, or shortly will be a director of all the companies whose shares you will be selling, I ought to appear unconnected. But Laura here will join your dealing team. She is a crack broker, knowing how to hardsell while at the same time appearing concerned for her clients' interests. She will, besides, be a useful link between yourselves and me. You can trust her. Now tell me how far the take-over has got.'

At that point the waiter arrived with the cappucinos. Gerard yawned, stirring sugar in his. 'It is down to making the right cash offer. Thompson & Thompson's showing a loss of several hundred thousand pounds a year. Norman Thompson makes out he is concerned for the future interests of his clients, but that is rubbish. He wants only money so he can walk away a rich man.'

'What we want is to buy him up as well,' said Dario. 'We'll pay him a bonus, partly in cash up front, partly in shares, so he will stay hanging around Thompson & Thompson's premises, reinforcing your brokers' recommendations to his former clients where necessary.'

'He will easily agree,' said Gerard cheerfully.

'As I am financing all this, I want results,' said Dario. 'You will need top-notch brokers. Now I could poach some from Johnnie Butler's team in Paris. It's an apt time since their dealing room has just been closed down by the police. All the lads must be looking for jobs. But we must proceed cautiously. We don't want the Stock Exchange to know we are taking on too many con men! We might be better off poaching from England Securities which has a lower profile. From what I hear, a new man is coming to run the company – John Falmouth.'

Gerard grinned. 'The safest thing would be to get England Securities closed down immediately.'

Dario frowned. 'No, our best plan is to inject the poison slowly, without administering the fatal blow until it suits us. That way we can divert public outrage from our operation onto his. There are journalists and MPs who will act on what we tell them . . . '

'We must watch John Falmouth,' said Gerard. 'He is known all over the continent as a business genius who will stop at nothing to mow down the opposition!'

'I could crush him with my little finger if I wanted to,' boasted Dario. 'He may have made millions from his scams, but he's a squirt who will sell his friends down the river and that makes him vulnerable.'

'He won't be our only enemy, and we should keep a low profile,' said Gerard.

'Agreed,' said Dario. 'We won't need to for long. That's the beauty of a grab and run operation like this. We will be done with it and out of sweet England before the authorities have woken up.

'The clients left holding the shares may make money from them, more likely they won't. By that stage, you needn't care.' He yawned. 'Now, will you excuse me *mes amis* if I retire. We are way past what in England they call the witching hour.'

As he paid the bill, he caught Laura's eye. Go after Daniel, he conveyed. She nodded.

Chapter 5

They all went back to the hotel together and dispersed in the foyer. Daniel made for the reception desk and Laura sauntered after him. Although it was 2.00am, there were many people standing about.

As Daniel was chatting up the receptionist. Gerard strode over and clapped a hand on his shoulder.

Daniel started and turned around. 'I might have known it was you.'

The receptionist who had been startled, smiled broadly. Gerard, perhaps not unwittingly, had let her off the hook.

'I'll say bon soir, mon frère. It has been a long night,' said Gerard.

'Haven't you forgotten something?' said Daniel.

Gerard grimaced. He felt in his pocket, took out a wad of banknotes, and passed them over. 'When you have squandered all this, come straight to bed. If you're not up early tomorrow morning there will be no more to come. And while we are talking business tomorrow, let's hear your input. You, too, will be a director of Thompson & Thompson.'

As he turned and left, Laura came into view. 'I'll join you for a flutter, Daniel,' she said. 'The night is yet young.'

He smiled at her. 'That's great. Gambling away my little wad will be so much more fun with you.'

As she accompanied him to the lift, she felt a strange helplessness within her, as if she was being whisked away on a magic carpet and unable to resist it, was lying back and enjoying the sensation. Dario had not needed to push her much to join Daniel, and it wasn't for sex.

'We'll try the hotel casino,' said Daniel breezily. 'It will make a change, and besides, entry is free.'

She nodded contentedly. What she wanted was to be with him.

'Why isn't Dario with us?' said Daniel.

Laura laughed as they entered the lift cage, and Daniel pressed the button. They shot upwards promptly. 'Dario can be, how shall I say it, a little staid. Sometimes I drive him mad,' she said.

He laughed. 'I knew it! We're birds of a feather. Like you, I need my fun and games. In my family I have for a long time been regarded as the black sheep.' He tossed his head. 'Huh! They don't understand.'

'Your relationship with Gerard seems strained,' she said as the lift shuddered to a stop.

He smiled as they came out into a hallway. 'How can I deny it? We are temperamentally poles apart. Gerard is the big businessman in the family. But it's muggins here who has to comfort him when he has lost favour with the authorities. It's emotional support and not money that he needs then. He has to offer apologies and rectify his wrongdoing, and it doesn't come easy. Gerard has probably been in more scrapes than you or I have had hot dinners. But there and again, he has made piles of money. Not that I see much of it in return for helping him like I do.'

They strolled towards the casino.

'He obviously needs you,' said Laura.

Daniel grinned. 'Yeah, as much as I need Gerard.'

The casino was instantly recognisable, with a yellow neon sign, and doors wide open. As it was into the small hours, only the serious gamblers were lingering at the roulette table inside.

'Let's try the fruit machines instead,' she said.

Daniel followed her to an arcade of enormous, glittering machines, each larger than a fully grown man. Daniel quickly changed some notes for coins, and they inspected the various games on offer. They were both aware that this was an infra dig form of gambling, but it was nonetheless all part of the fun. Eventually, Daniel motioned Laura to sit on a stool beside him so they were each facing a separate machine. He handed her some coins.

Together they inserted and played – long pulls, short pulls, in an effort to find winning formulae that would for Daniel settle the ball in the right hole, or for Laura produce the right colour combination. As in most gambling they had some wins and many losses. Daniel lost all his coins first, upon which Laura promptly handed him her remaining stack: 'Go on. You enjoy this more than I do,' she said.

He laughed. 'OK then.' When he had lost this last stake, he rubbed his chin ruefully, reminding Laura of a little boy who had just spent his mother's shopping money on sweets.

'I could change some more notes,' he ventured.

She laughed. 'Don't you dare!'

'That's what I need. To be kept in check,' replied Daniel, half to himself. 'I'm a spendthrift by nature, you see. Gerard keeps me in pocket so long as I support him in his business ventures. But tell me what sort of relationship you have with Dario.'

She shrugged. 'I'm his personal assistant. Dario is involved in a good many businesses. I travel with him round the world, handling his correspondence, his less important deals. There's another side to it too. He fancies me like mad.'

'And you?'

'I keep him at arm's length,' she lied.

Daniel looked at her hard. 'Like me, you're not a free agent. But I know that like me you will one day assert yourself. We're both destined to be free.'

Laura giggled. 'What sweet things you whisper in my ear, Daniel. I'm half inclined to get to know you better.'

Daniel leaned forward. 'In that case, let's quit the casino,' he said. 'Oh yes?' she enquired.

He glanced at her sharply. 'What's your problem, ma cherie? This is a hotel. There are more free bedrooms here tonight than a dozen couples could use on the spur of the moment. Come . . . '

After they had left the casino and had taken the lift back downstairs, she dawdled in the foyer while Daniel booked another room.

'Too bad we won't be gambling further tonight,' he said gleefully. 'The other two will be wondering where we are soon,' said Laura.

He laughed. 'Fuck them. We are cementing the business relationship between both parties.'

'I'll say we are all onto a good thing there,' said Laura.

'Don't count your chickens . . . ,' said Daniel, leading her back into the lift.

Their new bedroom was on the very top floor. Laura was incredibly excited as Daniel led her inside. He felt in his jacket pocket, took out a sheaf of papers, then lay on the double bed reading them, without bothering to undress.

Laura felt really turned on by his nonchalance. It was as if he was challenging her to seduce him. Very well then, she would do it! With a yawn, she kicked off her high heeled shoes, and lay alongside him. She snuggled against his shoulder.

'What are you reading?'

Daniel's eyes were glued to the page. 'This is a report I had prepared for me by my astrologer in Bayswater,' he said: 'I became a believer after following the vague astrological predictions in the newspapers. I'm no longer a beginner, so of course seek more comprehensive enlightenment, and I plan my life to fit in with what the stars foretell. It rarely turns out that I am wrong to do so.'

He pushed the report to her. 'See what my astrologer predicts.'

Laura read aloud: "You can look forward to a few months in which you will reap more than you sow. You will learn what it is to be prosperous. So longer as plenty falls in your lap, misfortune and strife shall appear to be things of the past . . . "

'Further down,' interrupted Daniel.

Skipping some lines, Laura read on. "Sadly before the year is out, all this good fortune will subside, culminating in ruin. Brace yourself for blood, sweat and tears, carnage and darkness . . . "

Laura slammed down the report. 'You don't want to believe that shit, Daniel.'

He chuckled hollowly. 'You think the take-over of Thompson & Thompson will end well?' he said. 'You imagine we are amongst good people? Put yourself for a moment in the shoes of your investors. Or look at the scenario through God's eyes.'

'Stop being so negative,' snapped Laura. She tried to get up, to return to Dario's side but her legs felt as dead as chopped wood. If her subconscious self was willing her to stay, it was because she needed Daniel. The prospect of returning to Dario made her feel drowsy and sick.

Daniel laughed. 'You know I'm right. But perhaps like the others we should look at the future with rose-coloured spectacles, meaning purely for its prospects of instant capital gain. I'm not really of a temperament for that however, and I don't think you are . . .'

He broke off as she touched him. They both undressed slowly, then came together again on the bed. Although she hardly knew him, Laura's instincts had been correct. Here was a man who cared. As he caressed her, she felt her whole body shudder in ecstasy, and she forgot about Dario, Gerard, the business relationship. Her thoughts drifted over her past, dismissing her tough thief's life, her prostitution, her father's beatings and his murder. Instead, she became aware of her deep love for her mother and her dead father, her care even for the men who were ruining her, her capacity to love a man. And she felt she was floating on air, dizzyingly, frighteningly happy as they explored each other slowly but thoroughly.

Afterwards she lay on her side, deeply jolted. This was the first time for years she had let her guard down, that she'd so enjoyed having sex with a man. Even as she felt deeply fulfilled, she was on a more superficial level disgusted with herself. She had briefly lost control, but now would retrieve it. Daniel was a weakling and a compulsive gambler. She should be looking to manipulate him, not to gratify her need for affection. She turned from him, staggered out of bed, and scrambled for her clothes.

'So early!' said Daniel.

She laughed. 'Who's a free agent? I must return to Dario. This is crazy . . .'

'Crazy?' he enquired, but she was dressed now. She slipped on her shoes, blew him a kiss at the door, and was gone.

Dario, as she had anticipated, was waiting up for her. Not that he made it obvious. He was lying in bed pretending to read the hotel's brochures.

'Had a good fuck?' he said without looking up.

She giggled. 'Jealous?'

He waited for her to undress and get into bed then he thrust the brochures aside. 'Did he tell you anything?'

She shook her head. 'He would not have been able if he'd tried. His brother Gerard is the brains behind their partnership. Actually, he's into astrology in a big way. I think the guy is a bit mentally unstable.'

Dario laughed. 'You want me to stay clear of him, don't you?'

Laura grunted. 'Keep your mind on business.'

He shook his head. 'Isn't it funny? You're giving me exactly the advice I ought to be giving you. Nonetheless, you may as well keep Daniel sweet for the sake of the deal.'

'He's putty in my hands,' said Laura.

'You will be dead before I'm ever that,' grinned Dario.

The following morning, Dario had to wake Laura up. 'We are scheduled to attend the business conference this morning,' he reminded her.

The conference hall was already crowded by the time they arrived, although the lecture wasn't due to start for another ten minutes. Gerard, seated near the front, had reserved seats for the group. They joined him gratefully, keeping a place free for Daniel.

Eventually, the conference organiser, a neat slim chap who with his clipped moustache and deferential manner resembled a head waiter, took the podium and announced. 'Good morning, ladies and gentlemen. Welcome to our annual business conference in Monte Carlo. We have a number of speakers to hear today, and so without any further preamble let me introduce our first one. Bruce Nixon, ex-chairman of Hitech Stores. Ten years ago his group took high streets all over the United States by storm!'

The heavyweight businessmen – and few women that filled the conference room – clapped wildly as Bruce Nixon ran up the aisle. It was a startling entrance and marked him as somebody different. With a wild Indian's call, he took his place behind the microphone. How he exuded energy, this tall thin man, jacketless, with a blue shirt open at the collar, and in grey cotton trousers. His pale but refined features under wavy brown hair appeared graceful, almost beautiful.

'Whoopee!" he shouted. 'It feels just great to be opening this conference and addressing you all here today. What I'm going to tell you during this short lecture is how to guarantee success in business. How to develop life long business contacts. How, after making your money, to keep it. And how never to pay any more taxes, for the rest of your life.'

The audience clapped again. He had aroused their interest as few speakers could. The whole room seemed to come to life in Bruce's presence. Few paid much attention to the latecomer slipping in through the closed double doors and taking a spare seat at the back of the hall. Only Dario was jolted.

He couldn't believe it at first. The man who had just arrived, the man in the blue pin-striped suit with unfamiliar steel-rimmed glasses lending seriousness to his plump red features was instantly recognisable as Lorenzo. The Franciscan in mufti caught Dario's eye, then looked away smiling faintly.

Concentration after that was difficult for Dario. Out of the corner of his eye he noticed Laura's attention to the incident. That girl was sharp and she'd be extremely useful to them in the months to come.

Right now he would bide his time, attending the lecture, and doubtless speaking with Lorenzo at the first break.

'Before you go into business with anybody, check him out,' boomed Nixon. 'If you have the right plan, you will succeed in the long term if you and your partners have integrity.

'Emerson points out quite properly that there is an unseen third party overseeing all our transactions. This means that any dishonesty will in the long run spark off its compensation, and you will suffer for it!

'We are all aware, ladies and gentlemen, that the business world is rife with crooks. Sharp practice is the short term solution my friends, and a counterproductive one. Let me tell you a little story from my own experience.

'You have already been told that as a young man I was chairman of Hitech Stores. At that stage, we were an expanding chain of retail outlets which specialised in cut price computers for the man in the street. Relying on low margins and high turnover, we worked our bollocks off, until we had gained a reputation for honesty, reliability, and speed of delivery.

'Profit figures soared over the first two years, and under my guidance Hitech Stores was in the forefront of a highly competitive line of business . . . '

At this point Daniel entered the conference hall. Gerard waved to him and he took the seat reserved for him. He was dressed in a blue business suit and his hair was neatly brushed. He glanced quickly at Laura; she flushed. He had almost entirely lost the previous night's dissipated look and she felt proud of him for it.

'I wanted to raise money on the stock market for Hitech Stores,' continued Nixon. 'My big mistake was to take a stranger's advice on a flotation. I have to admit I was dazzled with the vision of shareholders' funds flooding into the company coffers.' His eyes glistened. 'I saw how the financing would enable me to expand the company, and to improve its services too.

'So blinded was I that I didn't check out the calibre of persons I was dealing with. Quite simply, they were rogues. Our shares were pushed by broking firms in various countries at random prices ranging from one to five dollars. A sizeable discrepancy, for the same shares on the same day.

'The salesmen gave clients false information about the companies, provided by their managers, and, so clients were told, ultimately from Hitech Stores. Of course, I knew nothing of this at the time. Indeed I was led without knowing it into an elaborate web of fraud and deception. When trouble broke out I was, through no fault of my own, implicated.

'The rogues who pushed the shares syphoned millions of dollars of clients' monies into secret trust funds. Hitech Stores Ltd. had hardly seen a cent of it.

'The broking firms then went bust, and with the intake hidden away by crooks, the liquidators were unable to recover the substantial part of monies invested by willing stockholders.

'I sold Hitech Stores at a ridiculously low price to a predator. It was the worst possible time to sell, but I just had to wash my hands of the company and the bad reputation associated with it.

'The defrauders are currently at liberty, probably perpetrating similar scams. I am making no effort to catch up with the rogues. Justice, I am confident, will eventually track them down. These people have ruined not just clients and companies, but also themselves. Their karma is all negative.

'It is through hard smart work that I have made myself a millionaire several times over,' he continued. 'I know what the good life is like. I have lived in a mansion in Beverly Hills with horses, servants and several chauffeur-driven Rolls-Royces at my disposal.

'But even for honest people, the more worldly possessions you have, the more bother and unhappiness will befall you. While I was supposedly living a life of luxury, I had to keep seeing to the servants' problems, sorting out the maid's hassle with her lovers, or the porter's need for medical attention. It was a nightmare, but worse was to come.

'I have been married and divorced three times. Each wife had married me, I realised only in retrospect, for my money. My last wife, embittered after I escaped from her clutches, started proceedings for additional alimony.

'With that I sold up my several houses, my yachts, my cars, and other worldly goods at rockbottom prices to get rid of them, and I fled the United States.

'Fortunately I was prepared for the eventuality. My money was distributed in various accounts, funds, and safe deposit boxes throughout the world. Like the pirates of old, I had buried my treasure where nobody would find it.

'There is a lesson in that for all of you. Be prepared for an emergency and distribute your money so creditors cannot seize it. What the eye doesn't see, the heart doesn't grieve after and the courts cannot order to be distributed. So always assume the worst might happen and prepare accordingly. In doing this, it is essential to become internationalised.

'There is nothing that keeps one more alert, more intellectually vigorous than travel. Now I live where I please, never staying longer than three or four months in one country. In this way I am only ever regarded as a tourist by the fiscal fiends, and am never subject to a government's tax laws. In fact, I pay no tax whatsoever, quite legally, as I have renounced my American passport. I am what an eminent newsletter writer has termed an SI. This stands for Sovereign Individual. To become an SI is to live free. It is becoming the favourite lifestyle of the 1990s. It does not entail breaking the law, so don't muddle my advice with that of pedlars of false passports and ID cards, con men and rogue advisers to the criminal community.

'Ladies and gentlemen, I'm staying in this hotel all week. Immediately after this lecture, my personal assistant here, Carrie' – he paused and turned to the slim blonde seated to his right who smiled encouragingly at the audience – 'she will be waiting for you outside, booking appointments for any of you who require my advice on tax planning, on obtaining second passports, on tax havens like Monaco and Liechtenstein, on buying titles and regaining or renouncing citizenships, on becoming diplomats and avoiding being victimised by scam-merchants. In fact, on generally living a life unshackled by inefficient bureaucracies, thieving governments and con men the world over.

'My charge is around one thousand dollars an hour, although I will negotiate according to individual circumstances. I can also make myself available to you on retainer for a full year, either on the telephone or by letter. I like to enjoy my business relationships, and regard my many clients as friends. Indeed, it is my dream that we will grow ever stronger as a movement, becoming unstoppable.

'Remember, there is nothing to be ashamed of in fighting against the constraints of Big Brother. Every day in the USSR and America, businessmen are imprisoned for technical infringements of laws which they had never even heard about. It's a disgrace.

'Carrie will provide the box number address in Monaco by which I can be contacted. But anyone who visits here, don't expect to meet me in person. I'm a perpetual traveller. Nonetheless, my letters are always forwarded to me, although if I happen to be in Black Africa or South America for instance, the process might take six weeks or so. So be patient. You will get your reply eventually.

'I always check out potential clients, needing to guard myself against the occasional infiltrator. Who knows, there might even be an FBI agent in this very room. Well, if there is I am happy to let him know that Bruce Nixon isn't my real name.' He broke into laughter. 'Officially, I don't even exist . . . '

The audience howled with laughter, clapping hysterically as Nixon stepped down, and ran back the length of the room. Suddenly he set eyes on Lorenzo, and froze.

The multi-clad Franciscan briskly turned and lost himself amongst the crowds, but Nixon remained immobilised. His cheerful face was suddenly tense and his eyes bulged like a King Charles spaniel's. His fists were clenched, his torso half turned in a fighter's poise. Business people around him couldn't help noticing. They stared and murmured, searching for the cause of his distraction, but Lorenzo had already slipped out of the conference hall.

Suddenly, Nixon relaxed. He was himself again, affable and smiling. The entire room seemed to relax with him and he led the mass exodus, picking up his coffee from the table outside, and being charming to the wealthy businessmen who approached him. Meanwhile a queue was forming at the desk of his pretty blonde assistant, Carrie – an indication of the impact Nixon's lecture had made.

Dario, who had observed the whole incident, whisked Laura away to the far end of the conference room where Lorenzo stood drinking coffee, as invisible as a man in the flesh could be. Lorenzo sauntered over to them and murmured to Dario. 'Come to room 143 in ten minutes. Alone.' Then he was gone.

Dario's eyes focussed on the vestibule. Nixon, now half way across it, met his gaze for a split second then looked away. Dario pursed his lips.

He turned to Laura who avoided his eyes. She had seen all, and was doubtless speculating. 'That is my boss, Lorenzo,' he explained. 'You hold Nixon off while I go and meet him.' He laughed. 'They are old enemies no doubt!'

Meanwhile Gerard and Daniel had sauntered over to join Dario and Laura. Dario nodded briefly. 'Excuse me please,' and walked away briskly.

'What a lot of rubbish that lecture was!' remarked Gerard. 'How the hell are you to make a fast buck if you are thinking about integrity all the time? You will just get walked all over.'

'There is something in what he says, Gerard,' exclaimed Daniel.

'That's why you are so angry about it. How can you totally dismiss the idea that people will do repeat business with those they trust?'

'Trust might pay dividends in the long term, a condition even Nixon referred to,' growled Gerard. 'In the short term, it is a different ball game! I can't think why Lorenzo arranged for us all to attend this conference unless it's for the sole purpose of Dario's rendezvous with him.' He grunted. 'It's all a chronic waste of time if you ask me.'

'Is it?' murmured Laura, as nobody else seemed inclined to continue the conversation. 'I found Bruce Nixon's speech fascinating.'

'I'm going to meet him personally now, if I can barge my way through the crowds,' said Daniel. 'I'll obtain his correspondence address here in Monaco. You never know when we might benefit from his consultancy.'

Gerard shrugged. 'Do what you will with Bruce Nixon, only keep me out of it. I would prefer to exchange cards with the other businessmen. Think of the wealthy new clients for Thompson & Thompson we could find here. It's in that vein that you two should be thinking also. But I haven't any more time to waste now. Cheerio.'

Laura and Daniel both watched him merge with the crowds, already introducing himself everywhere and hustling for business.

The girl felt relieved that he had gone. There was an unspoken affinity between herself and Daniel which Gerard's presence had jarred on. She knew without asking him that Daniel felt the same.

Daniel smirked. 'He is practical, isn't he?'

'Like a bull in a china shop,' grinned Laura.

They drifted to the end of the queue in front of Carrie's desk, which had diminished now so they didn't have long to wait. When their turn came, Carrie glanced at her appointment book.

'The next four days are fully booked now, I'm afraid. Would next week suit you?'

Laura smiled. 'Isn't he popular? We won't be wanting his consultation immediately, but perhaps you would give us his correspondence address.'

As Carrie handed over his card, Bruce Nixon in person was coincidentally approaching the stall. He peered over Carrie's shoulder, smiling at the fullness of his appointment book, and yet there was a distracted frown on his face.

'Your speech was fascinating, Mr Nixon,' said Daniel.

He turned. 'You found it so? Good.'

'I'll pay attention to your advice as I make my way in business,' continued Daniel.

'It's only worth becoming an SI if you are already wealthy, isn't it?' asked Laura.

'That's right,' said Nixon. 'You don't need me now. It's when you have made it that you will use me. One warning though. You must be so careful to mix only with the right people on the road to riches. Sadly, your missing companion has struck up with the most unsavoury gentleman I've ever had the misfortune to encounter. Mark my words, if he's not careful, he will be ruined by him.'

Laura lowered her eyes. He had to be referring to Dario and Lorenzo. Why was it he spoke so forebodingly about Dario's boss? Any operation launched by Lorenzo might already be doomed to failure if the man was a known criminal. She felt dizzy with conflicting thoughts which she immediately pushed out of her mind. In speculating, she would only dissipate her energies.

As if reading her thoughts, he patted her arm. 'Allow me.' He took his card out of her hand and scribbled a telephone number on it. 'If you need any help my lovely, you can always get in touch with me, no charge,' he said. Then he was gone.

Gerard drifted over. 'Aren't you lucky!' he quipped. 'You have just had a free consultation.'

'Put a sock in it, Gerard,' said Daniel.

As the two brothers squabbled good-naturedly, Laura slipped away. She made for the ladies. Over the years the loo had become one of her favourite haunts – once for thieving, nowadays for thinking.

She sat on the lavatory seat, supporting her chin in her hands.

One thing was certain, Nixon and Lorenzo had fallen out over something big. Laura surmised that Lorenzo himself may have handled the flotation of Hitech Stores. Was he then the villain who had absconded with millions of dollars of investors' money? More disturbingly, was he on the brink of working the same trick again, this time using herself and Daniel?

Herself and Daniel. That relationship was what she cared about most. In her thoughts she dismissed Dario whom she knew so well and Gerard as well. They were not going to be a part of her long term plans. She had caught on that they were birds of a feather, and she was secretly hoping that they would one day receive their just desserts. Then she and Daniel might run off to be free, clean and honest.

Chapter 6

When Laura returned to the vestibule, Daniel was standing there alone waiting for her. The sun had come out in full and warm, glorious yellow was spilling through the large clean windows onto the grey floor. A lecture was in full swing, behind doors that were now closed.

Young waiters in white coats were stacking coffee cups on silver trolleys with amazing speed. Bruce Nixon and his pert assistant Carrie were strolling away from the hall. As they passed Laura, Nixon winked. She smiled back warmly, knowing that one day, Nixon could be useful.

Before she had time to communicate her thoughts to Daniel, Dario came rushing back. He nodded to Daniel. 'Get Gerard out of the conference hall,' he said. 'We must all return to London immediately. I'll explain in the car.'

Daniel nodded, and turned towards the lecture hall. Putting an arm round her shoulders, Dario swept Laura away. 'We'll talk as we walk back to the foyer,' he said.

Setting a fast pace, he curtly put her in the picture. 'Lorenzo came here for a reason. A new bid has just been made for Thompson & Thompson. The bidder has topped Gerard's offer substantially.

'The bidder is John Falmouth, using loan finance available through England Securities from shareholders in The Merden Group.' He stopped before the reception desk. 'We will go back to London to make a counterbid and to ensure we get our way. While I check us out of the hotel, you go and pack. Round up the others.'

Laura nodded and rushed off. He paid the receptionist, using his Amex Gold card. Every task he gave Laura was a further test. Lorenzo's suspicion of her worried him. 'She is the daughter of a Sicilian. One day she will want to avenge her father's death,' he had said, not for the first time, at their meeting that day. Then he had rushed off, to avoid confrontation with Nixon. He would be awaiting Dario and Laura in his Roman monastery, for business discussions, as soon as the takeover of Thompson & Thompson had been successfully engineered.

As he took his receipt from the receptionist, Dario heard a rush of footsteps. He turned, and with a start recognised Bruce Nixon, flushed and sweating, in a hurry to pay his bill and be gone. Close up,

Nixon's profile was more easily assessed. Dario placed him in his mid forties, some ten years younger than himself.

'You're not staying for your consultancies?' he remarked.

Nixon shook his head as he produced his credit card for the receptionist. 'I am cancelling all appointments. I have no desire to sleep under the same roof as one particular guest at this conference. There is an international fraudster and murderer in our midst. I warn you especially because you appear to be doing business with him. Well, God help you, that's all I can say!'

Dario smiled. 'Lorenzo is just a Franciscan. The poor fellow wouldn't hurt a fly.'

'Franciscan be damned! What a ploy to gain respectability. I wonder how much it cost him to buy his way in to that little game. He has even changed his name for the umpteenth time. Well, we all know of the corruption in the Italian priesthood, but if they are knowingly taking him in, they must be sinking to new depths. Do you think I don't hear about the scams perpetrated from that monastery of his? Do you imagine I don't keep an eye on him? The man rooked me for millions over the Hitech Stores flotation affair. If you are in his entourage, you can kiss your ass goodbye! The police in many countries are hot on his trail.'

'From what he tells me, it is you who were indicted for fraud, not Lorenzo,' said Dario. Lorenzo in that morning's meeting had predicted he might run into Bruce Nixon personally and had instructed him in exactly what, and what not to say to him.

'I cleared myself,' growled Nixon. 'I was an innocent dupe, as I explained in my lecture this morning. But your companion, I can assure you, escaped jail only on technicalities. What a nerve he's got, turning up at a conference like this for decent business people in the best policed state in the world! Well, whatever happens now, that crook has got it coming to him!'

After an amazingly short time, Dario was at the wheel of his Mercedes, driving out of Monaco with three excited passengers – Gerard and Daniel in the back, Laura in front.

'Norman Thompson has recovered from his nervous breakdown,' he remarked, as the Mercedes glided smoothly as a seagull along the Rower Corniche Road.

'I have heard there are discrepancies in his books,' said Gerard: 'I'll bet the accountants have unearthed a can of worms while we've been out in Monaco,'

Dario nodded. 'Taking over this company will be a cinch! As soon as we are back in London, we'll haul Norman over the coals. The old buffoon will be pleading for another breakdown before he knows it!

'As for John Falmouth, we must carve him up fast, before he does the same to us!'

Gerard grimaced. 'The next few weeks are going to be nasty, but we must stop at nothing to get control of Thompson & Thompson, and get our operation up and running. Soon, we will all be so rich we'll never have to work again! Just imagine!'

Daniel shook his head. 'Wishful thinking. Even fortunes don't last.'

'They do, if you invest them,' said Gerard shortly. 'Of course, if you squander our ill-gotten gains like you are accustomed to doing, Daniel, you will end up broke as usual.'

Laura turned to Gerard. 'What is money for if you never have fun with it?' she said. 'If you are going to stay young and sexy, you need to be a spendthrift from time to time.

'All these po-faced stockbrokers and accountants working in the City of London and other world class financial centres invest with so-called wisdom and live frugally, sensibly some might say. But their lives are one long wait for the day when they will retire and enjoy their nest egg.

'Only, that day may never come! They could die from stress long before they retire. Sometimes they will have hoarded millions. But what good is it to them then?'

Dario laughed. 'I somehow think none of us here will make that mistake. Only you, Laura, won't know what to do with your money. I'm willing to help you.'

'I'll manage thank you,' she said. 'You can be sure I won't throw it away on any more boarding school fees for instance.'

Dario laughed. 'It wasn't my money that went into your limited education, thank God!'

'For somebody who is not always responsible for me, you are fond of telling me what to do,' she said.

Dario grinned. 'I'm power crazy.'

'Some of us would prefer to live simpler lives, without being perpetually involved in scams,' said Daniel.

'Cut the bullshit,' said Gerard. 'You want the simple life of drinking, gambling and whoring until you run out of money. Then you are back knocking at my door.'

To Laura, London now seemed stuffy and mundane, full of crime and crowds. Business was business she accepted, but she would have enjoyed staying in Monaco a little longer. With Daniel, of course.

But this wasn't a time for sentimentality. Almost immediately, she was accompanying Dario to a firm of accountants near Chancery Lane.

The La Marche brothers greeted them in the waiting room. While Gerard had been reading *The Financial Times*, Daniel had been pacing about.

They were called into Derek Raybourne's room punctually. Derek, an affable northerner, was a senior partner of the firm, and his genius for bending the rules (and for understanding how others did this) was commended all over the City!

'I have good news for you, gentlemen.' Derek rubbed his hands as they seated themselves at the huge round table with its smoked glass surface.

'Corruption on a massive scale at Thompson & Thompson, I hope,' remarked Gerard.

Derek chortled. 'You are on the right track,' he said. 'The books don't bear scrutiny, that's for sure.'

'We can prove Norman is crooked, then?' said Daniel.

'Crooked is not a word we like to use in our profession,' said Derek loftily. 'Shall we say he has been far too creative in his accounting.

'For example, in the last fiscal year, a £500,000 loss was recorded in the annual accounts. At the time, the financial press took this at face value, but it should have been two million!'

Delving into a brown leather attaché case, he took out a file which he laid on the table. 'Here are the stock evaluations which led to last year's figures. Check through them at your leisure, and you will find they are based on distinctly over-optimistic profit projections. Naturally these projections have already proved ill-founded.' He flicked through the file to a neatly folded page from *The Financial Times*. 'These are today's prices. You can make the comparison for yourself.

'Not just last year, but for the past four years, Thompson & Thompson has survived as a result of shady accounting practices, including gross overvaluing of stock, and other assets. Losses were simply ignored for years. This has been kept from the public. I don't know how . . . '

Dario laughed. 'Journalists often don't dare to attack stock-brokers. Some reporters imagine stockbrokers are above reproach, but nothing could be further from the truth. Most stockbrokers are considerably more corrupt than the DTI authorised licensed dealers the newspapers attacked up to a couple of years ago before The Financial Services Act was implemented.

'Thompson & Thompson, struggling to survive, conveys the impression of being a respectable firm with courteous old-fashioned service. In the light of its books, this is totally misleading. They should have gone bankrupt years ago,' he continued.

Laura grinned. 'Norman would do anything to stop us exposing him.'

'We mustn't threaten him,' said Gerard.

'Quite so,' said Derek. 'Or rather do it very subtly, by implication, so you can't be said to be blackmailing him.

'In summary, Norman Thompson and the previous directors of Thompson & Thompson have committed peccadilloes here and there, and these are enough to ruin them.

'Make it clear to Norman that you would not dream of making your findings public, but that if the firm was taken over by some other party other than your good selves, news of the past discrepancies might leak. The safest thing, he should agree, would be to sell you the broking firm without further ado.

'Incidentally,' he added, showing them out with a smile, 'once you are established there, if you yourselves need an accountant who has – shall we call it – a flexible approach, then you know where I am.'

Meanwhile Lorenzo, constantly in touch by telephone, was insisting that The England Securities smear campaign couldn't start quickly enough.

While Dario and Gerard were concentrating on the takeover manoeuvre, Laura and Daniel found three press reports on John Falmouth's move to England Securities, which had appeared while they had all been in Monaco. The first, an anonymous article in *Truth Search*, a highly regarded satirical monthly, read:

> John Falmouth, who has just been appointed chairman of England Securities, was only some weeks ago negotiating with stockbroker and convicted fraudster Jonathan Butler. The proposed deal was that shares in the Merden Group, with which Mr. Falmouth is connected, should be promoted by Mr. Butler's Paris based stockbroking firm.
>
> Shares in the Merden Group are currently being promoted by England Securities. Jonathan Butler is awaiting trial in a Paris jail. Now, Mr. Falmouth when asked about him on the phone, can say 'Johnnie who?' instead of dropping the receiver back in place.

The second, from a middle of the road tabloid *The People's Herald* read:

> England Securities, the controversial City stockbroker, is taking on board a new chairman and managing director.
>
> John Falmouth, aged 38, claims to be concerned to clean up his new firm's dealing record. He says: 'From now on, England Securities' clients are going to be making money.'
>
> Wishful thinking? Clients should bear in mind that the Merden Group, whose shares England Securities are now pushing, has no track record to speak of, and conveniently has John Falmouth on its board of directors.
>
> The share price is currently at 60p with England Securities being the sole market maker for the Merden Group in the UK.
>
> Mr. Falmouth has great hopes for the Merden Group, which he claims some clients have already sold out of at a profit.
>
> Selling is a good idea. These days, investors are ill-advised to touch any shares that are not quoted on the London Stock Exchange.

The third article appeared in a rival tabloid, *The Examiner*, penned by City columnist Gerry West:

> England Securities welcomes a new chairman, John Falmouth, onto its board.
>
> Mr. Falmouth, aged 38, says: 'England Securities are one of the few stockbrokers serving private clients that are still running profitably. I will be improving its services and expanding its clientele.'

> This newspaper, which has always supported wider share
> ownership, wishes Mr. Falmouth the very best of luck.

After reading these, Dario grunted. 'Falmouth has got just one journalist on his side, Gerry West. What we must decide now, is how to obtain internal documents and memoranda from England Securities, so we can nail Falmouth.'

'If we start poaching their brokers, we can insist they bring such documents with them,' said Laura.

'We must snare their manager. Then the rest will follow,' said Dario.

'That's Simon Hall,' said Laura, who had checked this out. 'We had better fix a meeting with him.'

That evening, Gerard telephoned Dario with the good news. He had just made a million pound bid for Thompson & Thompson, saying this was his last word, and relentlessly hinting that Norman Thompson in person, as well as Thompson & Thompson, were facing imminent ruin unless they accepted his offer immediately.

'Norman panicked, discussed it with his co-directors for a few hours, then accepted,' said Gerard. 'He wants to see us informally to discuss arrangements. He is determined to keep a stake in the company.'

'Just what we want,' said Dario. 'He'll be a useful front man.'

At the boardroom meeting that followed, Dario set eyes on Norman Thompson for the first time. The old man was tall and strapping, with grey hair cluttered round his balding pate. Gerard of course was present, and Norman addressed him as the bidder.

'You will appreciate I am handing over the reins to you Monsieur La Marche largely because I am getting too old,' he said gruffly. 'I can no longer run Thompson & Thompson comfortably and see the company out of the red alone. Not that I wouldn't be able to if I was a bit more motivated and had access to an adequate line of credit.'

'We are delighted you still want to keep your hand in,' said Gerard.

'Yes, yes. I must keep some shares in the firm. It goes without saying I'll be pleased to help you all I can with the clients. I have known them for years. They will do anything I say at the drop of a hat. Of course I'll need remuneration, over and above the terms of the takeover . . . '

'You won't be disappointed,' said Dario.

The takeover proceeded smoothly. Dario, Laura, Gerard and Daniel forthwith started putting into order the firm's premises off Park Lane, Mayfair. Desks and equipment were in the process of being delivered to the luxury offices.

During the early days, Daniel ambled in to sign documents at Gerard's instigation, but otherwise stayed well clear. Whenever she saw him, Laura sometimes felt pangs of regret for what they were engaged in. She noted how uncomfortable he, too, was with it all. Then when Daniel disappeared again, she dismissed such thoughts as a distraction, and joined in the general slagging off of Daniel behind his back.

Gerard was the most scathing about him. 'It's not in Daniel's nature to help with all the donkey work,' he would sneer. 'He's probably out womanising all day. Well let him get on with it! He's a director and he is as liable as I am, although I will be making damned sure he doesn't make as much money as I do out of all this!'

Dario would say something else snide about him, then would usually change the conversation back to more practical matters. 'We must employ secretaries, account clerks and switchboard girls from a temping agency,' he said. 'It would be dangerous to have nationals. Let's have Australians. They are here today, gone tomorrow. When Thompson & Thompson folds, we can rely on them to be unavailable for police inquiries, then to flee the country at the first whiff of trouble.'

'I'll see to that,' promised Laura.

The interviewees, by her arrangement, started trooping in. Dario selected quickly, plumping for those whom he reckoned would be sexually available, loyal, were not too intelligent, and who would be too intimidated to speak should the whistle be blown. And so it came to pass that a covey of Australian quail became the new staff at Thompson & Thompson.

Twenty-three year old Sarah, plump, with curly brown hair, was his new secretary. Forty year old blonde-haired Susan was one switchboard girl. Thirty year old Tracey, with auburn hair and a sunny, freckled complexion, was the other. Twenty-five year old Jamie, with thin brown hair and acne, was the accounts clerk.

From another agency Dario hired twenty-nine year old Delia Lambert, a professional cook who, with her slender figure, her frizzy brown hair and pink lipstick looked like a fashion conscious teenager. She would be spending most of her time in Thompson & Thompson's kitchen, preparing sandwiches and coffee for the brokers or meals for the boardroom.

On their first day at work, the new temps were summoned by Dario and Gerard into the boardroom. 'Welcome to Thompson & Thompson,' announced Gerard. He was looking haggard with new lines starting to show on his forehead. 'My colleague here, Dario Abella, will now have a few words with you on company practice.'

'Thank you, Gerard.' Dario glanced at the new faces around the table: 'Thompson & Thompson is an old distinguished firm, and a long established member of the London Stock Exchange, which means we have passed stringent tests as to our suitability for trading.

'Our performance over the years has been monitored to ensure that we stick to these standards, and is still being monitored now. I am telling you all this so you understand you are working for a firm of repute.

'The clients of this firm sometimes engage in very large financial transactions. Anything that goes on under this roof is strictly confidential.

'In other words, you keep your mouths shut, and you do what you are told. That still applies if your leave the firm, for any reason whatsoever. Understood? Is there anyone here who can't accept these conditions?'

The group murmured its assent, then dispersed. At this point, Daniel entered the offices, whistling chirpily. He was dressed in casual brown cotton trousers and an open check shirt, whereas Gerard, Laura and Dario were all wearing business suits.

As Gerard came into the foyer, Daniel waved the *London Evening Standard* in his face. 'We're in the news,' he announced.

'Let's take a look.' Gerard ushered him into the boardroom, summoning Dario and Laura. The four of them sat round the table and scrutinised the article he indicated in the financial pages. It read as follows;

Take-over bid succeeds

Thompson & Thompson, the City-based stockbroker, has now changed ownership in a one million pound deal. The new chairman, Gerard La Marche, who cut his teeth on the Paris Bourse, hopes to be expanding the continental connections of Thompson & Thompson.

The stockbrokers has been running at an increasing loss over the past three years. John Falmouth, whose England Securities had put in a counterbid commented: 'Too many brokers are up for grabs these days. I wasn't going to pay over the odds for this one.'

Gerard glanced back up at Daniel. 'Popping in on a social visit were you?'

Daniel flushed. 'Come off it, Gerard. There's not enough work here right now to occupy all of us. I'm putting my name to this set up, aren't I? Even though, if you ask me, it stinks.'

'Nobody was asking you,' said Dario.

'It's too late for you to get out of it now anyway, Daniel,' said Gerard with a grin. 'You have signed documents, committed yourself. Nonetheless, as a gesture of brotherly love, I will lend you yet more money. Of course, I won't ever get any of it back – as usual. Take yourself off on another gambling holiday. Try Las Vegas this time . . .'

He started writing out a cheque. 'Don't come back for at least a month, then we will have this all set up. We will need you to participate properly.'

'That sounds fine by me,' said Daniel, pocketing the cheque. He picked up his newspaper and strolled off. Laura had a sudden crazy wish to be accompanying him, so she could restrain him from squandering money, and discuss the Thompson & Thompson situation with him in privacy. But she put the wish out of her mind.

The telephone rang. Dario answered to Susan, one of the new switchboard operators. 'Tim, for the dealing director. On the line from Paris.'

'Put him through,' said Dario. 'Hallo, Tim, I recognise your voice.'

'You heard about the raid on the Paris office?' said the loader.

'How could I not?' laughed Dario.

'Mike and I have been left high and dry. We have got heaps of clients, but nowhere to deal them from.'

'If you come here, you are both to keep a low profile. We're trying to be a respectable firm.'

Tim paused. 'Understood boss.'

'Nor do I want a fracas with Butler.'

'He's in jail now,' said Tim.

'So what?' said Dario.

There was another pause. 'Johnnie ain't gonna like your new set-up whether you take us on or not. It's better for you we're on your side, not his.'

'That is one good reason I'm taking you on,' said Dario sharply. 'You, Mike, the other loaders and any other brokers worth having – don't waste any time on mediocre ones – pack your bags now and catch the first flight into London. You all start tomorrow. And before you go, fill me in with what Butler wants from me in return for shanghaiing his Paris crew.'

Tim took a deep breath. 'A percentage out of all Thompson & Thompson takings. Or it's lights out, he says.'

'I will have to put it to my own boss,' said Dario, thereby terminating the call.

'I'm getting in some of Johnnie Butler's boys,' he announced breezily. 'They know how to sell shares, isn't that so Laura?'

She smiled. 'Thompson & Thompson wouldn't be the same without them.'

On the following morning, Dario welcomed the contingent from Paris into the new dealing room. Tim and Mike were there, with three others whom he remembered as particularly hardsell brokers.

'Remember, I want no one to know you are here yet,' announced Dario. 'Just get settled in and ring up your clients, letting them know you have moved to a highly reputable London stockbroker.

'Tell them there are some excellent share offers in the pipe-line, which should prove very lucrative to them, but that you can't say any more at this stage. Bring 'em to boiling point slowly . . . '

That evening Dario dined with Laura in the flat. Afterwards, he yawned. 'I must be off to Rome next week,' he said. 'You had better come, too, and meet Lorenzo, my boss. You didn't have time to talk to him at the conference.'

Laura hesitated. The thought crept into her mind that she could be with Daniel instead and it irritated her: 'I'll stay here in England right now. Thompson & Thompson needs me,' she said.

'Lorenzo insists you come,' said Dario. 'You will be able to see your mother too. She is working at his monastery.'

'Well I never,' said Laura.

Dario laughed. 'You'd forgotten all about her, hadn't you?'

'Don't you believe it,' she replied.

Chapter 7

It was primarily to see her mother that Laura accompanied Dario on the flight to Rome.

But it was Lorenzo whom she first set eyes upon as she emerged arm in arm with Dario from Leonardo Da Vinci Airport. The man of God was this time clad in his brown cassock which flapped in the breeze. Without a word, he opened the door of his little blue Fiat, slammed it behind his passengers, and drove at breakneck speed towards Rome.

'We don't want to stand around the airport,' he remarked. 'You never know who might be watching us. Italy is full of paid spies and mercenaries.'

Driving up the Via Applia Antica with no lapse in miles per hour, the Padre finally braked outside the courtyard to the catacombs. He ushered his guests into the monastery through a side door.

Laura shuddered at the whitewashed walls and scrubbed stone floors inside. It was practical enough, but so boring. The smell of polish made her want to sneeze. So much work was obviously going into looking after the place. Reading her thoughts, Dario smiled faintly.

'Anne must be doing a fine job as cleaner here, Lorenzo.'

'Lorenzo grinned. 'She works hard and well. To such an extent that I would say she can't miss her sex life.'

'That's my mother you are talking about,' cried out Laura.

'Anne is proud like you,' said Lorenzo, 'which is why she commands the Franciscans' respect. She lives in the visitors' wing, the only part of the monastery in which women are allowed. You two will be staying in the same wing, merely half a corridor away from her room. In separate rooms I'm afraid, but any sleep-walking you may do after lights out is nobody's business I'm sure.'

The visitors' wing was constructed of concrete, and jutted from the back of the monastery like a displaced limb. The large clean windows lining the corridor walls overlooked a garden in which a stony path crossed a showpiece lawn framed with flowerbeds. Beyond was the monastery's own vineyard.

After dumping suitcases in their bedrooms, Laura and Dario joined Lorenzo out in the corridor. He led them to Anne's bedroom and knocked on the door.

Pulling the bolt, Anne Soccolini opened the door. Laura gasped faintly. Her mother had lost weight over the previous months, but was still youthful looking and attractive. Her hair was tied well back and she looked the humble maid of work, albeit with a strong natural dignity.

The two women embraced for long seconds before Laura forced herself back to scrutinise her. 'How are you doing, Mama?' she demanded.

'Surviving, Maria. It's lovely to see you again.'

'I'm Laura Jones now,' said Laura quickly. 'And Roberto's now Dario Abella.'

'I will remember that.' Anne glanced at Lorenzo. 'Leave us alone for a while now please. We will join you at dinner this evening.'

Lorenzo nodded, turning to Dario. 'Come. We'll seize the opportunity to talk business.'

As he closed the door, Anne sighed. She sat on the bed. As Laura dropped down beside her, Anne hugged her tightly. 'There won't be much opportunity to talk here so let's do so now,' she said. 'I have stumbled upon so much that is evil, living here. There are some over thirty Franciscans in this monastery, and everyone of them is a nasty piece of work, with a past to hide. I find it all out by eavesdropping on their incessant gossip.

'Padre Lorenzo is a killer. He's known for it in this monastery, the bastard. The others all admire him for it. I believe he killed your father. Not that he or the other Franciscans ever mention Paulo, but I can sense the truth.

'You and I must join forces, Laura. We must find out from Roberto – or rather Dario Abella – whether it was indeed Lorenzo who killed Paulo. He knows, and he might let it slip. I'll try and get Dario drunk tonight, and you ask him afterwards. Pester him; there's nothing you do better than that.'

Laura set her teeth. 'If it was indeed Lorenzo who killed poor Papa, we must take revenge. It is a matter of family honour that we kill him in return. I'll pump Dario, but believe me it won't be easy.'

'Tell him casually you know it was Lorenzo who killed your father, and watch how he reacts,' suggested Anne. 'My job here is to clean floors and to tidy bedrooms. To keep the church and chapels spotless. I am given comfortable lodging here, excellent food and wine, as well as a subsistence wage. But I fear to assert myself or to walk out without help from outside. Help that could come from you . . .

'Padre Lorenzo is watching me like an eagle, all the time here. I feel like a prisoner under surveillance. I can make certain telephone calls, but I can't even be sure the phone's not bugged. Lorenzo says that if I ever speak to you on the telephone, I will never see you again. What a bastard he is! He doesn't deserve to live.'

That night, Laura and Anne joined Dario and Lorenzo outside the dining room. Before he ushered the guests in, Lorenzo whispered to them. 'Talk very quietly here. The Franciscans appear jolly and unbusinesslike, but they are eavesdropping during meals all the time. And they will gossip like old women.' He laughed. 'They are a lot of sanctimonious hypocrites really. I say this with inside knowledge so to speak!'

A separate table was reserved for the four of them. The waiter served well-heaped plates of pasta. Some thirty Franciscans sitting around them gorged themselves on this simple fare, eating with their mouths open, using fingers as often as their knives and forks, and all bending to eat like pigs in a trough.

There followed a stew and vegetables, in enormous portions. All this was washed down with a sweet and pungent home-grown wine. The diners were soon merry, not least the Padre Guardiano who was gobbling away, dribbling gravy over the bib tucked under his chin, his brow sweating with the exertion of it. From time to time, he glanced over at the guests' table.

'Eat up. Drink up,' he said fruitily in his broken English. Then in Italian: 'Lorenzo, I hope you are taking good care of our friends. We don't want them returning to Inghilterra, thinking that we Franciscans don't offer them the best hospitality, eh?'

Lorenzo always smiled back. 'You know me, Padre Guardiano. I look after them as well as I do myself.'

'Impossible,' the Padre Guardiano would chortle.

'Hark at him,' whispered Lorenzo. 'He's had a few too many already. We are always having to carry him, or another of the crew upstairs to bed!' He winked at Laura. 'You would never get into that state, would you?'

'Don't bank on it,' said Laura slowly. Without looking directly, she noticed Anne topping up Dario's wine glass.

Anne winked at her, then nudged Dario. 'How is my daughter faring in stockbroking Dario?' she asked.

'She is a genius at it,' said Dario.

'Ooh!' Anne smiled: 'You can't imagine how proud of her that makes me. Perhaps stockbroking is in the blood. Was not her father making some strides in it, before he was killed?'

'Too bloody right he was!' said Dario. 'Paulo was treading on a few people's shoes, from what I heard.'

'I knew nothing of it,' lamented Anne: 'Paulo never cared to confide in his women.'

'You must wish he was still alive,' said Dario.

She shook her head. 'Why should I? He was not a man concerned for his family. It may sound very wicked, but I don't miss him.'

Dario raised his glass. 'Well, your daughter is now striking it rich. Within a few months her life is going to be transformed. And so is yours!'

Anne glanced towards Laura. 'Did you hear that, darling?'

Laura flushed. 'I like stockbroking, that's all. Shares are easy money. I bet that's how you piled it up, Lorenzo!' she said.

Lorenzo cackled. 'You are a cheeky little thing, aren't you? Well, as it happens you are right. I've made a fortune out of stockbroking just as Dario and you are going to to.'

Dario started laughing, while Anne behind his back again refilled his glass.

'You look pretty tanked up, Dario,' warned Lorenzo.

'I'm only old once,' rejoindered Dario, picking up his glass and downing its entire contents in one gulp.

'None of us is getting any younger,' sighed Anne.

'The best way to stay young is to join the Franciscans,' said Lorenzo. 'I'm sheltered from the world. It's a dream life, despite the hardships of prayer.'

Dario shook his head. 'You have seen so much of life, Lorenzo, there's nothing more you can learn about it!'

Lorenzo smiled faintly. 'Dario considers me a worldly soul.'

'So do all the Franciscans here, do they not?' said Anne sweetly.

Lorenzo beamed, but his eyes were cold. 'There's too much gossip here by half. You should turn a deaf ear. Indeed, you have been told to, Anne.'

Shortly after this conversation-stopper, the four of them adjourned for the night. 'Be up bright and early to talk business,' ordered Lorenzo as he saw Dario and Laura to their rooms.

Laura found her bedroom chilly, its bareness not agreeing with her. She did, however, appreciate the solitude. She lay on her bed waiting some twenty minutes before she would be rejoining Dario and pumping him for confirmation that it was Lorenzo who had killed her father.

When a knock came on the door, she knew it was her mother's. Sure enough, Anne stood on the threshold, her features flushed and her eyes too wide, almost feverish. Laura smiled warmly, and beckoned her in, closing the door noiselessly behind her.

Anne had brought with her a cardboard box which she handed to her daughter: Laura glanced inside. It contained a bottle of Scotch, a bottle of soda water, and two tumblers.

'Offer Dario another drink,' said Anne. 'The more pissed he is, the more chance you have of bludgeoning out of him the information we need. Say freely that you got the whisky from your mother. The Franciscans allow me to keep alcohol in my room!'

Laura nodded. As Anne tiptoed out, she pressed her arm. 'Why not stay a little longer?'

'No. You have got work now with Dario. We'll talk again after you have done it.' She giggled. 'In the early hours of the morning, no doubt.'

Dario was in Laura's room before she got round to visiting his. He arrived just in his underpants, with a pronounced bulge in his crotch. Well, relief wouldn't come cheap for him, Laura told herself. He was walking unsteadily already. She saw that there was nothing a little more booze wouldn't do. Soon his tongue would be wagging like an old woman's, she would make sure of that.

'Come to bed, darling,' she said, and undressed herself quickly, as he swayed over the bed. He spotted Anne's box and looked inside. 'Ooh, a nightcap,' he said in delight, withdrawing the whisky bottle. He unscrewed the top, held back his head and swigged from the bottle neat.

'Leave that alone!' snapped Laura. 'I'll pour you a drink in a moment.'

'No water in it please.' He yawned and, throwing his underpants onto the floor, climbed into the bed, snuggling naked under the sheets. He gazed at Laura. She was naked too. Her nightdress lay abandoned over the clothes in her open suitcase.

She poured him a neat whisky, filling a tumbler and emptying around a third of the bottle. If that didn't make him blind drunk on top of all the wine he'd downed, what would? she asked herself. She poured herself a weak whisky and water, and brought the drinks over to the bed. She switched out the main light leaving on the little bedside one, then climbed in beside him.

It was a single bed and there was hardly room for the two of them. 'Budge over,' she said, and shoved him.

'Careful,' he said spilling a little whisky as he shifted. Then he drank half the tumblerful in one gulp. 'Just because the Franciscans are celibate, it doesn't mean their guests are. Lorenzo should have made special arrangements for a double bed.'

'If he did, he would be drawing unnecessary attention to himself,' said Laura. 'Not a good idea. Lorenzo has got a controversial enough reputation here as it is.'

Dario looked at her sharply. 'What do you mean by that?'

She shrugged. 'Mama was telling me how the Franciscans gossip about him incessantly. They know he is a killer, and that he killed my father. Had Papa been treading on his toes, Dario? Perhaps you could put me in the full picture.'

Dario lowered his eyes. 'What does it matter now? Your father had a flair for stockbroking. But he got too greedy and tried to blackmail his bosses.'

'Is that why Lorenzo killed him?' she demanded.

'Of course. He doesn't go around killing people just for fun. There now, I've let it slip it was he who did it. I should not have told you.'

'As I've just made clear, I knew already, so put it out of your mind Dario,' she said.

But Dario was already breathing hard. He was too drunk to stay awake. Too drunk for sex, much to Laura's relief. She took his glass before he could drop it. Mission accomplished, she told herself.

After he had been sleeping for a solid half hour, she inspected him. He lay like a rag doll, his eyes closed, snoring aloud. The lines showed on his ancient and lecherous face. An earthquake would not have awakened him!

She left his side noiselessly, tiptoeing across the floor, digging a dressing gown and slippers out of her case. Decently clad within seconds, she escaped from her own room.

Anne's door opened even before Laura could knock. The girl sunk into the shadows. Could a Franciscan be lying there in wait for her? But it was her mother who peered out, bright-eyed. Laura stepped forward again, and Anne beckoned her inside, closing the door so they were plunged into darkness. 'I knew you were in the corridor.'

Laura laughed. 'How could you have done? I was dead quiet!'

'Telepathy perhaps?' suggested Anne.

Laura sat on the bed. Anne switched the bedside light on. 'Well?'

Laura blinked. 'Lorenzo did kill Paulo. Dario let it slip, just as you hoped he would.'

Anne bit her lip. 'Whatever we thought of our Paulo, that's between ourselves. We cannot see him murdered, lying down. As Sicilians, we must take our revenge.'

'We will kill him,' said Laura. 'Don't give him any hint of what we are plotting. I'm going to make a bomb out of this scam, then we'll do it. I will have enough money for both of us afterwards to get the hell out of Italy.'

A dreamy look came into Anne's eyes. 'I knew you would help me again. You are a wonderful daughter. I'm not worthy of you.'

'What rubbish you talk! The monastery is having a bad effect on you,' said Laura. She kissed her mother. 'I had better rush back,' she said.

To her dismay, Dario was awake. She sensed it even as she entered the room. But it wasn't until she had closed the door that he sat up with a frown. 'Where have you been?'

Laura giggled. 'Can't I even go to the toilet without waking you and letting you know?'

Dario shook his head. 'You were a bloody long time.'

He resettled to sleep before she did. As she lay awake, she plotted gleefully. First she would make her pile. Then she would help her mother kill Lorenzo. She would stick two fingers up at her associates, and then run away to make a new life for herself. Alone, not even with her mother. She craved not to be encumbered with anyone, except perhaps Daniel. The girl who'd had too much responsibility thrust on her too young was now itching to be free.

The morning seemed to arrive before the night had begun. So busy with concrete plans and laden with anxieties had her mind been that Laura hadn't slept a wink. But when Dario awoke, she kept her eyes closed, pretending to snore. She was determined not to give him the slightest hint of her thoughts. If she did, he might catch on, and scupper her plans. Anything might happen. She could be killed. Anne could be killed. If ever a time for discretion was advisable, it was now, until she had achieved her objective.

If it wasn't for the money she stood to gain from the scam, she would be pressing ahead with killing Lorenzo and escaping from her associates *immediately*.

As she wasn't getting up in a hurry, Dario followed suit and turned over with a grunt, returning to sleep. Not unsurprisingly, they were up too late for breakfast, and so dispensing with it made their way straight over to the monastery library where Dario had confirmed they would be meeting.

This library, typical of its kind, did not seem quite right for business discussions. It was a large tidy room smelling of polish with huge wooden tables, and shelf upon shelf of old musty books. Dario seated himself at a table, picking up *The International Herald Tribune*, while Laura strolled about inspecting the books. The Franciscans seemed to have gruesome tastes: The Spanish Inquisition; The French Revolution; The Persecution of the Ancient Christians.

'They're a bloodthirsty lot,' she remarked.

But Dario was glancing towards the door even as it was being opened.

Lorenzo breezed in. His smile indicated that he had overhead Laura's comment.

'We read all that for release. In our practical lives, we have hearts of gold,' he said good humouredly.

A slim man with a moustache was accompanied the Franciscan. 'Georgio,' exclaimed Dario.

The two men briefly embraced. Georgio nodded to Laura, too. He was clad in a smart blue suit, and was looking, if tired, relaxed and happy.

'I was released from the Paris nick only yesterday,' he announced. 'Lorenzo picked me up at the airport very early this morning. I know of your new identities. I'm primed as to what is going on. Boy, aren't we all gonna make a lot of money!'

'Johnnie Butler is still in the nick, foaming at the mouth, but they won't let him out yet, even though he keeps offering them every deal, every bribe, every threat under the sun! He knows too all about Thompson & Thompson and wants his cut!'

'It's out of the question,' said Lorenzo.

'Yeah, sod him,' said Georgio gleefully. Only Lorenzo knew that he now at last had good reason to be confident. The Franciscan would that very day be contacting a politically well connected lawyer on Georgio's behalf, to get him a Brazilian passport. This would cost about $35,000 which Lorenzo had insisted on paying himself.

Once the passport was in his possession, Georgio Thomassino could always run away to Brazil, which might be desirable if England became a little hot for him.

Once in Brazil he could always pick up one of the women keen to marry a wealthy foreigner, or to bear his child.

There was an amazingly useful regulation that no Brazilian could be extradited. A quick way of becoming a Brazilian was to father a child by a Brazilian woman.

It was only with this escape route in hand that Georgio Thomassino was prepared to co-operate further in Lorenzo's plans. A spell in the Paris jail with the prospects of a stiff sentence had shaken him. Lorenzo's lawyers had negotiated his release, but this might not have been possible!

With all the preliminaries over, the meeting began quickly. While the others were seated, Lorenzo started the ball rolling, pacing the room as if fuelled by the sweep of his own oratory.

'Thompson & Thompson is indisputably ours now. We are in the business of selling our own shares. So let's pump out the shit immediately. You, Dario will be supervising the entire operation. All of you remember, assuming we are successful, you will be set up for life!

'Dario, under your new name, you will be Thompson & Thompson's financier. On the other hand, you are listed under your real name, Roberto Calafato, as managing director of Security Planning Inc., and as a director of every satellite company. Roberto Calafato in person will never be seen. The fact that Roberto Calafato, the company magnate, and Dario Abella, the financier are one and the same person must never leak out.

'If it does by accident, though, nobody will prove you have been financing Thompson & Thompson, since there will be no available record of it. Monies required will be paid from our Liechtenstein trust into Thompson & Thompson's secret Austrian bank account. How much more private can you get? We are avoiding a Swiss account since it can no longer be relied on for confidentiality. In addition, very few monies will be paid out. The cash flow will be one way traffic, Thompson & Thompson being largely run on credit.'

Lorenzo then switched his attention. 'You, Georgio, will be chairman of Security Planning Inc. We will get the papers signed up today, once Dario and Laura have departed for London.

'In your office off St. James' Square, you, Georgio, will be processing orders for new doors, alarm systems, security deposit boxes, in fact any product marketed by the network.

'You will have a list of the institutions we are expecting to sting, in which we have moles planted. Obviously, the firm's names are top secret, and I will not be revealing them in front of our colleagues here. No offence intended, but you are all only being told what you have to know.

'Even you, Georgio, will not yet know exactly when the robberies we are planning will take place, the methods we will be using, and the envisaged haul.

'We must ensure Thompson & Thompson has offloaded all the shares first,' said Dario.

Lorenzo allowed himself a tired grin. 'There will never be enough time, Dario.'

Laura half raised a hand, and Lorenzo glanced at her. 'After the robberies have been sprung, who will have faith in our security products again?' she said.

Lorenzo shrugged. 'The stock market is an unpredictable animal. Our group may retain credibility. The share prices may be sustained, may even go up.

'On the other hand, perhaps they will plummet. Who cares? Thompson & Thompson will have disposed of as many shares as it can by that stage. You three will then quietly vanish from the scene.'

'Leaving the La Marche brothers to carry the can,' said Laura.

'And old Norman Thompson no doubt,' added Dario gleefully. 'You're a genius Lorenzo.'

Lorenzo beamed. 'Believe me, I'm an old hand at the game. This scam will work. When I organised a similar one with Hitech Stores in the States we got away with several hundred million dollars in less than a year. The SEC is still trying to establish fraud, but doesn't know where to start. Regulations in the UK even more than in America are riddled with loopholes, which changes brought about by the Financial Services Act haven't even begun to eliminate.'

'I'm surprised you're not in hiding, Padre Lorenzo,' said Georgio.

'In a sense, I am,' said Lorenzo. 'This monastery is crawling with electronic security systems. I'm safe here, provided I keep my wits about me. There is always a risk of an attack from the inside. As for the world at large . . . '

He caught Dario's eye. 'Why do you think my appearance at the business conference in Monte Carlo was so brief?'

'The main threat to Thompson & Thompson clearly won't be the regulatory authorities,' said Dario. 'We have the most to fear from our business rivals like England Securities. We will be poaching England Securities' brokers, and attacking their firm on all fronts. John will want to crucify us.'

Lorenzo smiled. 'Falmouth will soon be facing criminal action in relation to his own inside dealings. The Department of Trade and the regulatory authorities are zooming in on him. If Thompson & Thompson can't thwart that raving coke addict, then you, Dario and the La Marche brothers aren't the men I thought you were.'

'Gerard is at this moment going it alone,' said Dario. 'He's sent Daniel on an extended holiday.'

'Daniel is a useful restraining influence,' said Laura.

Lorenzo shrugged. 'Once the millions start rolling in, nobody will be exercising any restraint.'

At this natural break, the door opened. Anne entered carrying a dust pan and brush. She raised her eyebrows politely at Lorenzo.

'We're finished now, so come in and clean,' he invited her.

At midday, Dario and Laura returned to the airport. London was only a few hours' journey away and they were back that night. By nine o'clock the following morning, it was as if they had never been away.

A laid-back atmosphere was to be found in the office as the brokers were waiting to start trading. All were sitting around with their feet up, drinking coffee and ringing up their own brokers for personal dealings. Even in their present idleness, these brokers in unison exuded a raw, uncontrollable power.

Laura, prompted to it by Dario, rang Simon Hall, the dealing manager of England Securities, from the boardroom. Once she had been put through, she could hear the bracing noise of his dealers. The shouts, the buzz, the excitement! How it made her mouth water! What lust to start dealing again it evoked in her!

'Simon Hall,' the dealing manager curtly introduced himself.

'Hallo, Simon. It's Laura Jones from Thompson & Thompson,' said Laura.

'What is it?'

'Would you be interested in tripling your income, for less work than you're doing now?' she asked.

He paused. 'I might be. What is this all about?'

'We would like you to meet us at Thompson & Thompson here off Park Lane, to discuss a new job we're offering you.'

'I'll be there,' he said.

They scheduled a time quickly and then he rang off. Laura felt thrilled that she was contributing in this way to the structuring of the new dealing room, and then guilty. When would Daniel be back? she wondered. She would have liked to discuss it all with him!

Meanwhile, England Securities was revving up for work. The dealing manager, Simon Hall, put down the telephone receiver and smiled. The proposal had come out of the blue and to be honest, it sounded hot. If it wasn't a wind-up, if he was really offered three times his present income, he would take it like a shot.

He got up and paced about. Simon was a bullnecked young man with broad shoulders and a heavy tread. Everything about him was solid and forceful. He knew how to scare the shit out of his dealers, which he regarded as synonymous with motivating them.

Like his colleagues in the City, what motivated him was money, pure and simple. He craved more of it all the time. Not that he hadn't already made enough to set him up for life. Not so much from his income as from the use he put his earnings to.

He had stumbled upon his biggest moneyspinner quite by accident. At a party, he had met a lawyer specialising in fiscal matters who urged him to become a passive underwriter at Lloyd's. All he would need to show would be that he had at least £250,000 in liquid assets.

Simon promptly made some independent inquiries, only to discover that 40,000 members were discreetly creaming off excellent returns over a period, despite some losses.

He selected a good underwriting agent, and duly had his sponsoring and nomination form (from the lawyer, who was an existing member) lodged with and approved by Lloyd's. This had been done as required before June 30th of the year preceding membership. During the following six weeks, his worth was verified by a Lloyd's approved bank, and he was accepted as a candidate. He signed various papers and syndicate underwriting contracts.

The next stage was an interview with the Lloyd's Rota Committee who stressed that underwriting was a high risk business and that his liability was unlimited, to the extent that his estate would inherit any losses (or gains) when he died.

He then provided the prerequisite standby letter of credit from his bank. As he was not considered a good credit risk (concealing much of his money, unknown to his bank manager, offshore), he had to place cash as collateral with the bank, equivalent to the face value of the letter of credit he was demanding.

He was sent regular reports on the progress of his underwriting syndicates. Cash was distributed to him from underwriting profit, from investment income, from reinsurance gains and losses, and from a Special Reserve Fund he was permitted. He found he was earning ten to fifteen per cent of premium income.

The biggest advantage of Lloyd's, he realised, was that his capital was employed to earn a double return, first by gaining interest benefits, and secondly by earning income as his assets backed the underwriting of insurance risks.

Cleverly, Simon had minimised the risks by going into Lloyd's at the maximum premium limit and by instructing his underwriter to spread his risk amongst a large number of syndicates.

All that kept him awake at nights these days was his fear of the risk of losses through fraud – although his stop loss insurance was a substantial buffer to that. He judged the professionals at Lloyd's by a few bad apples that had emerged from the basket in the past – and by himself. Cynicism, he told himself, was always healthy.

He returned the favour to the lawyer by giving him red hot inside tips on shares dealt at England Securities and elsewhere. His tax specialist duly made several killings on the stock market, with the result that the two became firm friends, and frequent partners in business deals.

Now Thompson & Thompson seemed to be offering Simon another chance to make a killing, and naturally he was interested. On the appointed day, he duly arrived at the premises of Thompson & Thompson, and paced about the reception area, until he was greeted by a smiling Laura (God, she was attractive enough) and taken into the board room to meet the big boys, Gerard La Marche and Dario Abella – foreigners by the sound of it. Well that didn't bother him, so long as they spoke the Queen's English!

They didn't beat about the bush, which impressed him. 'We want you to run our new dealing room,' announced Gerard. 'For joining us we're offering you a golden welcome of £30,000. This will be in cash, and unrecorded, so you needn't let our friendly Inland Revenue, or any other party for that matter, know about it.

'We will then pay you a basic of £2,000 a month, as well as fifteen per cent commission on all the business done in the dealing room. The target will be £750,000 worth of business a day.'

'That's a bit steep,' said Simon bluntly. 'We rarely do more than £500,000 worth a day at England Securities.'

'We are paying you and your brokers more, for better results,' said Dario. 'We will pay the brokers ten per cent commission on business achieved. The shares they recommend will be what Thompson & Thompson chooses to sell.'

'I would expect that,' said Simon.

'You will have to bring the best brokers from England Securities to work here,' said Gerard. 'You will have the power to hire and fire as you please. Any broker you bring can have £5,000 cash under the table after his first month.'

'That might not be enough,' said Simon.

'They will get that nowhere else,' said Dario.

'The good brokers are already earning big money,' said Simon.

'What do you mean by big?' asked Dario.

Simon paused. 'Perhaps fifty or sixty grand a year.'

Dario laughed. 'They will triple their income with us, just as you will.'

Simon frowned. 'They'll follow me,' he said finally. 'They all think the sun shines out of my arse!'

'England Securities are in hot water now. They must all know that,' said Dario.

'That doesn't take much working out,' said Simon drily. 'But is Thompson & Thompson likely to last?'

'Of course,' said Gerard. 'We have a good reputation. Ask anybody. Furthermore, the shares you will all be selling will stand up. There is serious money behind the company too. We're not living off overdrafts like England Securities.'

'OK. Hand over the thirty grand and you're on.'

'Steady on,' grinned Dario.

Simon took out a packet of Marlboro and offered them round. The two older men politely refused. He lit a cigarette, and inhaled deeply, blowing out a cloud of smoke like a dragon preparing to breathe fire. 'Now I know my men. I know how to run a dealing room,' he said. 'If you want this done properly, you must leave me to do it my own way.

I'm a hard man to please, and any broker who messes me about, he's out. But I'll get you the results.

'I've been in the stockbroking business for three years. At England Securities I've organised the selling of so much shit that some more of it won't give me any headaches.

'I've sold shares in an oil company that didn't even have a hole in the ground, in a recording company whose records were all losers. I have pushed little Australian and North American stocks that existed only on paper. A favourite of mine was a technology company that went bust overnight after we had offloaded £7 million worth of its shares.'

'What do you think of John Falmouth?' asked Gerard.

Simon laughed harshly. 'The man's a fire-fighter, staving off one crisis only to be confronted with another. But my God, he's clever. He likes to pretend he's one of the lads, off the dealing floor as well as on it. That way he discovers the brokers' individual weaknesses, so he can stitch them up the more thoroughly.

'A couple of his brokers are indebted to him to the tune of tens of thousands of pounds, which they are paying back in instalments deducted from their monthly commission cheques. This is money they lost on personal account trades, the fucking idiots. Those two won't be coming with me to Thompson & Thompson in a hurry . . . '

'Something else,' said Dario. 'Get us any written memos, bargain slips, pitches, anything that can be used in evidence against England Securities.'

Simon grinned. 'A smear campaign! There's nothing I like better. The timing is perfect too. The Department of Trade and the regulatory authorities are investigating England Securities' dealing in the Merden Group in particular. Our brokers appear to have the knack of selling to clients just before the price drops, with the firm buying back from them just before it rises again.

'There's clear circumstantial evidence of a breakdown of Chinese Walls. Whether the authorities can act on it is a different matter. But England Securities is vulnerable now, although nothing to what it will be once my men and I have deserted the sinking ship.'

'We intend approaching Dominic Gardiner,' said Dario. 'There is nothing like having in your court an MP committed to exposing corruption in the City.'

'He'll bite,' said Simon lightly.

'What makes you so sure?' said Dario.

'He is already a client of England Securities, and from what I understand, a dissatisfied one,' said Simon.

Chapter 8

On the way home that night, Simon felt lightheaded. He kicked several times at an imaginary football as he walked along the pavements. It was as if years had been lifted off his shoulders. Here was the opportunity Simon had been looking for to lead a coup.

He was particularly looking forward to the shock that it would bestow on John Falmouth's system. The chairman would be able to retrieve the situation only by forking out lots more money all round, which was out of the question given that England Securities was under investigation, even if he could force himself to overcome his usual miserliness. But Simon wanted bigger money, and he wanted it now. Hence he was leaving.

It was dark by the time he let himself into his six bedroomed house in St. George's Hill. His wife, Donna, was sitting in front of the TV, knitting. She was a sturdy girl in her late twenties with blonde plaits who was still pursuing her own career part-time as a nurse.

Their six year old boy Mark lay on the floor, doing his homework. After he had kissed his wife, Simon bent down and watched the child colouring in a map of England. Mark suddenly glanced up. 'Daddy,' he gurgled.

'Good boy,' said Simon running his fingers affectionately through his hair. He noticed Donna glancing at them with a strange expression on her face that he, just for an instant, interpreted as jealousy.

Before settling down with his family for the evening, Simon went to the telephone in the hall. He rang his top ten brokers one by one in their homes. He managed to get hold of only five. 'We're having a secret meeting after work tomorrow,' he told them. 'I'm saying nothing more now. Just make sure you are at the Riverside Inn at six o'clock sharp. No one will be made to stay late at work tomorrow.'

Next he telephoned his favourite West End escort agency and made a group booking.

He then slumped in front of the TV next to his wife, putting his arms round her shoulders.

She smiled at him. 'Did work go well today?'

'So so,' he said. 'I'm moving soon to another company.'

She started. 'Somewhere reputable I hope.'

'I hardly think so,' he grinned.

She pursed her lips. 'Sometimes I worry about you.'

'You're quite happy to live on my earnings, aren't you?' said Simon.

'Sorry I spoke,' she said huffily, concentrating again on her knitting. She was making a thick jumper for Simon.

That night, Donna went to bed early, checking Mark was asleep before she started undressing. When Simon followed suit, Donna was asleep on her back, snoring raucously. Undressing quickly, he shook her awake.

It was a typical late night session between them, with all the thrill of the rape. Donna enjoyed it as much as Simon did. Firstly she struggled like a cat in his grasp. She clawed his face, and pulled at his testicles, kicking, hitting and spitting, but he pitted his weight against her until she yelped.

She play-acted that the release he offered her was more than she had bargained for. Simon raised her nightdress in a twinkling, and she found herself forced to accommodate her husband's groping hands. Wriggle as she may there was no escaping his lust, and so, after holding out for as long as she had the strength to, she succumbed with an enormous sigh.

By this time it was Simon who was becoming a little tired. It was Donna's turn to be passionate, and she became as forward with him now as she had been reticent, mounting him greedily.

For Simon it was all tremendous. Lying back passively and letting it all happen counterbalanced his shouting and bullying on the dealing floor all day and every day.

After it was over, he settled to sleep. He'd had a long day and there was not much else now he was fit for. But he knew Donna once awoken wouldn't get back to sleep again so easily. She would lie there thinking about him and little Mark.

On her own admission, she longed for him to come home earlier at nights and to spend more time in her company, but he just couldn't.

If he was honest, Donna bored him. Family life was anathema to his aggressive temperament, although in small doses it could serve to complement it!

Before he knew where he was it was morning. Simon was up and out of the house after a hasty breakfast, arriving at England Securities for his usual eight o'clock kick-off in the 'football pitch', as John Falmouth termed his suite of rooms.

John was lounging in his swivel chair, his legs crossed under the desk. He was staring hard at the SEAQ screen before him. To his right, his brunette secretary, Louise, was pulling papers out of the filing cabinet.

'Morning, boss,' said Simon breezily.

John glanced up. His handsome blonde features had a dissipated look. 'That oil stock we have been selling for the past couple of weeks is nicely up in value,' he said. 'I've got a few million more of the shares on England Securities' books. I'll dump them in the market this morning. We should get 15p a share, just a penny below the screen price.

'The moment you see the share price plummet on the screen, tell all dealers to get their clients out of the stock immediately, and to reinvest the proceeds in the Merden Group. They can tell 'em there has been an announcement and the company could go bust. This is not untrue. There are always announcements, and any stock could go bust.

'Do nothing however while the Department of Trade inspector, Mr. Smith is in the dealing room. Fortunately, Mr. Smith will be spending most of the day down here examining the books.

'Also wipe all sales scores off the board. Remove my lovely incentives poster. I'm afraid brokers' cash incentives must be a thing of the past. We cannot be seen to be selling too aggressively or too competitively, this might be construed as against the client's interests, which is now a criminal offence.

Simon stared. 'You are effectively cutting brokers' earnings by about half, which makes it twice as difficult for me to motivate the floor. Turnover will drop like a stone.'

'It's your job to sustain it,' snapped John. 'Can't you see, Simon, we are being investigated on all sides? I must not be seen to be breaking the rules, or it's curtains.'

Simon shrugged. 'You will lose a lot of staff.'

'I can replace them,' said John. 'Even nowadays, with the Financial Services Act in force, wide brokers are two a penny. The dealing room needs a shake out anyway.'

Simon grinned. 'That's nothing new for England Securities.'

'Once I was a salesman like them,' said John grandly. 'I know the score. Here today, gone tomorrow, and back the next day. Anybody I fire just because he's done a dodgy deal can probably return when the client has stopped whingeing.

'Stockbroking is like bookmaking, a game of wits between the broker and his client. It's a gamble with the odds stacked against the punter.'

Simon laughed. 'That's the most accurate description of this game I have ever heard. The ideal of fair stock market investment is a myth. Amongst stockbrokers who stick around there are only sharks . . . and sharks.'

'The blueblooded stockbrokers are more corrupt even than the likes of us,' said John.

'They pay their staff less though,' said Simon: 'Speaking of which, it's time I had a pay rise.'

John sighed. 'Can't you see that is impossible now. I may even have to cut your income. But later, when the attention is off us, I will give you more money.'

'I will be waiting forever,' said Simon.

By the time he had returned to the dealing room, it was a quarter past eight. While brokers were trickling into work, Simon sat at his desk on a wooden pedestal, from which vantage point he could oversee the entire room.

He was responsible for some sixty brokers in this elite dealing room. In the dealing room beyond, there were another twenty under the control of Gordon Halcombe, his training manager.

As they came in, Simon called over several brokers whom he had not been able to get hold of on the telephone the previous night, and informed them of the rendezvous that evening. They left his side casually, but Simon could sense their excitement.

He turned to the white board behind him, and glanced at the previous day's sales scores recorded for each team in the room. The top team of three brokers had sold £120,000 worth of stock, the other teams each anything from £20,000 to £10,000. He wiped the board clean, wincing as he did so. A display of sales figures helped to motivate the room. Simon had little time for anything but aggressive selling of stock, regardless of its suitability for the client's investment needs. In his opinion, if "mug punter" was ready to buy it, that was his problem. The regulations of "know your client", and against "cold calling" when introduced by the Financial Services Act two years earlier had enraged Simon, until he realised that they were only cosmetic, still largely unheeded.

He turned next to the incentives poster pinned to the wall. Prizes were clearly listed on white cartridge paper: £50 cash for every £5,000 worth of stock sold in the day, £120 for £10,000 worth, £200 for £15,000 worth or above. These cash incentives had until now been paid out at the end of every day without argument.

Further down the list were the additional, more colourful incentives rewarding achievement of monthly targets. £1,000 cash. A holiday in Los Angeles, all expenses paid. Tickets to Annabel's and other top London nightclubs. Fortnum and Mason's food hampers. Bottles of champagne.

Simon ripped down the poster. He rolled it up swiftly and shoved it into a drawer. He would be smuggling it out for use against England Securities, once he and his team had left.

When by half past eight, all the brokers had arrived (latecomers were invariably fined), Simon shouted. 'This morning, we're all going to be goody-goodies. The DTI is in the building again. If our friend Mr. Smith wanders up onto the dealing floor, watch what you say to him. Speak carefully to clients in front of him. I shouldn't need to spell it out.

'For obvious reasons we won't any longer be writing up team scores on the board but I will still notice how much business each team is doing. There will be no more cash incentives . . . '

Most of the brokers groaned. 'It's not worth working here now,' said one, and his colleagues murmured in agreement.

'That's up to each of you to decide,' said Simon. 'Anybody who wants out, just hand me your box of client leads, and go now.'

Nobody took him up on the offer. Simon grinned faintly. 'From those of you who are staying I want in all written sales pitches, all memoranda, anything you have ever been given in writing. Team leaders, collect them, and bring them up to me. As soon as you have done this, get on with selling shares in The Merden Group.'

There were groans from the dealing floor.

'We've been selling The Merden Group for months. Our clients need something else,' shouted one broker.

'Give us some new clients, then we'll be glad to do it,' shouted another.

'You will be getting leads soon,' said Simon. 'There are also some new stocks coming up, maybe even this afternoon. So keep your clients sweet.'

'We've heard that one before,' shouted a broker.

'Tough,' shouted back Simon. He narrowed his eyes shrewdly at the heckler. 'You are a crap broker anyway. If you don't like it, piss off.'

Murmuring resumed throughout the room as the brokers fell to work, sifting through files and pulling out papers.

'I want no pitches or memos retained,' barked Simon. 'You will be getting them back later, or new ones to replace them. Team leaders make sure you get the lot. Anybody caught holding back material will be sacked.'

Team leaders left the papers on his desk. Simon stashed them without comment in a drawer. They would be going the same way the incentives poster was headed.

By nine o'clock, all brokers were on the telephone, pushing shares in The Merden Group to their clients. They were acutely aware of the entrance of Mr. Smith, escorted into the dealing room by John Falmouth.

The DTI inspector was a squat middle-aged man with a pasty complexion, pursed lips and steely grey eyes.

John Falmouth raised his hand and the brokers quietened. 'Mr. Smith will be asking a few questions,' he announced. 'Answer him freely. We have nothing to hide.'

John left the dealing room, and Simon shook hands with Mr. Smith. 'I'm the dealing manager here,' he said. 'And I'm a stickler for fit and proper practice.'

'Then why is your firm getting more complaints than any other in the City?' said Mr. Smith. 'I will be forming my own judgement. What stock are your brokers selling at the moment?'

'The Merden Group,' said Simon.

The Inspector nodded. 'Just as I thought. England Securities owns a more than five per cent stake in that stock, am I not right? Are your brokers informing their clients of this?'

'Of course they are,' said Simon. 'But if we do find a broker acting irresponsibly here, we sack him on the spot, as well as reporting the matter to the regulatory authorities.'

Mr. Smith smirked. 'It all sounds very ruthless. What with that and the decline of private clients' business, all your jobs must be constantly on the line.'

'The service we provide is too valuable for that,' said Simon.

'I hope you are right,' said Mr. Smith.

Simon watched him stroll across the dealing room, listening in on conversations with clients, then interrogating the brokers concerned. He was also scrutinising client record cards.

Simon walked through his dealing room, passing into the other adjoining, where his training manager Gordon Halcombe came over to meet him. He was a tall, broad shouldered man with longish, brown hair and beard, who before becoming a stockbroker had worked his way round the world, spending en route some weeks in a Greek jail on a suspected drug offence.

'Mr. Smith is next door,' murmured Simon. 'Get all your brokers on their best behaviour.'

Gordon nodded, glancing round at his brokers who looked up at him. 'A DTI inspector is going to be asking you about your business shortly,' he announced. 'Anyone who lets us down will be sacked.'

'Not that your lot has done much business for weeks,' remarked Simon.

'We have not had a chance,' snapped Gordon. 'All the good leads are distributed in your room, not mine.'

'I have a nice surprise for you,' said Simon. 'Come to The Riverside Inn at six o'clock tonight. There will be a few of us there. I'll do all the explaining then. In the meantime, don't breathe a word of this to anybody.'

With that, he picked up a trainee's telephone receiver, and made a quick call. Laura Jones agreed to wait behind at Thompson & Thompson that night for him.

After Mr. Smith had left the dealing rooms, Simon checked the SEAQ screen. The oil stock of which John Falmouth had spoken that morning was showing a drop in price over the last hour from 16p to 10p. Simon chuckled. John had obviously dumped all his shares. It was time to transfer capital. He announced to all brokers concerning the oil stock: 'Your clients are onto a loser there now. Ring 'em up. Get 'em to sell out, reinvesting the proceeds in The Merden Group. They could stand to lose a lot more money if you don't act quickly.'

While the brokers were frantically ringing their clients in order to effect the transaction, Simon slipped downstairs to see John

Falmouth. From outside the closed door to his "football pitch" he stopped short, recognising John's voice: 'I've lost a fucking fortune on this stock. My broker is refusing to take it back. Find me another broker, Louise darling, now . . . '

Simon knocked sharply and entered. He glanced at John who was seated with his face buried deep in his hands, the SEAQ screen looming over him like an electronic deity.

From her desk beside the door, Louise caught Simon's eye. 'Come back later,' she murmured. Simon hesitated, and John glanced up. His eyes were red-rimmed with stress and Columbian stimulation.

'No, I'll see you. How has business been today, Simon?'

'Guess,' said Simon.

John groaned. 'Mr. Smith is a real headache.'

'What the hell is he looking for?' asked Simon, knowing full well that it was evidence of insider dealing, syphoning of client funds into private accounts, and discrepancies in the books. He also knew in his heart of hearts that England Securities was guilty of all these and more.

'If I knew, I'd help him,' said John. 'He's just nosing about. If the DTI had to compensate for the loss of business they caused, they would be less ready to waste the taxpayer's money on pointless investigations. How they would crumple if they had to account for their time spent!'

'If they end up closing us down, they will take their time about it. We've got at least a year to play with,' said Simon comfortably.

John glared at him. 'How could you even contemplate the DTI closing us down? Whose side are you on, Simon?'

'You're treating me like a fool, John,' said Simon sharply. 'I know more of what has been going on here than you think.'

'Well as I told you this morning, we are strictly kosher now,' said John: 'Both you and the brokers will be taking home considerably less money, as well as conducting your business by the rulebook. Any of you who doesn't like it knows what to do.'

Simon dismissed his brokers early that evening, checking to his satisfaction that Gordon Halcombe in the next room was doing the same.

He slipped into his briefcase all England Securities' written sales pitches, memoranda, the incentives poster, etc. he had collected in that morning and he applied the combination lock.

He walked out with all this stolen property quite brazenly to his black company BMW.

He drove with all speed to a sex shop in Soho. He nipped inside, re-emerging in a few minutes with a carrier bag of metal and rubber apparatus, which he deposited on the back seat of the car. It was past six o'clock, but he was happy to let his brokers wait. That would show them who was boss. Many a time John Falmouth had kept him waiting. It was a trick Simon had picked up from him.

The brokers were seated around two joined tables in The Riverside Inn. As Simon entered, he saw Gordon Halcombe bang his hands on the table surface: '10, 9, 8, 7, 6, 5, 4, 3, 2, 1 . . . ' he shouted: 'Go . . . ' The brokers quickly downed their drinks. One short thin broker choked, and the two either side of him thumped his back. 'Buck up mate,' one shouted.

'I'll have to bow out,' he announced.

'Next round,' shouted Gordon Halcombe: 'Who's going to buy?'

When Simon came over, they made room for him, ceasing their "down it in one" game instantly. He sat down with his own drink, an orange juice, and glanced round.

Fifteen brokers were present, his favourites.

'I have invited you all this evening because you're the best brokers at England Securities,' announced Simon. 'You must keep this meeting strictly confidential from the rest.

'As you all know, the DTI has got its teeth into England Securities. This can only be because it has got good reason to suspect malpractice. The chances are Mr. Smith has found something untoward already.

'Like I told you all this morning, your bonuses have been squeezed out. England Securities is clearly winding down. John Falmouth is syphoning money out of the company and will probably sell it lock stock and barrel, as soon as he has offloaded all the shares he can in The Merden Group, which you know and I know aren't worth the paper they're written on.

'I've done you lot a favour. I have fixed a deal in that we will all be working for a top stockbroker. You are going to like it once you're there. You will be earning three times what you have been at England Securities. In addition every man present will be paid £5,000 up front merely for joining.'

'When do we start?' asked a broker.

'Not yet,' said Simon: 'We don't want John Falmouth, or the other brokers at England Securities getting suspicious, so we will vanish one by one. I will start by resigning. What you must do before you leave is to steal all the leads that you can. Don't touch those belonging to anybody here, for obvious reasons.'

He chuckled. 'We will be providing new clients too, if you can be bothered to open them up, but we'll be doing so much business with England Securities' clients that we will knock John Falmouth right out of the market.'

Gordon Halcombe frowned. 'For fuck's sake, nobody get caught nicking leads. The best way to do it, I can tell you from experience, is to work in pairs early in the morning. One broker keeps guard at the door, while his colleague rifles through others' lead boxes. Then you copy them on the Xerox. The best excuse for coming in early is to catch up on admin work.'

'You can say you have cleared it with me,' announced Simon. 'Now anybody who is not coming to the new firm had better tell me now.'

One tall broker with an angular face called Jeremy, who was a drinking mate of Simon, for which he was favoured at England Securities by being perpetually provided with good leads, half-raised his hand. 'What's the firm called?' he asked.

'I can't tell anybody that yet,' said Simon. 'If John Falmouth was to find out, he would try to put a spanner in the works. Not that he would succeed, but I can do without the hassle.

'But what I can tell you is that it's a much longer established stockbroker than England Securities,' he continued. 'These are career positions you will all be going into, and you will stay in them I hope for the next ten years at least, long after England Securities will have gone under. It really is time you all started thinking of your long term futures . . .'

He sipped his orange juice, and the brokers started murmuring. Simon cleared his throat. 'You lot are in for a treat tonight. You are invited to a meal at the Italian restaurant down the road, with women laid on too. It's all at the new firm's expense.'

'That's great.' 'Yeah.' 'Good thinking.' The brokers, with a few exceptions who left for arrangements they could not forestall, adjusted their plans for the evening and stayed around.

A slight young dealer with black hair called Sammy Dean looked at Simon very hard without asking any questions, then murmured an excuse and followed the few who had left. This made Simon uneasy.

The rest proceeded some minutes afterwards down the road alongside the Thames. It was a calm evening, with dusk already setting in. The water appeared dark and murky, its waves hardly stirring.

Upon arrival at the elegant restaurant, brokers were helped off with their coats, and ushered to a trestle table near the window.

The escort girls were already waiting in elegant flowered dresses, or in skirts with blouses of intricate design. One more girl was needed, so a blonde beauty sitting next to the window took a mobile from her handbag, and telephoned her agency.

Chapter 9

Starting with aperitifs, then moving onto a pasta course, the brokers ate fast, chatting up the escorts sitting opposite them. A few brokers, after weighing up the attributes of what was on offer, nudged each other and swapped places.

A brunette in white shorts and low cut frilly blouse, a 'new model' as one broker put it, entered the restaurant and walked salaciously over to the table, taking her seat opposite Gordon Halcombe who had been without company.

Simon Hall alone now lacked a female escort. This was as he had planned. While he was eating, he eyed his new team. Going like lambs to the slaughter, he thought grimly. He, Simon, would be making more money out of this bunch of prats than they would ever realise, and while they thought they were carving out proper futures for themselves, they would be screwing up any chance they had had of surviving in stockbroking.

And there they would hang on the edge of the cliff until their fingers were prised from its edge, the greedy stupid bastards. He too might suffer, but he could live in luxury off the interest from his earnings afterwards, possibly for the rest of his life, while they foundered in a job market which would have closed its doors to them. Simon smiled slowly.

The brokers were forever ordering more drinks, their voices getting louder. Customers at the surrounding tables stared. The brokers started up a sing-song. The blonde girl sitting next to the window climbed onto the table, unbuttoning her blouse as she writhed to the sound of their voices:

> We top brokers of England Securities are,
> Sell your house, get rid of your car.
> Think it's funny, lost your money.
> Oh what a cunt you are!

The brokers started clapping as she stripped off her bra, kicking some plates. They all rushed to move closer when she showed a glimpse of her private parts.

Simon slipped away after the main course. One of the brokers turned. 'Where are you off to Simon?'

Simon noticed it was Jeremy. 'I'm going off for a better fuck than any of you will have tonight,' he yelled.

Jeremy turned back to the others. 'He's going home to his wife,' he said. Gales of laughter issued from the table, as Simon left the restaurant. Many of his brokers would be taking their escorts home for the night, and paying extortionate extra charges for the pleasure.

Laura buzzed him into the premises of Thompson & Thompson. Upstairs, Simon smiled at her. She looked supercool in blue corduroys and white blouse. Her blonde hair was blowing in the breeze he had let in. He didn't close the front door.

'This way, please,' he invited, ushering her out and waiting patiently while she locked up.

'You've got the goods?' she asked.

'Yes.' He shook his briefcase in one hand, his carrier bag in the other. 'I'll show you shortly,' he added, accompanying her down out of the building, then past his parked car towards The Richmond Hotel in Piccadilly. He escorted Laura through the sumptuous entrance hall, collecting his room key from the impeccably groomed redhead at the reception.

'You've got a cheek, haven't you?' gasped Laura.

He laughed. 'Two, actually.'

She nonetheless accompanied him, apparently without qualms. The lift took them up several floors, landing them almost outside their room. Unlocking the door, Simon was smiling still. The bed was large and inviting, with a pink spread. The French windows led onto a balcony overlooking the streets far below, but no noise of traffic penetrated the glass.

Simon closed the door behind them, and facing Laura quickly, tapped his briefcase. 'The documents you need are in here,' he said. 'Only I know the combination lock. You will have to force it out of me.'

'What is this game?' she cried.

'It's up to you how you play it,' he said, and upturned his carrier bag on the bed. The contents dropped out. Black metal handcuffs, four short whipcords, a ball cage, a blindfold, and a metal bar for keeping the ankles apart. A black leather whip and paddle. A thin, curved cane.

Laura recalled the day she had accompanied Georgio Thomassino back to his hotel room in Rome. He too had produced the instruments of bondage and humiliation, as a preliminary to a horrible kidnap. Georgio, like Dario had been, still was, answerable to Padre Lorenzo, who had killed her father. Simon was becoming linked in this network, but she would make sure she kept the upper hand over him.

She handcuffed Simon, tying him to the bed, and applying the other implements, including the blindfold so he was stretched out on his stomach, immobilised.

She started to whip him hard. He groaned in blissful agony, flinching as the welts appeared on his thighs. After some five minutes' sustained torture, he cried out, 'Enough. This is the number of the combination . . . '

Leaving him trussed like a chicken, Laura opened his briefcase. Removing the papers she found inside, she shuffled them together and left them in a neat pile on the desk behind her.

Laura then picked up the cane. 'Let me go now,' snapped Simon, but she started to lay into him afresh. The bamboo cut into his skin, already raw in places. He wriggled and cried out.

She then dropped the cane on the floor, picked up her bundle of documents, and turned towards the door.

'Release me,' he screamed. Sweat gleamed on his forehead, and his teeth were bared in a peculiarly ferocious manner.

She laughed. 'Sleep well, lover boy.'

He struggled, but his wrists and ankles were well tethered, while his legs were inexorably parted by the steel bar.

'You will pay for this,' he roared, but she had already closed the door behind her.

Downstairs she pressed two £50 notes in a round-faced page boy's palm. 'Find me a taxi,' she said, 'then release my prisoner.' She handed him keys. 'These are for the handcuffs and ankle restraint. For the whipcord you will need a sharp knife.'

The boy grinned faintly and bowed.

Her taxi was there almost immediately and sped Laura away from the splendid hotel to the small flat she shared with Dario.

As she entered, she could hear her guardian splashing about in the bath. The bathroom door was open a crack, so she pushed her way in.

Dario was sitting upright in the tub humming to himself. His face was wet and wrinkled like a turtle's, and his chest was covered in white lather. 'Soap my back, darling,' he said.

She put down her bundle of papers on the lavatory seat, and gave him one of her best shoulder and back massages, making him groan with pleasure.

'You have hidden talents, Laura,' he insisted.

She smiled. 'I have Simon's documents here, straight out of England Securities.' She indicated the pile on the lavatory seat. 'We'll look at them once you have had your bath.'

He sat forward and stretched out a dripping arm. His eyes glinted. 'No, I want to see them now.'

'You will get them wet,' she protested.

But he was out of the bath already, shaking his hairy body dry. Wrapping a towel round his waist, he seized the papers and made for the living room. Laura trailed after him, seating herself by his side on the sofa as he scrutinised them.

Here was sales pitch upon sales pitch for various penny stocks, all forecasting amazing price rises and mooting take-over prospects, all generous on projected earnings and reticent on previous years' figures, unless the stock was being marketed as a "recovery situation", in which case the past losses and failures were presented as a reason for buying.

'This reminds me of the pitches we had in Paris,' chuckled Dario. He turned next to internal memoranda. His eyes bulged as he scrutinised these. 'My God, how indiscreet,' he said. Taking a red pen from his pocket, he used it to circle extracts showing England Securities in a less than favourable light. Such items included:

> Too much stock has been coming back onto England Securities' books. This is not acceptable and from your point of view is unproductive, since you will only be off-loading it again. Brokers who allow their clients to sell stock will be penalised. Any who perpetually bring unwanted stock back onto our books will be dismissed!

> Remember, every day, in every way, our clients' boots are getting fuller and fuller.

> Today we're offering our clients still more shares in The Merden Group, on the grounds that they are getting them at a penny below screen price. £1000 cash for the top salesman today. £500 each for the next two.

> There have been reports in the national press on the high incidence of drug taking and alcoholism in City firms. To protect England Securities' good reputation, it must be made clear that alcohol and drugs are forbidden on the dealing floor. Any broker who is suspected of being drunk will be breathalysed and fined.

> It is not England Securities' business to intrude on brokers' private dealing arrangements. This only becomes our business when brokers get into massive debts, which they cannot pay off, as John Falmouth then usually gets lumbered with them. It seems extraordinary that brokers at England Securities will gamble three or four times their annual salary on one account trade. Any broker whose private dealings adversely affect the good reputation of England Securities will be instantly dismissed.

> Brokers have recently been making huge profits from personal dealings in stocks we have been offering to clients. This is a dangerous activity which leaves them open to charges of insider dealing. Such dealings may not take place without permission in writing from John Falmouth.

There were other papers in the bundle listing brokers' names, with sales scores alongside them, together with critical comments: "A good week," or "Needs to try harder," were typical. There was a memo addressed individually to a broker that read as follows: "You need to do bigger deals. Try pitching your clients to buy £5,000-£10,000 worth of stock at a time. Tell them that your other clients deal in this quantity."

Dario took a deep breath. 'We will tell Dominic Gardiner to start campaigning against England Securities immediately,' he said.

An appointment was fixed, and Dario arrived early on the scheduled evening at the House of Commons.

After the MP had been tannoyed, a young girl with hazel eyes and long brown hair in a turquoise dress came to meet Dario. 'I'm Nicky, Dominic's assistant,' she announced, shaking his hand briskly. 'Please follow me.'

Dario accompanied her to the lift. 'Dominic can only spare fifteen minutes,' she pointed out as they ascended.

'That is quite enough for this visit,' said Dario casually. 'I know he is a busy man. In the public eye all the time.'

'He enjoys it,' said Nicky.

The MP was sitting at his desk as they entered. He half arose, waving his guest into a chair. Dario recognised him from TV, and from press photos. His round face with bushy eyebrows and a shock of blond hair was memorable enough. He started rubbing his hands. 'What have you brought to show me?'

Dario rummaged in his briefcase and took out a file of the documents he had previously been examining. 'I have some damning evidence on the dealing practices of England Securities,' he began.

The MP leaned forward. 'Of whom?'

'England Securities. You know them?'

'I do. Go on.' The MP's face was red with excitement.

'This for a start.' Dario handed him the documents. Gardiner started skimming through them, his eyes widening with horror. 'Gosh, it's the same old story,' he commented. 'The same bloody con. I can hardly believe it's still happening in 1990, after the implementation of the Financial Services Act, and after all my efforts to clean up the City.'

'I know your reputation . . . ' began Dario.

'Call me Dominic. Everybody else does,' said Gardiner.

'The public is dependent on you once again, Dominic,' said Dario. 'This time, to close England Securities down.'

Gardiner frowned, pondering for a short while. At length, he glanced up. 'I don't mean to appear rude,' he said, 'but where is your interest in it? Surely you are not acting purely for philanthropy's sake?'

'Ha ha ha!' Dario fairly shook. 'I wouldn't pretend to be a saint, Dominic. I'm a company director, and my companies are in the process of being floated. I hate to see the stock market's reputation being dragged into the mire by John Falmouth and his England Securities.'

'Which broker is sponsoring your flotation?' asked the MP.

'Thompson & Thompson. A long established and eminently respectable firm,' said Dario.

'Ah yes,' said Dominic Gardiner. He reached into a box of cigars and offered one to Dario who raised a defensive hand. He lit one himself. Nicky passed him a black ashtray. 'I'll tell you a secret,' he said. 'I deal personally with England Securities, and I'm fed up with their service.'

Dario smirked. 'They weren't perhaps your wisest choice of stockbroker.'

'I have found that out the hard way,' said Gardiner. 'I enrolled with half a dozen brokers a year ago, as part of my investigations into the City. I kept England Securities for my personal dealings. Ironically they turned out to be the least scrupulous of the lot . . . '

'You ought to try Thompson & Thompson,' said Dario. 'I'll send you our forms to fill in. They are rather lengthy I'm afraid, but we like to "know our clients" thoroughly. Our best broker is Laura Jones.'

'I'll try her,' said Gardiner.

'Laura is your girl,' said Dario. 'But going back to the subject of England Securities . . . '

'They have had it coming to them for a long time,' said Gardiner. 'Leave them to me.'

As soon as Nicky had shown Dario out, Dominic Gardiner stood up with a yawn and stretched himself, then opened his filing cabinet, and removed from the England Securities cuttings file an American newspaper dated 1 October 1975, reporting the sudden crash of Utah based Commodity Enterprises Ltd. of which John Falmouth had been a director.

His co-director, one Charles Borley, had absconded with private clients' funds. To what extent had Falmouth connived in this scam the MP wondered. He had in fact been waiting to act on this information. The time was now ripe to stir the shit.

When Nicky was back, he dictated her a letter to John Falmouth. As the words rolled off his politician's silvery tongue, he smiled, and taking her cue, Nicky smiled too.

At ten o'clock the following morning, John Falmouth was feeling just great. While his assistant, Louise had been keeping an eye on the door, he had sniffed a line of cocaine and had made a few grand on the market, before the day had even properly started. Then Louise handed him Dominic Gardiner's letter which she had herself already opened and read, as she did with all of his mail.

He groaned when she told him who had written it and pushed it aside. 'It's too early in the morning,' he said.

'Read it,' she insisted. 'Get it over with.'

Falmouth scrutinised the letter, re-reading it three times, and grinding his teeth to see how the wording minimised libel risk. The contents were as follows:

Dear Mr. Falmouth,

It has been brought to my attention that your stockbroking firm England Securities has been attracting criticisms In the circumstances, I would be glad if you could answer the following questions:

109

1) Is it true that England Securities holds stock on its books until the price rises substantially, then sells it off to its clients?

2) Is it true that your brokers are instructed to stop at nothing in parting investors from their money?

3) Is it true that your clients are not generally allowed to sell out of stock?

4) Is it true that in 1975 and earlier, you were a director of an American company called Commodity Enterprises Inc.?

I look forward to your reply.

Yours sincerely
Dominic Gardiner, MP

Falmouth gazed into space.

This MP was the only serious threat to England Securities at present. Why such a man should bother to be getting at him was, in Falmouth's opinion, simple. He was striking at an easy target, a small firm that had limited means of self defence.

He turned to Louise who was watching him calmly. She was a loyal little bitch. 'Is Dominic Gardiner still dealing with us?' he asked.

'I'll check.' She made a quick telephone call, and Kate, the credit control clerk, a dour grey-haired Scot in her middle-age, duly appeared in the office. 'Dominic Gardiner? He owes us some £10,000, on stock purchases and a failed account trade. He is Sammy Dean's client, and I've warned Sammy to do no further business until the MP's outstanding debts have been settled.'

'Send Sammy down to me, Kate,' snapped John. 'As for Gardiner, he had better pay up, or we'll sue the arse off him. Make sure you quote me on that, too.'

Kate gave him a strained smile and was not able to get out of the room quickly enough, which made Falmouth grin.

Sammy was down promptly, looking nervous as he always did, his black hair awry, his shirt noticeably crumpled.

'What have you been doing with Dominic Gardiner?' said Falmouth. 'He's threatening us.'

'I know whom you can look to for that,' said Sammy coolly.

'I suppose you are going to put the blame on Kate now,' said John.

Sammy shook his head. 'Listen carefully, as what I'm about to say will come as a shock to you,' he said. 'Simon Hall is plotting a coup. He is taking Gordon with him, and all the top brokers. They are arranging to leave one by one, stealing leads and anything else they can. They are all going to the same stockbroker; Simon won't tell them which one!'

'One of this lot must have been whispering in Dominic Gardiner's ear. All it takes is a telephone call!'

'I don't believe this,' shouted Falmouth. 'You're making it up.'

'You know I'm not,' replied Sammy quietly. 'Ask Simon Hall . . . ' he pronounced the name with a sneer: 'why he collected in all sales pitches and internal memos. Why he took down the incentives poster on the wall.'

'It was probably for the DTI visit,' said Falmouth.

'Oh yeah?' Sammy smiled. 'All I've got to say is this. If the others leave, I would appreciate being made a team leader as a reward for my loyalty.'

Falmouth took a deep breath. 'If what you say is correct, you shall have that and more. Now don't mention our conversation to anybody, and I won't. Nor will Louise . . . ' He glanced at his secretary who shook her head obediently.

'Who besides Simon is in this ring? I need to know,' he continued.

Sammy half closed his eyes, reciting the names as he remembered them, while Louise wrote them down.

'I was invited to the initial meeting at The Riverside Inn this week,' said Sammy. 'Afterwards, Simon treated the brokers to a free night out, with escort girls.'

'He's trying to buy you is he?' said Falmouth grimly. 'I'll check this out. In the meantime, Sammy, take the rest of the day off. I'll see you again first thing tomorrow morning.'

As Sammy left, Falmouth was already on the internal line to Simon, his voice sweet as honey. 'Pop down and see me the moment you can,' he said.

When Simon entered the chairman's room, his step faltered. Something seemed wrong. Falmouth's eyes fixed on Simon's face. They sparked off his scorn. 'You bastard,' he breathed. 'It's a small world, Simon Hall. I'll get you for this, you see if I don't.'

'What have I done?' said Simon calmly.

'You know what,' snapped John.

'What about you?' said Simon. 'Reducing our earnings. England Securities was getting on fine until you were made chairman.'

'I saved this firm from going under,' rasped Falmouth. 'I pumped in money, and instilled respectability. Is this how you repay me?'

'You're referring to my looking elsewhere for a position?' inquired Simon.

'It's not so much that. You're disposable,' sneered Falmouth. 'What I object to is your playing the Pied Piper, trying to whisk away my staff, under my very nose.'

Simon laughed. 'You can't stop them leaving you. Give your staff credit for having minds of their own . . . '

'It's you who are doing this to me.' Falmouth stood up and hit out without warning.

Simon staggered from the blow on his chest and stumbled, but was on his feet again, cat-like, wriggling to dodge Falmouth's savage kicks. The chairman stood in front of his desk screaming. 'By the time I've finished with you, I'll be sweeping your remains into the rubbish bin, you deceitful bastard! You're fired, without your last month's wages! You're fucked over references! I'll hound you wherever you run to, you disloyal skunk . . . '

Wham! Simon's fist caught John's nose, then his teeth. Next his jaw. John wavered and fell, his temples swelling like a steamed-up pressure cooker.

Louise hovered, crying aloud. John sat up against the wall. His desk was dislodged, and his papers were scattered everywhere.

Louise stepped forward. 'I'll call the police,' she shouted. 'I'll have you charged with assault.' She took a step towards Simon, her eyes bulging, her brown hair flying asunder, her arms reaching for his throat.

Leaping nimbly back, Simon shook his head. 'You are as crazy as your boss, darling,' he said. 'If you call the police, it's John Falmouth you'll be screwing, not me. In fact I might even ring the police myself.'

'Get out,' she panted hoarsely, and leant down, offering Falmouth a helping hand. He staggered to his feet, using her arm as a crutch. Simon laughed shortly and left, slamming the door so hard that it shuddered in its frame.

Falmouth fingered his sore mouth, while Louise dabbed his nose to stall the flow of blood. John's face was swelling, and he could keep his bruised eyes open only with an effort as he staggered to the door. Louise followed him like a shadow.

Simon was standing, waiting for the lift. 'You go down, and straight out,' spluttered John: 'You will never be seeing the dealing room again.'

'There won't be much of it left soon,' sneered Simon.

The lift arrived, and as Simon stepped inside, John shouted, 'When you find you're earning no money at your new firm, you will be crawling back to me with your tail between your legs.'

'I'm getting more money up front there than I would earn in weeks with you,' shouted Simon.

John stood by the window and watched as his dealing manager emerged from the building. He blinked to suppress his tears. Simon was a diamond in the rough, not yet having reached his potential, but hard to replace. Then sentiment gave way to annoyance as he noticed him standing like a statue on the far pavement outside. Why couldn't the bastard just leave?

The reason became painfully apparent. Simon was signalling to brokers still in the dealing room above. Horror or horrors, he was beckoning them! John anticipated the mass exodus frantically before it happened.

Simon's cohorts clattered down the stairs like a machine gun burst. None had waited to summon the lift. They joined their leader out on the street.

In this emergency, the plan to leave one by one had been abandoned. How breathless they all were. So exhilarated!

One broker noticed John Falmouth at the first floor window and thumbed his nose at him. Some of the rest noticed and sniggered. John backed from sight. They were a pack of kids, he thought to himself. And yet it was definitely kids who were needed to sell shares, young 'uns who didn't know how to pity clients, to spare them, who were as hard as nails at prising money from them. Stockbrokers, like terrorists, did their best work while they were young.

Chapter 10

John Falmouth, his heart palpitating, made his way up to his dealing rooms. The atmosphere in each was mayhem, as he had anticipated. Most of the best dealers had followed their Pied Piper out. The others were lounging about speculating as to their futures, even whilst they marvelled at the event. So bemused did they appear that John realised the plot had been kept from them too. That was logical. Simon would have to know to trust no one in the hothouse of the dealing rooms, where there were informants to John himself and to the national press as well as perhaps spies sent in there from other firms.

'Get on with your work as usual,' shouted John. He appointed a temporary dealing manager then returned to his office. Seated once more at his desk, he telephoned the MP Dominic Gardiner with determination in his heart. He was put through to him instantly. 'I received your letter this morning,' he declared. 'Your concerns are unfounded. I don't know who has been talking to you . . . '

'It's not important,' said Gardiner cuttingly.

'I've just sacked some disloyal brokers. You shouldn't listen to malicious rumours.'

'Malicious rumours be blowed,' sneered the MP. 'I have hard evidence . . . '

'Someone has been stealing from my office, I suppose,' said John. 'I'd better call the police.'

'At the rate we're going, so had I, Mr. Falmouth,' said Gardiner.

John slammed down the phone. He sat cupping his head in his hands. This was all proving more than he could cope with at once. Louise hovered over him and he glanced up at her.

'Brokers are queuing to work here. We'll build a new team in an instant,' she said.

John shrugged. 'I'm going to ruin Simon and his crew, to show them who is the kingpin in stockbroking.'

Louise locked the door of his suite, a preliminary which in itself heated his blood. He would have liked to have Simon and the renegade brokers in front of him, so he could shake them into quivering wrecks. But that was just a pipe dream, and Louise was a very real substitute.

She instructed him where to unzip her dress and was still and passive as he caressed her naked body. Finally, she undressed him.

He entered her standing up in a frenzy that left her gasping and cringing. Afterwards, he seated her on his chair and paced the room still naked like she was.

'Does Cynthia know about us?' asked Louise.

John laughed harshly. 'My wife. She doesn't know we have sex, and she doesn't care. Out of sight, out of sound is the way she's staying, so long as she remains a director of The Merden Group, that is.'

'I don't know why you don't divorce her,' said Louise.

John shook his head. 'You're a great secretary Louise and attend to my needs in every sense. But don't mistake being a very good fuck for the kind of arrangement she and I have.'

Meanwhile, the renegade brokers had the rest of the morning free, meeting up again at lunchtime in a pub. Simon addressed them there. 'The new firm is called Thompson & Thompson,' he said' 'We'll go in this afternoon. Be ready to start ringing your clients.'

They all piled into taxis and arrived at the offices. Simon left his brokers to find their feet in the new dealing room while he took Gordon Halcombe outside. We won't let them deal yet,' he told him. 'Let's make sure our new bosses deliver the monies up front they promised.'

Gordon accompanied Simon down the corridor to a second dealing room. The sound of laughter and gossip issued from the half open door. Brazenly, Simon peeped inside.

The brokers were sitting about playing cards and heaping their bets – £10 and £20 notes kept in place under pound coins. The topic screen, looming over them, showed stock prices. They all glanced up at the intruders.

'You must be Johnnie Butler's lot,' said Simon.

'Yeah,' lisped one of the brokers.

'Aren't you dealing?' asked Gordon.

'Do we look like it?' he replied. The others laughed.

Simon then noticed Laura watching him nonchalantly from the corner of the room. 'Don't you know when you're beaten, Simon,' she called out.

'I wish it was more often,' he called back.

He and Gordon turned away. Gerard, approaching along the corridor, shook Simon's hand cordially. 'It's great to see you all here early,' he said. He led them both into the boardroom and closed the door, pulling out chairs. As they sat down he strolled about. 'I want you lot to start work immediately,' he said. 'On Thursday evening we are holding a dog and pony evening for clients at a top hotel. So get your brokers to invite their clients.

'It's at half past seven, with drinks and eats. We will be having a director of Security Planning as a guest speaker, on not just his own company but the satellite ones too. It will be a most profitable evening for all of us!'

Simon nodded. 'Fine. I assume you will be settling all the golden welcomes before we start work.'

'Tomorrow,' said Gerard. 'Dario Abella and I will also give an official welcome to your brokers then.' He waved towards the second dealing room. 'We could put you in with the others, but they might distract you. They have already been selling shares in Security Planning Inc. at six dollars, and are waiting for some new clients.

'You will be selling them at five and a quarter dollars. We will be guaranteeing the clients a small profit. They will be in and out quickly, the shares then going to a new dealing team to offload. But leave all that to me.'

'The dealers are self-employed?' said Simon.

'Yeah. Don't talk to them about that yet,' said Gerard. 'We don't want the Inland Revenue on our scent before we have even started. We will just pay them all gross at first. Later, they can sort out the tax . . .'

'None of 'em will give a shit,' said Simon. 'So long as they get their money and the cheques don't bounce. My brokers were trained at England Securities. They are not bothered how Thompson & Thompson does its bookkeeping. It was not until today that I even told them this firm's name.'

Gerard started. 'You certainly don't believe in letting them know any more than they need to.'

Simon grinned. 'They are my dogs, and I keep them on leashes. When I say "go", they go. When I say "bite", they bite.'

There was a sharp knock at the door and Dario pushed his way in. He came up beaming, and smacked Simon gently on the arm.

'Laura told me right. My saviour's here already, eh?' he said. 'Your golden welcomes are all ready. It will only take a day to transfer monies into the company bank account.'

'Did Laura tell you I gave her my England Securities documents?' asked Simon.

Dario nodded. 'She tells me she had to practically beat you up to get them. But that was one of your little games, she says, and that I'm to keep out of it.'

He chuckled. 'Laura is very loyal to me, you know. She gave me the documents immediately, and they are now in Dominic Gardiner's hands. Falmouth's for the high jump, believe me.'

'He's had it coming to him,' said Gordon cheerfully.

Dario looked at him quizzically and Simon made the necessary introductions. 'We will get back to the dealing room now,' he said.

Later that afternoon, as the locksmith was banging away on the outside of their dealing room door, fitting a combination lock, Simon addressed his team. 'Start inviting your clients to the dog and pony evening. We won't be making 'em invest until we have got our golden welcomes and cleared the cheques, so don't you worry about being stitched up. I'm making sure it doesn't happen . . .

'Put your clients off continuing to deal with England Securities, but do it subtly. Rather than slag England Securities off, hint that they are all safer dealing with a highly reputable firm like us. Offer a convincing explanation as to why you left England Securities. Above all, keep them on the boil.'

Brokers hesitated to pick up the phones. 'Anyone who wants to go back to England Securities, sod off now,' said Simon. 'If you can't stand the heat, get out of the kitchen.'

One short plump dealer called Kit shouted out, 'We could go back for a month, just to get the last commission cheques they owe us.'

'Falmouth will never pay up unless we take legal action,' said Simon. 'We will send 'em fucking solicitors' letters. We will squeeze England Securities dry before we sink 'em for good.'

The brokers were finally bulling into their clients when Kit answered a call. 'Hallo John,' he said. The others became silent. The room was suddenly charged, as if extra oxygen had been pumped into it.

'You had us followed did you?' Kit was saying. 'You want me back? How large is the incentive? Hold on . . . '

Simon snatched the telephone receiver from his hand. 'You won't be getting any of my brokers back Falmouth, so what do you want?' A note of surprise entered his voice. 'It's me you wished to speak to? You could have fooled me. All right I'll meet you. Friday lunchtime at the Tower Hotel. Ta-ra . . . '

Putting down the receiver, he burst into laughter. Clutching his sides, he rolled. The brokers roared hysterically with him. 'Falmouth is trying to make deals now,' gasped Simon. 'He's taking me out to lunch. I'll sort him out then.' He glanced round at his brokers. 'How have your clients been responding?'

'They are wary,' said one broker.

'England Securities have been giving them the pitch already,' said another.

Simon smirked. 'Any damage England Securities does us will be repaid, triplefold!'

That evening, Simon hooked his finger at Gordon Halcombe, indicating him to remain behind. The others left for home, talking excitedly amongst themselves. Thompson & Thompson appeared to be giving them a chance to assert themselves. In reality, Simon knew, they were doing only what he told them.

Gordon came over. 'Is it something important? I'm taking the wife out to dinner tonight.'

'Ring her, and say you will be late,' said Simon. 'You and I are popping out for a drink. I'm sorry I have given you no notice, but business is business.'

After Gordon had made the call, he accompanied Simon out to a wine bar, a few hundred yards from Thompson & Thompson's premises. They sat in a dark corner over a bottle of '78 Chateau Latour.

'I'll come straight to the point,' said Simon. 'How loyal are you to Thompson & Thompson? More importantly, to me?'

'I'm surprised you even ask,' grunted Gordon.

'What I'm about to ask requires the deepest loyalty in you,' said Simon.

'Tell me more.'

'I want you to defect tomorrow. Go back to England Securities. Tell John Falmouth you were misled by me and swear your allegiance to him.'

'And if he doesn't take me?' said Gordon.

'You would come back here immediately. But he will take you. I think you can guess what I want further. You will be the spy in the enemy camp. Your job will be to keep an eye on what is happening there. What stocks are they selling? How many new dealers are they taking on? What pressures are the DTI and regulatory authorities exerting? Above all, what manoeuvres is John plotting against Thompson & Thompson? I'll need to know everything immediately.'

Gordon downed his glass, the wine bringing a flush to his cheeks. His eyes brightened, then narrowed, calculatingly. 'What is it all worth to you in hard cash?' he demanded.

Simon cackled. 'You Shylock!'

'Look who's talking!' said Gordon evenly.

'£300 a week, provided that you keep giving us useful information. More if you tell us something crucial, or if you have to snoop around. Remember, that is on top of the eighty grand or so you will be earning at England Securities. When the time is ripe, you'll quit again, bringing with you another bunch of brokers to fill a third dealing room at Thompson & Thompson. So, are you game?'

Gordon nodded slowly. 'I always fancied myself in the role of a spy.'

'Remember, this is our secret,' said Simon. 'Tomorrow, I'll be cursing your treachery, with the brokers . . . '

'That's best,' said Gordon. 'We'll all laugh about it together one day.'

'Shake on it,' said Simon, offering him his hand. 'We will make history in the City by this.'

The following morning, Simon's crew gathered in the dealing room. 'Time for breakfast,' said Kit.

'Ring the cook, then,' said Simon.

'OK. What's her name?'

'Just call her Cookie.'

'Cookie,' the brokers repeated delightedly, and Kit, ringing through to the kitchen for 'Cookie', ordered breakfast all round.

Delia Lambert, the new cook, brought plates of egg, bacon and sausage into the dealing room, two at a time. Brokers sat eating at their desks as they flicked through *The Sun* and *The Financial Times*.

'Let's get cracking with our breakfast meeting,' said Simon. As Dario and Gerard entered, he glanced at them. 'Before you address the brokers, let me give them their cheques. I want each and every man present to listen to you with full attention.'

They nodded as if to say, "You're in charge. Handle your brokers as you see fit." Simon handed round the cheques. Each amounted to £6,000 per broker, consisting of £5,000 up front, and £1,000 for the first month's basic. The brokers' eyes gleamed. It seemed to be an enormous sum for thus far doing nothing. Enough to keep them at Thompson & Thompson for a bit, without asking too many questions, assuming the cheques would clear.

Simon for his own part was relieved to have received his cheque, with the others early that morning from Gerard. He would be speed clearing it within an hour or two, shoving it into the offshore bank account of a company he had set up purely for tax avoidance purposes.

'Where's Gordon?' asked a broker.

'He's defected,' announced Simon loudly. 'Back to England Securities. He didn't have what it takes. Just forget about him now.'

'What a cunt!' said Kit.

'Deceitful wanker. We're better off without him,' said another broker.

'Treacherous bastard,' said another.

'Hear, hear,' said Simon grandly.

Gerard smiled. 'You certainly have got a loyal team, Simon.'

'Not that we can't see that a mile off,' said Dario.

'My brokers are all hand-picked,' said Simon. 'Anyway, back to business.' He turned back to his team: 'We are getting clients to a top hotel on Thursday night for a presentation. The following morning you prime them. On Monday you sell the fucking stock.'

'The other dealing room put in a crap job,' said Gerard. 'The only one in there who has made any effort is Laura.'

'There is no room for passengers amongst you lot, this isn't a gravy train,' said Simon grimly. 'You have not been paid a handsome sum up front for nothing. If you work your arses off, you'll be millionaires. If you don't, I'll boot you out.'

After this meeting was over, Simon and his brokers left for the banks to cash their cheques.

In the other dealing-room, the umpteenth game of vingt-et-un commenced. Laura felt vaguely uneasy. Why were Dario and Gerard restraining her lot from selling more stock?

News had filtered through to them that Johnnie Butler had worked a deal with the French police, and was now out of custody.

'We'll be hearing from him,' predicted Mike. There was a tremor in his voice.

The entree when it came was as swift and sudden as a lion's attack in the jungle. Four men in smart business suits with a determined glint in their eyes were let into the building by Dario.

'We have an Anton Pillar order to search your premises,' announced the ringleader. 'Mr. Jonathan Butler has good reason to believe his property is here.'

Before they entered the second dealing room, Tim and Mike frantically gathered up the little blue cards lying on desks. These were client leads, which they and their colleagues had filched from their Paris office. Stupidly, as they now saw it, they had not bothered to copy them and destroy these originals.

Mike thrust a carrier bag of these leads at Laura. 'Quick, darling,' he said. She walked smartly out of the dealing room and slipped away through a back exit, even as the men approached.

Out in the street, Laura popped into the nearby wine bar. She rushed downstairs nodding at the waiters who smiled courteously, recognising her. Her favourite young barman was cleaning the tables. She handed him her bag of leads, while pressing a £50 note into his palm. 'Look after these for me,' she pleaded.

Trepidation flashed across his face. 'It's not drugs, is it?'

She laughed. 'Nothing like that. Don't you worry, I'll collect it later.'

The offices, when she returned to them, were in turmoil. She had whisked away the booty none too soon. Brokers were standing around watching the four visitors make a thorough search.

Laura wandered out into the corridor. She had made serious money since she'd been here, and would be making some more, but she felt depressed with the situation.

She was terrified by the knowledge that Johnnie Butler had organised the raid. He was a dangerous man!

She left the offices once again for a breath of fresh air. A smart blue Peugeot estate car was hovering outside. The window slid down. At the wheel was a familiar face.

'Daniel!' she shouted, smiling out of genuine delight.

'Ssh.' He thrust his finger to his lips, beckoning her into the seat beside him. She hesitated, then obliged. When she had explained to him what was going on, he whistled. His face, red and puffed, lit up like a halloween mask reflecting horror. 'I saw the raiders go in,' he said. 'I'm glad I didn't follow them. I don't want to get caught up in all that.'

'How was Las Vegas?' asked Laura.

'Exciting to say the least,' said Daniel. He pressed the accelerator, and the car shot down the road. 'Let's get the hell out of here. The stars warned me to beware the unexpected today, and my God they were right.'

Over lunch in a Chinese restaurant in Soho, Laura went for the jugular. 'How much did you lose gambling?'

Daniel sighed. 'Tens of thousands of pounds this time, I'm afraid. I'm up to my neck in it now with moneylenders. My dear brother knew exactly what he was doing sending me out there. I must now make Thompson & Thompson work so I can pay off my debts. Only I don't like it.'

· 'Are our clients really going to see a short term profit from Security Planning Inc.?' she asked.

Daniel frowned. 'We'll soon know.'

'We should both quit Thompson & Thompson and run away together,' said Laura.

Daniel smiled warmly. 'Yes. Let's get some money together first.'

'From Thompson & Thompson naturally,' said Laura. Before they went for lunch, she picked up the leads from the winebar, leaving them safely under the seat in Daniel's car.

Meanwhile, Thompson & Thompson was in a state of upheaval, although the raiders had discovered neither leads nor any other property of Johnnie Butler's firm on the premises. Directly after lunch, Simon's dealing room was invaded by the original team of brokers, spearheaded by Tim and Mike. The door, normally locked, was temporarily on the latch, so they all barged in.

'What stock will you lot be selling?' demanded Mike.

'We don't know,' replied a broker.

'Blue Chips,' said another. 'Glaxo, ICI and Guinness, I think.'

'Like hell,' said Tim. He looked hard at Simon. 'You'll be selling Security Planning won't you?'

'Fuck off will you?' said Simon.

'What price will you be doing it at?' persisted Tim.

Simon took a deep breath. 'You're barking up the wrong fucking tree. Now get out of this dealing room with your mates before I kick your arse all the way out, down the stairs, and out of this building.'

Simon took a step forward and his brokers gathered around him. Here was an army of superior size and strength that could beat the invaders to a pulp.

'Cool it,' said Mike, retreating to the door, and holding it open. The invaders were herded out like cattle. Simon closed the door, and it locked automatically.

He returned to his desk, smiling faintly. Laughter rippled round the room. 'We don't want to be associated with that lot of crooks,' said Simon. 'When we start selling, don't leave paperwork about. Don't tell those fuckers a thing. Remember to keep our door closed and locked. Hopefully they will all piss off in a week or two.'

He wandered over to the window. Glancing idly down on the street, he noticed Daniel and Laura strolling into the office block together. Some sixth sense made him bristle at the sight.

Simon turned back to his brokers. 'Who has a regular Pakistani or Indian client?'

A broker called Jim Mahon raised a hand. 'I've got Mr. Patel,' he ventured.

'How big a client is he? How often did he ring you at England Securities?' inquired Simon.

'He would ring up every other day,' said Jim. 'He would deal around £5,000 a time on all the duds. He holds £20,000 worth of shares in The Merden Group. Of course he has lost most of his money invested, but I don't think he realises it yet.' Jim grinned, smoothing a cowlick of brown hair off his forehead. 'He's always ringing in and trying to sell out. He gives a different reason every time, the daft prick. One day, he's moving house. The next day he's buying a new car. A week or two after, he needs funds to pay off his options broker. It's all lies of course.

'I kept the dickhead locked in by spinning him the same old crap every time.' Jim put on his posh broker's voice. 'The shares are about to go up, sir. An announcement is expected soon. Your portfolio is at a low ebb at the moment, and it would be crazy to sell out. Wait until the market goes up.

'He's mug enough to fall for it every time, the afterbirth. He's only loaded because he inherited his father's all-night supermarket, and has just sold it off. A fool and his money are soon parted, that's what I say. I will be dealing him big here at Thompson & Thompson.'

'Does he speak like this?' Simon puckered his lips, parodying a Pakistani accent. His words spilled out slowly, and the brokers clapped and cheered.

'That's almost it,' said Jim. 'Sound more flustered, as if you are about to go bankrupt, and you'll have it perfect. Vary your tone. Plead and threaten in turn.'

'I'm not wasting any more time practising,' said Simon: 'Presumably I would pass for him on the phone to England Securities.'

Jim nodded. Simon dialled England Securities' telephone number. He knew it by heart as did his brokers; they would never forget it. (The combination lock on the dealing room door was the England Securities telephone number, too).

The dialling tone sounded. After a full ten minutes, there was still no response. The brokers giggled, as Simon, propping the telephone receiver on his shoulder, put his feet up on his desk and lit a cigarette.

'Now I know how England Securities' clients must feel,' he said.

'Wait until you've hung on another ten minutes and then a broker cuts you off accidentally on purpose,' said Jim. 'Or worse still, puts you indefinitely on hold.'

Sure enough, Simon counted aloud, one by one, another twelve minutes before the telephone was answered.

'England,' came a sharp voice to which Simon listened carefully, recognising it as belonging to Arthur Gales, a seventeen year old broker who was too naive to recognise a trap.

'Good afternoon. I must speak with Jim Mahon,' said Simon in a painstaking Pakistani accent. There was a pause.

'Mr. Mahon has left us now. Who's calling please?'

'It's Mr. Patel. Jim left a message with my secretary this morning. Are you sure he's gone?'

'He was sacked,' lied Arthur. 'I'm dealing with his clients now. He's probably tried to get hold of you from his dodgy new firm. If he approaches you again, my advice to you is to slam down the phone.'

'Why?' said Simon.

'The new broker he works for is really crooked. They are pushing unquoted stocks. They have stolen our lists, and are approaching our clients. You will lose all your money on any investments you make with them.'

'This sounds terrible. How do I know you're not pulling my leg?' asked Simon.

'Of course I'm not! You can check with our chairman, John Falmouth. Or with our dealing director Gordon Halcombe if you like.'

'I thought your dealing director was Simon Hall,' said Simon.

'He was sacked too. He's with Jim Mahon. Now if you will tell me what stocks you are already holding with us, I'll give you a run-down of current prices. There's actually a stock I'm recommending urgently at the moment . . . '

Simon unceremoniously cut him off. 'They are slagging us off bad,' he said. 'We must start playing dirty. Anybody who wants to help me prepare material for the newspapers against England Securities, come and sit over here. The rest of you, ring your clients. Tell them it is now urgent to sever all dealings with England Securities . . . '

Chapter 11

The buzz in Simon's dealing room was as impassioned as it was instantaneous. Brokers had taken to their telephones, pouring into the ears of their clients the most concentrated doses of venom Simon had ever heard from them, and he had heard much.

'England Securities are crooks, sir. That's why we left them. How much money have you ever made on their recommendations? Steer clear, I urge you.

'All the criticisms you have ever read in the newspapers or heard about England Securities are only half the story, sir. Never have any dealing with that firm again.

'My advice to you, sir, is to sell all the stocks you hold with England Securities, immediately. If you try to do it on the telephone, the brokers will either downright refuse to buy back, or they will make it so hard for you that you will give up from sheer frustration at the deliberate delaying tactics on their part, coupled with the sheer expense of holding indefinitely on trunk calls. The easiest way for you to sell out is to send in a registered letter, listing your holdings, and instructing that they are to be sold. England Securities will have to sell the stock then, although they will certainly rip you off on the prices.

'Don't pay them for stocks they misrepresented to you. Just say you are cancelling. Make sure, too, you threaten to report their sales tactics to the Stock Exchange, the Department of Trade and the national newspapers.

'Your best tactic, sir, is to insist on being put through to John Falmouth, so you can complain about your broker. That will really put the wind up them.'

Meanwhile, following discussion with a few of his brokers, Simon telephoned various national newspaper journalists, offering material for a news feature. 'Top brokers walked out of England Securities to set up a new dealing-room in a top-notch stockbroking firm. The reason was that they were fed up with their clients losing money on stocks whose prices were rigged. Furthermore, England Securities offered cash bonuses to sell certain stocks at certain times, which was against the law of agency, etc . . . '

Simon spoke clearly and evenly, as if with total objectivity, althought it was precisely in this quality that he was lacking. He was deliberately omitting to mention that he and his brokers had been enticed away by golden welcomes, and prospects of far greater remuneration.

The next morning, Simon came into work clutching several national newspapers. 'They've put it all in word for word, the prats,' he said triumphantly. 'These financial journalists haven't a clue. You feed them information and they print it without even checking the sources. They must really be amongst the laziest parasites on this planet.'

The brokers laughed and cheered. Several dashed out to buy their own newspapers, but were quickly back in the dealing-room empty-handed.

'What the fuck is wrong with you all? You look as if you've seen a ghost!' said Simon.

'There's a fucking photographer standing outside the building. He focussed his camera on us as we were coming out,' growled a broker.

Simon started. 'We all know who's behind that.'

He strode over to the window and peered out. The photographer was standing on the far pavement below, tubby, red-faced and leaning relaxedly against the wall. A single lens reflex camera with a telephoto lens protruding like a phallus hung round his neck. He caught Simon's eye and grinned faintly, all but waving to him.

Simon gritted his teeth. He turned back and went to the corner of the room, dropping into a broker's vacant chair. He made a quick telephone call, whispering in staccato down the line. Then he grinned slyly at his team. 'Just stay inside and watch the action,' he said.

Shortly afterwards, he beckoned his brokers to the window. They clambered around him, entranced by the spectacle in the street below. Two heavyweights had the photographer in their grip, pinioning his arms behind his back. One of them turned to face him. His knee jerk into his crotch was swift, unexpected and lethal. His mouth contorted, the photographer crumpled to the ground like a scarecrow in a hurricane, banging his head.

His other assailant promptly ripped the camera from round his neck, opened its back, and pulled out the film cassette, deftly pocketing it. He then threw the camera hard on the road where it landed with a crack. He stamped on it for good measure, smiling grimly all the while. As the two thugs walked smartly off round the corner, the street appeared void of witnesses. The heavies had done their work with professionalism.

The photographer lay flat on his back for long minutes, then stirred. With an almighty effort, he heaved himself to his feet. He picked up his smashed camera gingerly by its strap, and limped off out of sight.

Simon grinned. 'Now you can go and buy your newspapers,' he announced.

While a few of the brokers were out, one of those remaining in the dealing room telephoned his bank. Afterwards she turned to Simon in a fury. 'Thompson & Thompson's six grand cheque has bounced.'

Simon frowned: 'The rest of you check with your banks if it's happened to you.' In the meantime, he dialled his own. Sure enough, his cheque too had bounced. 'That fucking does it,' he screamed, slamming down the telephone receiver. 'Thompson & Thompson is trying to put one over me, and if they don't rectify their tricks immediately we will fucking screw this set up and run our own show instead. Until further notice, nobody do any work. Nobody ring your clients, or even take incoming calls from them.'

As he sat deciding what to do, out of the corner of his eye he noticed a broker taking incoming calls. About to reprimand him, he stopped himself and listened: 'RSPCA,' the broker was saying. 'No, we're not a stockbroker. We're the RSPCA. Would you like to make a donation?'

Simon laughed as he saw how abruptly that particular telephone conversation was terminated. 'That's the way, kid,' he shouted out. 'The rest of you can do the same.'

Other brokers started ringing up the continental sex lines, chortling at what they heard, then handing over the receiver to colleagues.

Two brokers disappeared to the gents, to snort coke, Simon knew, a habit they had initially picked up from him. Nowadays, he encouraged brokers in taking any sort of drugs because it kept them too stupefied to care much what stocks they pushed on whom. He delighted in conning the con men.

Drug abuse on the brokers' part had the further advantage of eating up their money, which made them hungry, some would say desperate, to earn more.

Finally, it gave him a hold over them. Not that Simon would use it except as a last resort, but if brokers were being awkward or tried to leave at a time when they were needed, he was not above a little discreet blackmail. It was said that no one knew better than Simon Hall how to apply the thumbscrews. Indeed, his exploitation of this talent was he had got where he was now.

For lunch he joined Dario and Gerard, as arranged, in the boardroom. He noticed to his slight annoyance that Laura and Daniel were present. Besides not trusting them, his opinion of Laura, as of all women, was that her activities should be confined largely to the bedroom.

Simon was deliberately maintaining an ice-cold demeanour so that the ultimatum he planned to drop later should stun the others the more.

When everybody was seated and the cook had served a first course of oxtail soup, Gerard turned to Simon who was sitting next to him. 'We've sacked all the brokers in the other room, except for Laura here.'

'She'll be there on her own will she?' said Simon, throwing her a glance and annoyed that she returned it.

'Out of the question,' laughed Gerard. 'I hope it's all right if she joins your lot.'

Simon grimaced. 'So long as she understands I hold the whip-hand. But there's an obstacle that must first be surmounted.'

'Now is the time to bring it up,' said Gerard.

'The cheques you gave us all bounced,' said Simon grimly. 'My brokers are now assuming that this is going to happen every month. It will take quite a lot to disabuse them, I'm afraid.'

Gerard looked at Dario grimly. Dario reached across the table, touching Simon's forearm lightly. Simon shook him off and looked straight in his eyes, with raised eyebrows.

'I'm so sorry, dear boy,' said Dario. 'I've been transferring monies into the firm's accounts, and our bank was doubtless waiting for these to clear. You must have speed cleared the cheques, which simply hasn't given us enough time. You had better all re-present the cheques, without speed clearing them. In the meantime, I'd like to see your lot doing some business . . . '

'My lads had started contacting clients,' said Simon. 'But I've now told them to stop altogether until they have been paid . . . '

'I think we have sorted out the problem now,' said Gerard. 'Let's get onto more important matters.'

'There is nothing more important than pay cheques,' snapped Simon.

'Agreed,' said Gerard lightly. 'That's why I'm offering you personally another twenty grand, in cash, this afternoon. All I ask in return is that you make yourself a director of Thompson & Thompson.'

Simon stared. 'What's the point?'

'It's simple,' said Gerard. 'I'm not hanging round these offices each and every day. I have other business to attend to. Daniel here is even less likely than me to become a fixture here. At certain times you need authority to sign cheques, and gain access to the firm's bank account, as well as to make big decisions. If you're a director, you can do all these things yourself.'

'Yeah, and I'm made liable,' sneered Simon.

'Only for what you do. No one is telling you to break regulations,' said Gerard.

'None of us will be doing that if I've got anything to do with it,' muttered Daniel.

'All right, it's a deal,' said Simon. He was making a show of consenting almost against his will, but deep within himself he rejoiced. Being power-hungry, he had always craved a directorship.

If he had stayed at England Securities, John Falmouth would almost certainly have offered him one, but on his terms. Here, at Thompson & Thompson, Simon would be running the show more or less as he pleased. The stockbroker might almost as well be renamed Simon Hall Ltd., so thoroughly would he stamp his personality on it.

Back in the dealing-room, Simon showed Laura a desk next to his own. 'Sit there,' he said.

'It's occupied,' she said.

He laughed. 'I'll soon rectify that. From now on it's yours.'

She smiled impishly. 'I see you're a real dictator. In the office, anyway.'

A knock came on the door and the handle rattled. Simon walked over slowly and opened up. Norman Thompson stood there.

'Good afternoon,' said Simon gruffly.

The former chairman of Thompson & Thompson smiled cheerfully. 'I understand you have just been appointed a director here. Congratulations son,' he said. 'I'm here to help you with the firm's old clients, as you know. I have some written records to update for your benefit. You won't mind if I occupy a small corner of the dealing room, will you?'

Simon frowned. 'There isn't enough room for us as it is.' You had better find somewhere else.'

Norman's eyes smouldered. 'I must use this room for a day or two, if I'm to remain on the premises.'

Simon let him pass to a desk in the corner, where he sat down, opening out an accounts book he had been carrying under his arm. He ignored the young brokers who were staring at him as if he were a creature from outer space.

That afternoon, new screens were delivered up to the dealing room in boxes, one for each desk. The brokers assembled them, then sat playing with the remote controls, and making patterns appear.

Simon glanced round the dealing room. 'Re-present your cheques,' he said. 'We will do no business until they are cleared. But invite your clients to our presentation on Thursday night. Talk to them about nothing else. OK, get on the phones and do it now . . . '

That evening, as Laura was putting on her coat, Simon caught her eye. 'I've arranged for Dominic Gardiner to come to the presentation,' he said: 'You're the one who will be escorting him.'

'He had better be worth it,' she said.

'Perhaps you would rather leave him to me?' said Simon.

She smiled coyly, taking the hint. 'How do you suggest I play it then?'

He looked round. The other brokers had left, but Norman Thompson remained, in Simon's opinion listening hard, although he was frowning over accounts.

Simon glanced back at Laura. 'Put him in some Britelite Industries. I have it on reliable source that there will be a bid for the stock. Don't say anything to the others. It will be a quick in and out. Pick up a few of the shares yourself too, if you like.'

She grinned. 'I suppose this is priming Gardiner for the big deal?'

'Bright girl,' said Simon.

In his hearing, she put through a call to Dominic Gardiner. He agreed that she should pick up for him, first thing the following morning, £250,000 worth of Britelite Industries on the account. 'I don't know why I'm doing this,' he growled. 'It must be your charm that persuades me.'

'Surely not,' giggled Laura.

'But yes,' said the MP. 'I don't much care for the profits. On the other hand I am a ladies' man, as my assistant Nicky could tell you.'

In the background came a female voice. 'You're a bloody gambler.'

'All right Nicky,' sighed Gardiner.

On Thursday evening, the brokers arrived early for the presentation and waited apprehensively in the hotel lobby while Simon distributed name badges for their lapels.

All then wandered into the smart reception room, getting their own drinks and snacks from surrounding trestle tables. The light was subdued and shadowy on the polished parquet floor. Adjoining through double doors was the large presentation room.

This was a low key but chic set up, the best this fashionable West End hotel had to offer.

Clients coming in were faltering at first as they hunted down their brokers whom they often didn't know by sight. Amazingly for them, the authoritative voice down the telephone turned out often enough to belong to a youthful individual who lacked the social graces to deal with his client face to face.

Simon turned on a few brokers who were standing around doing nothing. 'Where are your clients?' he demanded.

'We're still waiting,' they said.

'Balderdash,' said Simon. 'Go and meet clients who aren't yours. There are enough lost lambs here, I'd say. As for you Laura,' he turned to the girl, 'your best prospect has just arrived. Get your arse in gear. If he's kinky, you'll need it too.'

Glancing in the direction he indicated, Laura recognised Dominic Gardiner with his shock of blond hair, sporting a white rose in his lapel.

Passing Simon in her high heeled shoes and slinky black evening dress, she deliberately trod on his toes and he yelped. Standing on tip toe she hissed in his ear. 'Why don't you hide in the toilets and wank yourself off, Simon Hall?'

He grinned. 'I don't fucking need to, you bitch. By the time this party gets underway, I'll be fending off the ladies!'

Without giving him a second glance, Laura glided away. Introducing herself to Dominic Gardiner with a warm smile, she ushered him through the room, fetching him a vodka and tonic.

'You never told me you were a femme fatale,' he said.

She simpered. 'I'm a business woman, too, Dominic. I'm making you money already on Britelite Industries. They are up 3p on the day. I'm looking for you to make a killing . . . '

'That's just what I want to do with you, Laura,' he crooned.

As she switched onto automatic, acknowledging his further blandishments, Laura noticed out of the corner of her eye that a slim young lady with dark shoulder length hair in a shimmering white dress was engrossed in conversation with Simon. There was something disturbing about her.

Laura concentrated on giving Dominic her best attention, but was uneasy in her heart. Just as she was thinking it would never come, the presentation was announced. Brokers escorted clients into the vast auditorium where everybody sat randomly, filling not even half the available seats.

Daniel, Gerard, Simon and Dario stood at the podium before them. A little further along stood Georgio, beaming all over his moustached face.

Seeing him made Laura shudder, reminding her sharply of their encounter only a few years back on the streets of Rome, leading to the confrontation with her father's corpse. For a wild moment, she wondered if it was planned that she should suffer Paulo Soccolini's fate.

'Good evening, ladies and gentlemen,' announced Daniel. As he spoke, he swayed slightly, as tipsy as the rest of them, which added sparkle to his performance. No one appeared more exciting than he did that night!

This director of Thompson & Thompson appeared the archetypal playboy, and his audience was all the more favourably disposed to him for it. Was not rubbing shoulders with the rich the way for them to get rich themselves?

'Welcome to this presentation on behalf of Thompson & Thompson,' he announced. 'We will be showing you tonight the goodies we have got in store for you, so you can envisage the massive profit you should be making by sitting back and letting us do all the work.

'I'm Daniel La Marche. Let me introduce my colleagues: my talented brother, Gerard La Marche. Simon Hall, our whizzkid dealing director. And this is Georgio Thomassino, chairman of Security Planning, who will be talking to you about the investment of the decade, available exclusively to all of you, as private clients of Thompson & Thompson.'

Georgio then came forward to speak. In a brilliant assumed American accent that never faltered, he exhorted the merits of Security Planning and of its related companies in investment terms. 'Today, with crime and mugging statistics rising, who can honestly sleep at nights without a nagging fear of burglaries? Bear in mind that raids on domestic properties and on businesses alike are becoming increasingly sophisticated.

'What is the answer? We must use the best locks. Indestructible doors. The most reliable safety deposit boxes. Our security system must be planned and updated by experts.

'Ladies and gentlemen, our group of companies is operating in one of the few truly expanding fields for the 1990s, security.

'In the States, people have flocked to buy our shares. The companies have now opened branches in the UK. Have you not seen the products advertised on TV? Have you not considered buying shares in these companies for yourselves . . .?'

There were murmurs of interest from the audience.

'Raise your hands anybody in this room who really wants to be rich,' continued Georgio.

Good-humouredly, most of the audience, brokers included, raised their hands.

'Here's your chance,' boomed Georgio. 'The shares will not be available tonight. Nor will they be available tomorrow. Dealing, I'm informed, starts first thing on Monday morning, and what I would suggest is that all clients here arrange for their brokers to ring them first thing, to secure their shares.' He paused. 'Ladies and gentlemen, let's strike gold together . . . '

A tremendous clapping and cheering echoed around the huge auditorium. Dominic Gardiner was sitting next to Laura, and, as if inadvertently, his hand had strayed onto her lap. In her own mind, she tried to assess what this was worth to her.

He caught her eye, and gave her the slow wink. 'Let me take you home.'

'That's very good of you,' said Laura.

As she left the hotel in his company, Laura noticed out of the corner of her eye that Simon was still keeping company with the girl in the white dress. Simon caught her eye, grinned faintly, then looked away.

Driving Laura in his white Rover past Big Ben, Dominic slowed by the kerb. 'My London pied-a-terre is in Pimlico,' he said suggestively. 'I stay there during weekdays throughout parliamentary sessions, returning to my family home in Kent at weekends.'

'Let's see it,' said Laura.

He shrugged. 'If you want to.'

It was very much what she might have expected, being small and tastefully furnished with antique chairs and tables. In the bedroom, a Georgian four poster bed took up most of the floor space. To see it made Laura yawn. 'I'm sleepy,' she announced, and flopped onto the mattress, stretching out her limbs like a cat before the fire. Her show of innocent relaxation seemed on the one hand to embarrass the MP, and on the other hand, to amuse him.

'How old are you, if you don't mind my asking?' he said.

She smiled teasingly. 'That's not a polite question.'

Clasping his hands, she pulled him on top of her. He grinned as she turned him onto his side and started unbuttoning his shirt.

'It doesn't look as if I'm going to be driving you very far home tonight,' he said.

When she had undressed him and herself, she snuggled against his chest. 'Are you still dealing with England Securities?' she asked.

He stroked her hair. 'No way. That reminds me, John Falmouth still hasn't answered an accusing letter I've sent him. I'm hearing complaints about his business by the score. I'm going to have to take a hard line . . . '

'You want to close down that bastard's firm for once and for all,' she said sweetly as he switched off the light.

Dominic scrambled back into bed. 'Got a bone to pick with him, have you?' he said.

'Not at all,' she said sweetly.

In bed, he was surprisingly clumsy, fumbling too desperately and thrusting too hard. She ended up steadying him and guiding him teasingly into her. Afterwards he lay back panting. 'What an improvement on my wife you are,' he said. 'She's shut up shop these days.'

She smiled. 'Perhaps you should divorce her?'

He grunted. 'Nothing is easy for a man in my position. I stick my neck out too far in the course of professional duty as it is. It leaves me open to public criticism. But why am I telling you all this . . ?'

'Why not?' said Laura.

He yawned. 'Make me some money on my shares, Laura. Then I'll be very, very happy with you.'

Laura awoke late the following morning. When she glanced at her watch, she noticed that it was already a quarter past ten.

Fully naked, she pranced out of bed, and walked down the corridor. The ubiquitous white carpet was soft under her feet.

Light radio music was blaring from the kitchen. She knocked on the door smartly and pushed it open. Dominic was seated at the kitchen table, reading *The Times* over cornflakes and coffee. He smiled warmly at his guest, as if a girl younger than his daughter walking about naked was the most natural thing in the world. 'Breakfast?'

'Just coffee and toast please,' she said. As he bustled about preparing it for her, she returned briefly to the bedroom, bringing back her handbag, from which she took out her mobile. After making a brief call, she smiled. 'Good news, Dominic.'

His eyes widened. 'The shares?'

She nodded. 'They are doing fantastically well. Up 30p on the day. Bid speculation is rife. Institutions are queuing to snap up Britelite Industries. The small client isn't going to get a look in . . . '

'I'll sell out now,' said the MP. 'I believe in taking a profit where I see it.'

Laura shook her head. 'Let the price run. I will sell your shares once they appear to have reached a peak.'

Chapter 12

Laura caught a taxi back to the office, arriving on the premises at mid-day. 'You're late, Laura,' barked Simon as she entered the dealing room.

'Never mind, I'm doing the business,' she retorted.

He grinned. 'It's more than the others are.' He glanced up at his screen. 'Britelite Industries are up 38p on the day. My sources told me this would be around the peak.'

Laura telephoned the MP, selling him out. He thanked her profusely. 'That's £9,500 you have just made me. Tell me of any other hot tips, won't you?'

She giggled. 'We will make some real money next time.'

Simon meanwhile was mouthing off to the others. 'This gorgeous bird I met last night, she just wouldn't leave at the end, so we booked into the hotel. Phew, she was hot in bed.' He looked at Laura, who had just put down the telephone receiver. 'You could learn from her, darling.'

Laura smiled disdainfully, but it was lost on Simon. The brokers around him were all laughing. When he answered his telephone line, he beamed down the telephone wire. His caller, as it turned out, was Gordon Halcombe. 'What's it like being dealing manager?' asked Simon.

'You should know,' said Gordon. 'You should also know what it's like to be duping John Falmouth at the same time. Anyway I'm ringing for a reason. You made one big fucking mistake last night, Simon.'

'Yeah? Tell me the measure of it.' Simon's voice was casual, but his smile had vanished.

'You took one of Falmouth's harem to bed, a lass who works for his wife. He's paid her off this morning. She was wired up, you know. She has even produced photos of you she took while you were asleep.'

'Get hold of them for me.'

'I will try. Something else. Falmouth is sending solicitor's letters to all your brokers. I don't know what's in them.'

'Thanks Gordon.' He put down the receiver. 'That girl who latched on to me last night. Who let her into the hotel?' he asked.

The brokers looked at each other, and shrugged.

'Why?' asked Laura.

'It doesn't matter,' said Simon. He stood up and stretched himself, yawning. 'I'm going out to lunch with John Falmouth now. You lot must spend the rest of the day priming clients to buy shares in Security Planning Inc. Tell 'em nothing at this stage except to make themselves liquid for Monday.'

John arrived twenty minutes late in the foyer of the Tower Hotel where they had arranged to meet. 'I'm so sorry I've kept you waiting,' he said with all his usual charm. 'My chauffeur took a wrong turning.'

They sat at a corner table in the carvery, with loaded plates. Secretly, Simon was flattered at being invited to lunch with this wealthy man who had mere weeks earlier been his boss.

'How is business doing?' asked John.

'We haven't started yet,' said Simon cheerily.

'Aren't my brokers getting bored?'

'They are too well paid for that, John. And they're no longer yours.'

'They had better not deal our clients,' said John.

'You own the clients?' said Simon.

'Let me buy up Thompson & Thompson,' said John. 'I'll boost turnover, and take the worry from your shoulders.'

'Not a chance John,' said Simon. 'And I'd leave me alone if I were you. I'm a lot younger than you. I'm going to be around for a lot longer. And I'll fight . . . '

'I'm sorry it's come to this,' sighed John. 'England Securities will fight too.'

'We don't want to be associated with you,' murmured Simon. 'You are known to be crooks.'

'If that's so, my dear chap, who has been our dealing manager for the last couple of years?'

Simon shook his head. 'Ask yourself why I and the brokers have left. It wasn't just because you've cut the commissions . . . '

The bill for the lunch was substantial. John looked at Simon: 'Well?'

He laughed. 'I didn't even bring my cheque book.'

As he returned to his offices, Simon felt secretly nostalgic for the old England Securities days, but he concentrated his thoughts on the fortune he was already starting to make at Thompson & Thompson.

Back on the dealing floor, he noticed that his brokers had all gone home early. While the cat's away, the mice will play, he concluded.

At home that evening, Simon read in *The London Evening Standard* about a new private motion proposed by MP Dominic Gardiner in the House of Commons: That this House believes that England Securities' dealings are based on deception, and that clients should cease dealing with the firm forthwith.

All evening his brokers were ringing him to discuss this welcome development. 'England Securities have had it now,' sighed Simon happily. 'We will probably end up hiring all their brokers as well as getting their clients' business . . . '

By eight o'clock on Monday morning, the brokers were all in the dealing room, breakfasting. Daniel and Laura were sitting together whispering. Norman Thompson was scrutinising his account books at the far end, his grizzled head bent low, as if to emphasise that he was playing no part in this meeting.

'The day has finally arrived,' announced Simon. 'Has anyone here not had his cheque cleared.?'

None spoke, and several grunts of satisfaction indicated that all was well in that department.

'No excuses now,' he thundered. 'There is no stopping us. We are going to show our fucking clients what we're made of. We're gonna wipe the floor with England Securities. We're gonna load these clients with stock until it's leaking out of their arses.

'The pitch? Write it down lads . . . ' He paused while they produced pens and pads. 'Security Planning Inc. A company handling all security arrangements for businesses, and homeowners alike world-wide.

'A contract with a major European bank has created substantial City interest in the shares. Buy now at $5.25 while stock lasts. Come in really big on this one. It's a once in a lifetime investment opportunity. . .

'OK you lot, start selling now. And hurry up. There's only a limited amount of stock available, so you will be competing with each other to place it.'

At that point Dario put his head round the door. 'Simon. Daniel. Norman. A word please,' he called out. 'I had better not say it here. Perhaps you would come outside.'

Dario ushered them into the boardroom where they joined Gerard at the table. He beamed around the group. 'I'm offering you as directors an early chance to pick up stock in Security Planning Inc., and its related companies,' he said. 'I don't for a moment suggest that you do it in your own names. Use nominee names and transfer purchasing funds from untraceable accounts.

'The shares are yours for ten cents each. What you may wish to do is buy big now as Gerard here has done and sell the lot when we have offloaded enough of them to justify a major price rise.' He winked. 'This is quite legit, but it still pays to be discreet.'

'Count me in on this,' said Simon.

'Are you sure it will be so profitable?' said Daniel.

Dario chuckled. 'As sure as we ever can be with shares. Take a look at the facts. We are controlling the market. All dealings in these particular shares will be done without involving the Stock Exchange.

Eventually, Thompson & Thompson will be dealing in listed shares as well, to pull the wool over the Exchange's eyes.'

'OK. Count me in too.' said Daniel.

'I'm not so sure. This sounds to me like insider dealing,' said Norman.

'Why should that worry you?' said Gerard. 'You are up to your neck in all this anyway. You might as well make some extra money out of it.'

'I don't like it,' said Norman. He stood up. 'I will be in the dealing room if you want me,' he said. He strode out briskly.

'The uncooperative cunt,' said Dario.

'I'll talk to him,' said Simon. He got up, too, and returned to the dealing-room, Daniel following closely. The brokers in there were working frenziedly. Their ears were glued to the telephone receivers, even as they tapped away on their calculators and scribbled out bargain slips.

'How much money have you all got in, I wonder,' growled Simon.

'I'll count it,' said Daniel, gathering up the bargain slips that lay loose on Simon's desk.

After ten minutes of totting up on his calculator, he stretched himself in his chair and yawned. As bargain slips continued to pile in, he added their value to the total. Brokers remained late that evening, still doing deals.

Eventually, at eight o'clock, Daniel stood up. 'You have all done over £1 million worth of business today,' he said. 'And I'm going home.'

'Well done. If all your clients pay up,' said Simon.

After raising a cheer, the brokers trickled out, leaving him and Daniel with Norman who had emerged from his corner like a snail from its shell.

'We will do twice this tomorrow if we can,' said Simon. 'Believe me, we will all end up millionaires.'

'That's more than the clients will,' said Daniel.

'If they are let down, they won't be dealing with Thompson & Thompson again,' said Norman.

'There are always more clients,' said Simon.

Mid-week, Simon called an emergency meeting. As Gordon Halcombe had warned him would happen, letters had arrived from England Securities' solicitors – at Simon's and the brokers' individual homes. Their old firm was demanding that they cease dealing its clients in compliance with a clause in the contract of employment they had all signed for John Falmouth.

'We will sort England Securities out. Just put them out of your minds,' announced Simon. 'Keep selling Security Planning. We haven't given you each five grand up front for nothing. If you object, piss off home and don't come back.'

'We should be offering less speculative stocks as well,' shouted a broker.

'We're arranging that with the Stock Exchange,' said Simon easily. 'Now get on the phones.'

As his brokers continued to sell, Simon sat back in his seat. So England Securities, currently being criticised in public by Dominic Gardiner, was now trying to turn the tables and force Thompson & Thompson into closure.

Simon was more worried than he let on. John Falmouth was a man of iron will, resourceful and ruthless in business. He was likely to fight Simon to the bitter end, long before which Simon hoped to have made his million and absconded. Perhaps Dominic Gardiner would close John down, he speculated.

The call that came through to him next almost knocked him out of his seat. 'Gerry West here,' came the cheery voice of the only financial journalist in the national newspapers who was partial to England Securities.

'What do you want?' snapped Simon.

'What is this Security Planning Inc. I hear you're selling?' he demanded. 'Where are they quoted? Are you sending out prospectuses? Has the Stock Exchange approved the stock?'

'We are not selling the stocks yet, we are just taking orders,' lied Simon. 'We're sending out prospectuses to interested parties.'

'I've heard different from all this. Can you send me a prospectus, please?'

'OK. But if you libel us in *The Examiner*, we'll sue. We are a reputable stockbroker.'

'Let's hope your clients have no cause to dispute that. I'm naturally unable to promise you what I will or will not write. My first responsibility is to my reading public.'

Simon grimaced. 'Don't trust anything John Falmouth says about us. He's trying to close us down.'

As he replaced the telephone receiver, Simon noticed that the brokers were all eyeing him uncomfortably. They seemed to have run out of steam. Had they heard too much, and conjectured still more?

'What are you all gawking at?' he shouted. The brokers quickly averted their eyes. 'I'll handle these journalists. Just get on with the selling, but watch for trick calls.

'If anybody you don't know enquires about these shares, get them off the line by taking an address and saying you will send them information. If you become greedy and try to sell to them, you might be putting a noose round your own neck. These journalists tape their telephone conversations, and you might find your own words quoted back at you in the national press.'

Laura caught his eye. 'I had a call from a woman who claimed that she had been recommended Security Planning Inc. shares at a party,' she said. 'I heard share price announcements in the background, and just knew she was a journalist. She kept asking, "Can you guarantee a profit?" I told her, "We can't guarantee anything, it wouldn't be legal, and I promised to send her information – which of course I won't.'

'You've got the idea, Laura,' said Simon. 'But in future, nobody here is to talk to suspicious characters about the stock at all. Just say it's a private placing, and put the phone down on 'em.'

That morning Gerard popped in and Simon brought him up to date with events. 'We'll consult Dario,' he said, and they went to find him, Daniel characteristically trailing after them. They tracked him down in the boardroom.

Upon hearing about the solicitor's letter, and Gerry West's call, Dario laughed.

'These are just teething problems,' he declared. 'Gerard, fix a solicitor to visit us on the premises, and we will sort out England Securities. Simon, I will want you to see Security's prospectus proofs in a minute, before I have them printed.

'And tell the brokers to go easy for a bit. We will see what the national press says about us. Meanwhile, don't send out any more contract notes just yet. Tell clients that you are holding off due to fluctuations in the dollar, or the uncertain American markets. It doesn't much fucking matter what the brokers say, provided it sounds plausible and in the clients' interests. We'll send all outstanding contract notes at the same time as the prospectuses.'

As Dario temporarily left them to fetch the prospectus proofs, Gerard winked at Simon. 'With the shares selling at $5.25, think of the profit we're showing on ours.'

'On paper!' said Simon curtly.

Gerard laughed. 'Perk up. Even if we are never able to sell back our shares, what have we lost? Look how little we paid for them.'

Dario was back quickly, and laid the prospectus proofs out on the table. He flicked through the pages. 'Notice this mention of contracts under negotiation with major companies.' He winked. 'Not finalised yet, of course.

'The small print here, which few will read thank goodness, emphasises the high risk nature of the stock, pointing out that it is unquoted on any recognised Stock Exchange. Clients will never be able to say they were not warned.'

Gerard sniggered. 'They will still complain, if the shares go under.'

'We hope that will never happen,' said Simon with a glimmer in his eyes.

'Of course, in shares there are never any guarantees,' quipped Dario.

The next morning, Gerry West's newspaper contained an article he had written, with the damning headline: "Stay clear of Security Planning Inc."

The brokers were almost rabid. Was their beloved new firm collapsing about their ears?

'We've having a rest from dealing,' announced Simon calmly. 'Just play cards or read magazines for the moment.'

'It's your fault, Laura,' shouted a broker, staring at her with hate blazing in his eyes. 'You talked to the Press. You have even admitted it.'

'Yeah, you're too young for this job, Laura,' said another.

'You don't know the game because you were never at England Securities,' another accused her.

Laura scowled. 'I'm as good a broker as anybody in this room.'

'Cool it, everybody,' snapped Simon.

As they settled to play cards for money, Norman Thompson got up and walked out of the room. Daniel La Marche soon followed suit.

After a week of idling, the brokers started protesting their boredom. Clients were still ringing in daily and asking why they hadn't received contract notes.

'We are waiting for more favourable market conditions,' or, 'We are waiting for the dollar to improve,' the brokers would say.

Simon knew that if he failed to keep them stimulated his brokers would not bother to come into work, and might even start looking for alternative employment, as a result of having too much time to examine the consequences of what they were doing and their consciences.

'You are all miles better off here than you would be in any other job,' he told them. 'You are still getting your basic salary. In addition, you have each had five grand up front. You will make more money here than in your wildest dreams, but you have got to be patient. At times when you're paid to come here and do nothing, then you can damned well come here and do nothing.'

To divert them, he introduced strip poker. The office girls, Sarah, Susan and Tracey, as well as Delia the cook were cajoled into joining in. When in the game one of the girls stripped off a vital garment, the men wolfwhistled. This beat selling shares.

As Susan and Tracey were no longer on the switchboard, all incoming clients' queries were directed to an answering machine. Letters started flooding into Thompson & Thompson. Investors were complaining bitterly of their brokers' evasiveness.

When the novelty of strip poker had worn off, Simon sent the office girls packing, back to their duties. 'I reckon we've got another four or five weeks before we are dealing again,' he told his brokers. 'Old Norman has left us to ourselves too. What we'll do is take over a company. I would suggest we go for The Merden Group, which will be one in the eye for John Falmouth.

'I happen to know a bit about them because I had access to privileged information as dealing manager at England Securities.

They have been looking for a buyer for some months. I reckon we'd get them for under £1 million. No prizes for guessing how we would raise the finance . . . !' Simon beamed round the room. Smiles appeared on the brokers' faces.

'From our clients?' one murmured.

'You've got it,' yapped Simon. 'You lot with your England Securities training all ought to realise that the best money to use is always other people's.'

One broker grinned. 'If we own The Merden Group, we'll gain some control over England Securities too.'

'I was wondering who would catch on to that,' said Simon: 'It's true, provided they haven't gone under by then. We might even save England Securities, pump in capital and use it to push shares in The Merden Group ourselves.

'OK, now we will need a bank loan, on the back of clients' monies we'll be raising. Every broker here will be a director of the new take-over vehicle in direct proportion to the equity he's raised for it.

'We also need a written proposal,' he continued. 'And an Extel card on The Merden Group. Furthermore, I will be setting up a company as a take-over vehicle. If it's successful, Thompson & Thompson can go and fuck themselves. I will be discussing the take-over of The Merden Group with my accountant, and I will need someone here to accompany me . . . '

He broke off abruptly, as the door opened. Dario glanced inside. 'The solicitor is ready,' he announced. 'You lot had better see him in the boardroom one by one.'

When he had left, Simon grinned at his little team. 'For the time being, we will keep all possibilities open. If the sale of all these shares takes off, that's great. If it doesn't, we'll have an alternative plan, so keep your fucking mouths shut. While you're each giving testimony to the solicitor, I'll be there to help you . . . '

The solicitor was a keen young dark-haired Oxbridge type with a brisk smile and a courteous manner. Dispensing with small talk, he fired sharp pertinent questions at each broker in turn, in private session.

He took notes as the brokers explained why they had left England Securities, taking their clients with them. Simon prompted them all to tell the same story, constantly breaking in with. 'Go on, tell how the stocks we sold at England Securities always seemed to go down in value. How shares in The Merden Group were ramped. How brokers and managers alike there were put under such pressure to hardsell dud stocks that it was no longer possible to act in the clients' interests.'

The brokers poured out all the atrocities they could muster about England Securities. After they had all seen him, the solicitor snapped shut his notebook. He stood up, offering Simon his hand. 'We will sort England Securities out,' he said in his posh accent. 'It's highly unlikely they will try to enforce their employment contacts by taking court action. Look out much dirt would come out if they did!'

A few days later, the solicitor had drafted a proposed reply to England Securities, which he sent to Simon and to every broker individually for reference.

Early most mornings, Dario would put in a brief appearance in the dealing room, propose solutions to any problems Simon put to him, and then leave. Immediately then discussions for the take-over of The Merden Group would proceed.

One morning, Simon bumped into Laura in the corridor. She was just coming back to the dealing room from the loo. 'Darling,' he said, clapping his hands on her hips.

She flashed him a scornful smile. 'You want another thrashing?'

He laughed. 'Perhaps I do. But more importantly for now, how much have you told Dario about our plans to take over The Merden Group?'

She flushed. 'I've told him nothing. My loyalty is to you.'

'You had better come with me to see my accountant,' he said. 'You can smile at him sweetly if need be.'

'Fair enough,' she said.

He was letting Laura in on too much, reflected Simon, as they sat in his accountant's office. But he wanted her with him for other reasons.

The young dark haired accountant they saw was one of several Simon juggled for his various business interests. He was probably the dodgiest of the lot.

He listened while Simon explained his take-over plans, then he grinned: 'When you told me on the telephone that you were looking to take over a company, I figured it had to be The Merden Group. It was the logical choice. So look what I've got here.'

Opening a cardboard folder, he removed The Merden Group's latest annual report, its Extel card, and various brochures and documents relating to the company's products. 'The Merden Group is in a cash flow crisis, there is no doubt about it,' he said. 'Its chairman has been looking for a buyer over the last nine months. Furtheremore the company's dealings with England Securities' corporate finance department are under investigation by the DTI. Meanwhile the chairman and directors are open to offer . . . ' He laughed. 'It's a goer. If you can raise the finance.'

'That's the least of our problems,' said Simon.

Laura smiled at the accountant. 'With your help, of course.'

As he drove Laura back home, Simon deviated from the route, parking down a leafy surburban alley. 'Lover's Lane,' he announced.

She shook her head. 'Wishful thinking,' she said grimly. 'You had better drive on.'

'Spoilsport,' he said. He groped her breasts impulsively, brushing aside her defensive hands. She wrenched herself free of him, and wriggled smartly out of the car. He was after her immediately, seizing her waist, swinging her round to face him, no longer with gentleness.

The pain that shot through his testicles was so sharp that it left him doubled up and howling involuntarily while tears stung his eyes.

'What did you knee me there for?' he asked after she had half dragged him back into the car.

'You're a waste of space, Simon,' she said. 'Your brokers are doing nothing. You are dreaming about a take-over that will never happen. If you use client funds for it, you and your team could be charged with a criminal offence, as the accountant would have explained had you put him properly in the picture. Besides, I'm bored with you as a man and I don't like to fuck failures.'

Dario confronted Simon as he came back to the office with Laura. 'Been out bonking, have you?'

'No such luck,' said Simon.

'Stick around now,' said Dario. 'I want to talk to you.' He led him alone to the boardroom, closing the door behind them. 'How is the smear campaign against John Falmouth going?' he asked.

'Dominic Gardiner has attacked England Securities in Parliament,' said Simon.

'That was yonks ago,' said Dario impatiently. 'What's been cooking since then?'

'Give us time,' said Simon.

Dario laughed. 'Get your skates on, kid. I want him wiped out. At the same time, we've another target.'

'Gerry West?' inquired Simon.

'Spot on! You've started on him already?'

'Yeah,' lied Simon. 'Is that all?'

'No.' Dario glared at him. 'I don't walk about with my eyes closed, Simon. Your brokers are losing their edge. Don't leave the building for hours again, unless it's on company business.'

Chapter 13

Back in the dealing room, Simon called over a broker still hanging about, a short chunky lad with an ill-shaven chin who had been smoking his umpteenth cigarette while scrutinising the racing pages of his tabloid newspaper.

'Go to a newspaper library tomorrow,' he said. 'I want copies of every article that Gerry West has written about England Securities or John Falmouth in *The Examiner* for the last two years. We want evidence that he favours them, so highlight any parts which indicate this.'

The three other brokers left in the room, including Laura, overheard the conversation and gathered round.

'Remember Gerry West's book, *How to Survive in The Post Crash Stock Market*,' said one. 'England Securities was distributing free copies to its brokers immediately after John Falmouth was appointed chairman.'

'Remember, too, Gerry West used to be a client of England Securities,' said another broker. 'He was sold some decent stocks, then mysteriously his name and client details vanished from the computers.'

'Which stocks were they?' asked Simon.

'The best one was Xavier Investments. The little third market company over which John Falmouth has been accused of insider dealing.'

'I remember now.' said Simon.

'Also he came to John Falmouth's birthday party. The news spread all over England Securities, remember. John went around boasting he had him in his pocket.'

'We must get sworn testimony of all this,' said Simon. 'Our solicitors will prepare an affidavit. We'll take Gerry West to the cleaners. Not only will he not dare to rail against Thompson & Thompson, but he will be lucky to have a job left, by the time we've finished with him.'

Back at home that night, Simon slumped in front of the TV, trying to wind down. He had dined well and was lost to the world. More problems than he had anticipated were arising in this Thompson & Thompson lark and he needed respite. For the time being at least, he resolved that the takeover plans should be set aside.

His wife, Donna, went off into the kitchen to make tea, which they were both in the habit of drinking during the long evenings together. She had just put Mark to bed.

Suddenly, she swung back into the living room, wringing her hands. Her eyes were wide and her pupils dilated. She was frowning intensely.

'What's up, love?' demanded Simon.

'There's a man in the garden with a video camera, filming the house.'

Setting his lips, Simon sprang to his feet. Nervous energy zipped through his veins like a current.

'Don't go outside,' said Donna quickly. 'Ring the police instead.'

'The police!' Simon snorted. 'Wake up woman. By the time they arrived, the film crew would have done its dirty work.'

Dressed as he was in his business suit, without putting on a coat, he rushed outside, trying to slam the front door behind him, but his wife ran after him, stopping it from closing with her foot.

Simon discovered the intruder lurking in the garden. The man, a shadowy figure in the darkness, didn't attempt to run away, but instead turned the video camera on Simon, filming him in his wrath.

Simon seized him by the upturned collar of his coat. He grabbed at the video camera and missed it. His victim dropped the camera on the lawn and took a grip round Simon's waist. Simon squeezed his throat. 'You're working for Falmouth, admit it,' he said.

The man grimaced. His bull-dog face was coarse and red, his skin crinkled and weather-beaten. His nose was smashed in, his jaw swollen. A gap in his front teeth made his mouth look ominous. His black hair, greying at the temples, was crew cut.

Simon squeezed harder and his victim choked. 'Admit it,' he repeated.

Suddenly Donna was running before him. 'Simon, look behind you!' she screamed. 'Run!'

Releasing his grip, Simon tried to bolt, but the cameraman in his own turn was clinging still to him. Even as he writhed, the cloth-wrapped brick came crashing down on his skull. The inside of his head might have burst into flames, so intensely did he feel the pain. He sagged, collapsing onto the lawn. The cameraman and his rescuer savagely and continuously kicked him, before vanishing into the night. They had made a good team.

The police arrived minutes afterwards, summoned by Donna. Before the ambulance came, a police officer asked him who he thought had organised the attack.

'John Falmouth, the chairman of England Securities,' said Simon sullenly.

'Did you recognise your attackers?'

Simon shook his head.

Upon inspection it turned out he was not badly hurt. Almost incredibly he had escaped with sore ribs and a black eye.

Back at work, his co-directors were unsympathetic.

'You should never have confronted him,' said Gerard.

'Why didn't you just call the police immediately?' asked Daniel.

'What was the use?' snarled Simon.

Dario alone considered the implications. 'We'll fix extra locks on your front door by courtesy of Security Planning Inc.' he promised. 'And we will have a security guard in the offices here.'

'I'll second those proposals,' said Simon.

The new security guard whom Dario selected certainly looked ideal for the post. He was a muscular bruiser of a fellow in his late twenties, some six foot four in height, who in his turbulent youth had been variously a bouncer in nightclubs, a rugby player, a football hooligan, and a small-time professional boxer.

His chubby red face appeared permanently bruised, and his nose was smashed in from several angles making him snuffle and wheeze. Flexing his muscles, he would speak curtly and gruffly, conveying that he was a man of few words and much action.

'Strangers are never allowed on the premises except under the escort of a member of staff,' Dario told him. 'Don't hesitate to throw them out.'

'A pleasure, sir,' beamed the security guard, clearly meaning it.

Over the next couple of weeks, a solicitor's letter went to Gerry West's newspaper, threatening legal action due to his inaccurate writings and his partiality to England Securities.

Some days afterwards, Dario came into the dealing room. 'Gerry West's editor has apologised to us,' he announced. 'Gerry's going to be on a leash from now on.'

After being approved, solicitor's letters were sent to John Falmouth from Simon and from every broker there, each saying the same: His client had resigned because he could no longer tolerate England Securities' attitude towards him and his clients. He had been forced into using dubious techniques to sell often worthless stock. Consequently, he did not feel himself bound by the clause in the contract he had signed which would impede him from contacting his old clients.

The letters elicited no response from England Securities' solicitors. Subsequently, Thompson & Thompson's solicitors sent another batch of letters to this effect: Since England Securities had not refuted the points raised, Simon's team of brokers would now resume approaching its clients.

The sales campaign at Thompson & Thompson recommenced with a bang. The brokers all telephoned the clients whose purchase orders had not been put through, reconfirming before sending out contract notes. To Simon's annoyance, many clients were cancelling.

'I simply no longer have the money,' they would say, or 'If you contact me again, I will make a formal complaint.'

'England Securities have been warning the clients off us,' said Simon impatiently. 'Just drag as many as you can back into the net. Any who listen to John Falmouth's boys will end up getting stung by them, I'd say.'

Upon hearing Laura speaking on the telephone with Dominic Gardiner, Simon hovered. 'You made good money on the Britelite Industries account trade,' she was saying. 'This is a less risky deal. I can virtually guarantee a 75 cents profit, and your money will only be tied up for three or four weeks so come in big . . . in this case £250,000 isn't enough. Double it. It really is worth it.

'I'll be glad to look at John Falmouth's letter, but don't accept his invitation to visit his firm. He's a master con man and would pull the wool over your eyes. Everything would appear above board.

'Right, I'll collect your cheque from you in the Commons. Tonight . . . '

As she put down the receiver, she glanced up at Simon triumphantly.

'I'd better accompany you,' he said.

At five o'clock, shortly before they left, Simon checked the day's turnover. With Laura's sale to Dominic Gardiner it amounted to a cool £750,000 worth, not taking into account any cancellations to come.

'We have a long way to go yet, lads,' he announced.

As he and Laura were passing the switchboard desk, Dario sauntered over. 'How's business?'

'Just great. And it will be even better tomorrow,' said Simon.

Dario nodded. Hanging about until Simon and Laura had left the premises, he promptly entered the dealing room.

A few brokers lingering there, exchanging boastful stories about their sexual exploits, turned to look at him.

'How much business have you guys done today?' he demanded.

A broker gestured towards the bargain slips, piled on Simon's desk under a paperweight. 'Three quarters of a million quid's worth,' he said.

Dario nodded. 'We'll never run out of stock. So keep your clients panting for more.'

'You bet,' said one broker.

'So long as the pay cheques keep coming in,' said another.

The brokers laughed to a man.

'We're all in this for the fucking money,' said Dario. 'That's the most realistic attitude we can have.'

'I like the deal we've got,' remarked one broker. 'Ten per cent plus basic is cute.'

Dario chuckled. 'So long as you keep doing the business, we'll look after you. And remember Thompson & Thompson is here to stay. We're not a fly by night sharepusher like England Securities.'

'We won't be going back there in a hurry,' said another broker. Again, they all laughed.

'We'll have them treading in their own shit so deep that they'll drown in it,' said Dario. He turned away, leaving the brokers in stitches, any faltering loyalties reinvigorated. Dario wanted all the brokers to stick around for as long as the operation would last – which was likely to be only a few months, his principal reason for suddenly now setting off to visit Padre Lorenzo.

Catching an early morning flight, he was in Rome at midnight and at the monastery by 1.30pm. At 7.30 in the morning, he joined Lorenzo in the dining room for breakfast.

'I'm concerned about the loyalty of the brokers, even of my fellow directors,' he declared. Laura, too, is keeping secrets from me. She and the broking team were plotting a company take-over using clients' funds. I found this out only by eavesdropping, Laura never told me anything. I've noticed too she is fixated on her dead father. How far should I trust her? I'm worried that the worm may turn.'

'You don't have to keep her or any of them on the boil for much longer now,' said Lorenzo. 'Just keep stressing how they must trust you, how they must be loyal to you and how much money they will make. And get them to work fast. Remember, a silent time bomb is ticking, until it all folds.'

Dario nodded. 'They'll do what they are told only as long as they think they will be well paid for it.'

'Listen to me carefully how you should handle that problem,' said Lorenzo. 'Give Simon charge of the client account. He can pay in clients' cheques, and out of these, once cleared, he can pay himself and his brokers monies due. When the chips are down, it is him the Serious Fraud Office and the regulatory authorities will have by the balls for mixing client and company funds.'

'I'll know nothing,' announced Dario.

'By that stage you won't even have to face questioning,' urged Lorenzo. 'You will have done your disappearing act.'

At this point, Anne approached their table, and started wiping down its surface with a damp cloth. Throwing back her scarfed head, she glanced at Padre Lorenzo. Her features subtly conveyed a loathing which made Dario flinch.

Two of the other Franciscans who had just come in for breakfast sat alongside Padre Lorenzo, where they were conveniently placed for eavesdropping.

Like a lady with her skirt, Lorenzo gathered up his cassock. 'Let's get some fresh air,' he said.

At this early hour, they had the courtyard to themselves. A harsh sun glared in a cloudless sky.

'My time as a Franciscan is coming to an end,' said Lorenzo as they strolled. 'For safety's sake, I need to find another nest, another identity. My enemies will find it harder to hit a moving target. But you, Dario, are unidentifiable in England, are you not?'

'True,' said Dario. 'My South Kensington flat is leased in Thompson & Thompson's name. All my expenditures are on the company credit card. Only Laura knows my real name . . . '

'Make it clear to her that if she puts a foot wrong, her mother will have a fatal accident,' said Lorenzo.

'Ha ha.' Dario couldn't restrain himself. 'Perhaps she should have a fatal accident, anyway.'

Lorenzo grinned. 'After Laura has fulfilled her task, perhaps they both will.'

The conniving Franciscan touched Dario's forearm, his cowl flapping in the breeze. On the road nearby, some hundred labourers were plodding to work with glum faces. There but for a life of crime go I, thought Dario, and smiled smarmily back at the Padre.

'You and I speak the same language, Dario,' sighed Lorenzo. 'That's why I care for you. Now when you do your disappearing act, it will have to be sudden. Don't expect the luxury of notice. You will need to start making your preparations now.

He tightened his grip on Dario's arm, leading him onto the road. They followed its course for a few hundred yards alongside the thickets. The scent of wild flowers and hay filled Dario's nostrils and he shook his head like a horse shaking off buzzing flies. It was going to be a scorcher of a day.

In Lorenzo's presence, he felt strangely guilty about being absent from Thompson & Thompson at this crucial stage. Was he not ducking his responsibilities? Would he not have years of his life afterwards to travel continents?

As if reading his thoughts, the Padre spoke briskly. 'You may only have a few weeks left at Thompson & Thompson. So get Laura out of your flat. If she kicks up a fuss, offer her a cash bribe of say £300 and moving expenses, *after* she has moved out with all her possessions, and you've fixed a new lock on the door. Bear in mind that under UK law she's a tenant with rights.'

'Your next step is to move out your own possessions. Hire some "no name" movers from outside London, and have all your stuff transferred to a private store where you control access. Do this quickly, and don't go later to check on your stored items.

'Give a specially made up name and address, and a misleading reason to the agents who rent the storage space to you. The next time you go back there will be to transfer all your stuff to another storage premises.'

Lorenzo led Dario back towards the monastery. Down through a back way, he led him into the heart of the catacombs. Unlocking the creaky door that led to the disused chapel, Lorenzo ushered him inside.

He outspread his new documents over the altar. 'You will be going straight to Los Angeles after the scam. It's a big anonymous city with enough resident freaks and crooks for Uncle Sam to concentate its attentions on, without adding you to the hit list. You will open several bank accounts.

'When you're asked for your Social Security number, make one up on the spot. Just remember it has nine digits. The IRS won't bother to check it for a year or two.

'This is a new driver's licence. A phoney state ID card. Fresh passports, under your new name, Dale Gatsby. There is a real person of this name, of about your age and size, with a divorced wife of about Emily's age. The guy is confined in one of America's more discreet crazy houses. He's a human vegetable. You will become him.

'What you must do is get to the Canadian border on your British passport, then put it in a safe deposit box in Canada. Next pass into the United States, saying you are an American citizen who'd been day-tripping. Study your profile,' – he tapped some papers – 'so you can answer basic questions. If they are suspicious, you may need to show your ID card.

'You will obviously have to perfect an American accent so start practising now, before you adopt your new identity. I'll give you some tapes to listen to and imitate. We can speak on the telephone at nights, and I'll advise you on how authentic you're sounding.

'Remember, say nothing about your plans. Assume even your friends, if you have any, will sell you down the river. Ninety per cent of arrests are made through "helpful co-operation" of neighbours and relatives. Need I say more?'

Dario opened his mouth, but Lorenzo silenced him with his hands. 'From what I hear, Johnnie Butler is no longer your friend. And you'll never want to meet anybody connected with Thompson & Thompson again. You will need to keep the lowest profile you can.'

Meanwhile, back in London, Thompson & Thompson's offices were buzzing with activity.

Simon and Laura had met Dominic Gardiner, and he had showed them samples of the many letters of complaint about England Securities, promising that he would be pressing further for the stockbroking firm's closure.

Gardiner had believed Simon and Laura's testimony that England Securities was spreading malicious and misleading rumours about Thompson & Thompson, and that the firm alone had instigated the "ill-conceived" bad press on Security Planning Inc.

More importantly, Gardiner had paid a cheque for £500,000 for his shares in Security Planning Inc., on the understanding that he would be sold out of the shares within five weeks. The cheque was currently in the process of being cleared.

Back in the dealing room, Simon screamed instructions to his brokers. 'Tell your clients they will be out of their Security Planning

Inc. shares within five weeks, and that we're guaranteeing a minimum profit of 75 cents a share. It's a fucking licence to print money, so they should all be coming in big . . . '

Taking their cue, the brokers all shouted down the blowers like madmen. 'Sir, if it's the last investment you ever make in your life, this is the one. Come in heavy. Throw your chips on this recommendation. Don't listen to what your wife says about it. What's it to do with her? . . . '

The bargain slips, hastily filled in, were again arriving on Simon's desk in droves. In the midst of all the activity, Daniel came in lugging with him the new prospectuses for Security Planning Inc., which he proceeded to drop on Simon's desk.

Simon picked one up. The prospectus was contained in an expensively produced, glossy grey folder. 'OK you lot,' he shouted. 'Get off the phones and start sending out these prospectuses. Don't waste any more time on it than you have to. We're here, after all, to sell stock . . . '

While the brokers were addressing envelopes, many grumbled amongst themselves.

'What the fuck is up with you all now?' demanded Simon.

'Johnnie Butler's brokers in Paris have been contacting our clients, warning them against dealing with us, and using up their available funds by loading them with worthless Canadian stock,' said a broker.

'The brokers from the other dealing room must have photocopied our leads before they were kicked out,' groaned Simon. 'For fuck's sake, you lot, take your leads and records home with you at nights. There may be other traitors within our ranks . . . '

By late that afternoon, Simon had estimated some £800,000 worth of business had been done that day. The brokers were still selling and putting prospectuses into envelopes.

'Anybody who doesn't send out prospectuses is running his own risks,' he announced. 'These days, you are all personally open to prosecution for failing to take account of your clients' interests. If you're going to break the law, do it in a less obvious way, as I've no doubt you all know how to!'

'We've run out of clients,' declared a broker. The others murmured their agreement.

'Next week, you can offer a new stock to clients who have already bought shares in Security Planning Inc.,' said Simon. 'For the time being, I'll get you all some new clients.'

He quit the dealing room, seeking out Gerard, and found him looking over some accounts in the back office.

'My team is desperate for business,' he said. 'We must have Norman Thompson's – the firm's – old clients.'

Gerard nodded. 'We may have to twist Norman's arm though. All his clients are cautious pensioners used to investing accordingly.

Don't sell them straight shares in Security Planning Inc. Sell them the debentures instead.' He rummaged in a drawer, and brought out a sales pitch which he handed to Simon.

It read as follows:

Security Planning Inc. Debentures.

Security Planning Inc. Debentures are an investment vehicle specifically designed for clients who don't wish to be exposed to the uncertainties of the regular stock market.

These debentures are convertible into shares at any time you choose. Over the forthcoming six months, a 75% mark-up in share price is anticipated. Over the next 12 months, 200%.

For so long as you are holding the debentures, you will be receiving 15% interest a year, which is considerably more than current building society rates. Interest will be paid to you in the form of a monthly cheque.

Simon glanced askew at Gerard. Both men grinned faintly. It wasn't necessary to comment. 'Let's find Norman,' said Gerard.

Thompson & Thompson's former chairman was in the adjacent office. He looked at his two colleagues as if to say, "What are you two after, talking to me?"

'We would like to approach your old clients,' said Simon.

Norman shook his grizzled head. 'They're just not liquid at the moment. Their funds are tried up in unit trust, gilts and equities they have bought through the firm over the years . . . '

'Some may want to convert,' said Simon.

'It's our right to have access to them,' said Gerard.

Norman opened his mouth and closed it again. He pointed to a green filing cabinet in the corner. 'You'll find my client records in there. My name mustn't be quoted in any of these transactions.'

Chapter 14

In the dealing room the next day, the brokers were lounging about. Simon didn't reprimand them. In his opinion, they needed the respite. He distributed Norman's old client records.

The brokers were startled and pleased. Thompson & Thompson was at last offering them something. Here was an opportunity to give their established clients a long overdue rest.

'Anybody who doesn't feel like dealing these, give 'em back to me, and I'll pass them to someone who will,' announced Simon.

Everybody laughed. They all smelled business.

'What you do is simple,' continued Simon. 'You ring these suckers up. Ask them what they are holding in the way of unit trusts and other fixed interest investments, checking it all against their records.

'Then tell them you're a broker at Thompson & Thompson, with our good friend Norman Thompson . . . ' He smirked, and the brokers tittered. 'Tell them that with their permission, you will be taking all funds out of their current spread of holdings, and will reinvest them into Security Planning Inc. Debentures which pay fifty per cent higher interest than they are now getting.' He paused while a broker distributed the new written sales pitches. Everybody was looking distinctly uneasy.

'Remember, act as if you're switching the funds anyway, and you'll get the client's consent,' added Simon.

The brokers read the pitch, scrutinised the new client records, then hummed and ha-ed. Simon grimaced. The longer they were given to think about it, the more likely they were to become conscience-stricken.

'Right, on the phones. I want all these new clients sold debentures in the next hour, before Norman comes in and takes all the client records back,' he shouted. 'Come on. All those expensive cars and houses you want. All those holidays, those nights out. Here's your chance to make your fortunes. You get 10p on every pound's worth you peddle!'

The brokers did the business. Nonetheless, hardened as they were, their faces registered their distaste for it. The transactions were all over within minutes, most of the 'old fogeys' telephoned agreeing to the switch over, Simon was relieved to note. A few, though, wanted a word with Norman Thompson first. 'Forget them,' ordered Simon.

After their evil deed was done, the brokers started playing cards or reading magazines. The atmosphere was loaded. They had just indulged in blatant misrepresentation, although this would be hard to prove. Most nonetheless would not have done it, had not Simon pressurised them to act without giving them time to think.

The average portfolio of these clients was worth £60,000-£80,000 usually spread over eight to ten investments, each of which had in varying degrees appreciated in value over the previous few years, providing a small but regular overall interest return. It had been wise and cautious investment. So clearly in the interests of the client.

The ten per cent commissions accruing to brokers for sale of the debentures meant they earned an average £6,000-£8,000 on each completed transaction. Most managed around ten transactions. In what other field of business would they earn £60,000-£80,000 each, for an hour's work?

Simon himself was ahead more than £600,000 from the manoeuvre.

The following morning, he was notified by Thompson & Thompson's bank that a substantial number of clients' cheques had now cleared. In accordance with Gerard's instructions, Simon wrote out wage cheques for brokers from the client account. He knew vaguely that this was illicit, but didn't care. He took pride in considering himself a pragmatist.

When they saw their cheques, the brokers started yelling for joy. £20,000-£30,000-£40,000. It was incredible, they were saying, and Simon grinned. It was nothing compared to what he was making out of them, the poor, stupid sheep.

The brokers nipped out to bank their cheques. 'Don't be long,' said Simon. 'The moment you're back, we have new stocks to sell. All the satellite companies in the network.'

'It's all the same stock,' quipped a broker. Everybody laughed.

On her way back from the bank Laura stopped to buy a newspaper. She was in no hurry. The truth was that the previous day's work in her view signalled the end for Thompson & Thompson, for news of the ill-fated debentures sales would surely leak out.

Inside the newsagents, she saw Daniel standing at the magazine stall, reading an astrology journal. Laura tapped him on the shoulder and he started, looking round. 'Phew,' he said, recognising her. 'I thought my number was up there.'

'It will be for both of us if we don't take a grip on what's happening at Thompson & Thompson,' she said.

When she had bought her paper, Daniel put his arm round her shoulders and led her out. As they strolled down Oxford Street, an anonymous couple in the crowds, Laura was aware that they resembled lovers more than business partners and it pleased her.

'What have my honourable colleagues done this time?' said Daniel sarcastically. For all his gambling ways there was a straight streak in him that Laura found touching.

'If you'd been in the office recently, you'd know,' she said.

As she related to him the events of the debentures campaign, she felt his whole body shudder. Daniel pursed his lips, frowning as if to corrugate his features irreparably; then he said in a gritty measured tone, I've spent more time and energy keeping Gerard out of jail than in achieving anything positive in my own life. Once again, I'll be coming to his rescue. The debentures bargains must be cancelled before we're all ruined instantly. I'll have a word in Norman's ear.'

'What can that senile old twit do?' demanded Laura. 'He's been bought out, anyway.'

'He can ring his old clients and tell them to cancel the transactions,' said Daniel.

'That's clever. He'll do it, because he will be scared you'll otherwise implicate him in fraud,' said Laura.

Daniel nodded. 'The running of Thompson & Thompson, like anything dear Gerard involves himself in, is getting out of hand. I wouldn't advise you to stick around much longer.'

'I'm only here for the money . . .' muttered Laura.

He laughed. 'You must have made a fortune already.'

'I've had about forty grand. I'm owed another £100,000. Or £35,000 if you exclude commission due on the debentures sales I made yesterday.'

'Take what you've got and run,' advised Daniel. 'This is bound to lead to trouble. I'd be off like a greyhound, if I wasn't my brother's keeper.'

'I'll bet Thompson & Thompson owes you money, too,' said Laura. 'And with your gambling habits, Daniel, you need all you can get.'

'You're smart, I'll give you that,' said Daniel. Laura had to lengthen her step to keep pace with him.

'They keep me dangling,' he continued. 'Dario owes me forty grand, and nobody even knows when he will next grace the premises.'

'You must confront him,' said Laura. 'We've really landed on a pirate ship.'

She slipped back into the dealing room, where brokers were all drinking champagne by courtesy of Kit.

'What is there to celebrate?' asked Laura, as a glass was pressed on her. The brokers were curiously reticent. One then whispered to her: 'Kit's taking £40,000 in clients' funds to invest in a Docklands flat he's picked up at a rockbottom price. He's expecting to make a bomb on it, once the property market picks up.'

'That won't be for a while yet, with interest rates being as high as they are, and with all the sackings in the City. But I suppose the clients know what they're doing,' said Laura.

'This is it, they don't. The clients assume their monies have gone into Security Planning Inc.,' grinned the broker.

Simon sauntered over, but not in time to catch the tail end of the conversation. He looked at Laura. 'You were a long time going to the bank.'

'I had an urgent meeting with the manager,' she lied glibly.

At that very moment, Dario was touching down on British soil. He was not ready to return to the office on that day. He had other work to do. Returning to South Kensington, he found himself a public telephone box. He knew never to make important calls from home, in case his line was tapped.

He telephoned Dr. Rubens, his personal lawyer, who was a partner in one of the City's most prestigious firms.

'Operation A in five weeks or so,' he announced. "A" was understood between them to signify "Abroad".

'Very good.' Dr. Rubens' upper class accent had a lively American twang to it. He had worked for some years as an attorney in New York. It was indeed for his expertise in international law that Dario was hiring him.

'Once I'm gone, I may be back within weeks. But it could take months,' Dario spoke slowly to maximise clarity. 'Until or if you get further instructions from me, pay the rent on my South Kensington flat from the Jersey account.'

'Suppose I need to get in touch with you?' said Dr. Rubens.

'I was coming to that,' said Dario. He dictated the address of a mail receiving service in Hong Kong.

As he put down the telephone receiver, Dario chuckled to himself. That Hong Kong address was the first link in a chain of communications and he was safe, he knew, in giving it to anyone.

The mail receiving service in Hong Kong had already been instructed to open and fax any communications to him in South Africa. The South African address was another mail drop, which in turn would fax anything to him in Canada. Canada in its turn would fax anything to him in Brazil.

The Brazil mail drop was instructed to hold all mail for him until further instructions. Dario planned to phone the Brazil service periodically to check if there were any messages, and if there were to have them faxed to him at a message centre in some hotel within easy access but where he wasn't actually staying.

Padre Lorenzo had given him the blueprint for this, further instructing that he need only use two links for sending out his own outgoing messages, as this would be sufficient to conceal his whereabouts.

That afternoon, Dario gathered up his new passport, in the name of Dale Gatsby. Wrapping this in carbon paper so it would survive X-ray checks, he sent it by unregistered mail to the address of one of Padre Lorenzo's contacts in San Francisco.

Many of the records he might require as to Dale Gatsby's phoney past had not yet been manufactured. Lorenzo had explained to him that he should recreate all the records he wanted at his leisure, should provide the address of a mailing forwarding service as that of the source of those records, and should handle the correspondence himself, photocopying altered documents, offset printing and rubber-stamping where appropriate.

Next, Dario took a taxi to the prestigious modern flat of Andrew Jordan, his landlord, off Kensington High Street.

Jordan, himself ex-eurobond dealer turned property and antiques trader, opened the door. He was wearing overalls, and smelt of turpentine. 'Come in, Dario,' he said. 'I was just staining a bookcase.'

Inside the living room, he pushed a sherry on Dario while he removed his overall and had a wash. He was back again in a twinkling. 'How can I help you?'

'I'm afraid my business requires me to move,' said Dario. 'You will be receiving regular cheques from my lawyer for the rent, and eventually I'll be back.'

The landlord nodded. 'What about your mail?'

'I'd be very grateful if you could forward it on to me.' Dario pressed a £50 note in his hand. 'My lawyer will let you know as soon as I've gone. He will give you a forwarding address, and £10 for every item of mail you forward me. I'm also giving you power of attorney so you can sign for registered and recorded delivery. If you need to get in touch with me urgently, please do so through my lawyer.'

'Very good.' Jordan showed him out courteously, knowing better than to ask questions.

Dario was at last ready to flee without notice if he had to, although there remained a number of preparations to complete.

He rang Lorenzo that evening from a public telephone, and the Franciscan confirmed that he had booked him five weeks hence into an international hotel in Los Angeles under the name of Dale Gatsby, where he would be staying as a long term guest by special arrangement at half price: 'If you need to arrive earlier, just ring the hotel with a date,' he said. 'There will be a room all right. It's not yet even Christmas. It's only in the high season that the hotel fills up.'

Dario stayed chatting to him, trying out an American accent which Lorenzo found some fault with, although generally applauding him for it.

Before hanging up, Lorenzo instructed him to visit Georgio Thomassino the following morning. He could now reveal that their "Big Bang" as he had jokingly rechristened the grand robbery, was scheduled for 1st November, six weeks ahead.

'Georgio is trying to defer the date. Tell him Thompson & Thompson won't last long enough for that luxury,' said Lorenzo.

As Dario let himself back into his flat that night, Laura greeted him in the hall. He kissed her cursorily. 'How's business been in my absence?'

'Good,' she said. 'But Simon and the other brokers are slowly going off the rails. The firm's starting to take too many risks.'

'I'll check out what you're saying tomorrow,' said Dario, coming into the living room. 'Right now, I've some news for you.'

He settled himself into a chair, while Laura took his coat.

'I'm quitting this flat,' he announced. 'Too many people know of it. I'm making other accommodation arrangements, which I'm keeping private. You will have to find somewhere else to live. Take a leaf out of my book and be discreet . . .'

She nodded sagely. 'It's all coming to a head now, isn't it?'

'I didn't say that,' said Dario cautiously.

She laughed, and left him there.

Dario closed his eyes. It didn't appear that she would be creating any fuss. More urgent a preoccupation was how he would set about concealing his monies and assets in preparation for leaving the country.

Thompson & Thompson's client funds, following initial pay-offs to directors and staff, were being regularly and swiftly transferred to a confidential trust in Liechstenstein. He would retain personally a sixth of the sum accumulated, which should amount to well over a million pounds. Invested, it should be enough to keep him for life. With the aim of increasing overall monies accumulated, he would soon be witholding staff commissions, never in fact to be paid.

Furthermore, Dario would be withdrawing all funds from his personal UK bank accounts, then redistributing them into various foreign bank accounts under phoney names, using different passports as evidence of his identities. Lorenzo had warned him to feed his new bank accounts only with cash, so that origins of transactions would prove untraceable.

Eventually, he would convert some of his share of Thompson & Thompson's ill-gotten gains into gold bars which he would store in a safe deposit box currently booked under a false name on his behalf in an Austrian bank. It was a local bank with no branches in the US or UK, so pressure could not be brought to bear on it by those respective governments to break bank secrecy and reveal details of his hidden treasure, should anything go wrong in future and an investigation be mounted.

Finally Dario would be distributing monies from the sale of his shares in Security Planning Inc. into the keeping of a discreet Hungarian bank, used to handling capitalist money successfully, and offering a totally confidential service that was, ironically, denied to Hungary's own citizens.

Now that he was getting his affairs in order, Dario was quite cheerful as he visited the grandiose offices of Security Planning Inc. off St. James' Square the following morning.

Georgio Thomassino, looking dapper as ever, embraced him

inside his magnificent suite. He waved him towards the brown leather sofa. The two men sat down.

'All ready for "Big Bang" are you?' grinned Dario.

Georgio nodded. 'We would virtually double the takings if we had another six weeks' preparation.'

'Lorenzo insists it's on 1st November. Thompson & Thompson will be hard put to last even that long,' said Dario.

'I understand. Well, soon we'll be retiring, eh?' said Georgio.

'Which companies are the happy victims?' asked Dario.

Georgio stroked his moustache. 'I have no idea . . . ' he said.

Dario laughed. 'I was just testing your loyalty. You get ten out of ten.'

'So I should,' said Georgio. 'How are the shares selling?'

'Like hot cakes,' said Dario. 'Like you, I don't know specifics . . . '

After Dario had left, Georgio Thomassino paced his office like a caged animal. With Lorenzo he had been playing for time as a strategic move, so that he would not get taken for granted.

In fact, he had the raids fully planned, and they would work like a charm if the day was put forward to tomorrow, although there was no risk Lorenzo would thrust that on him.

He mulled over the details in his own mind. The first victim institution would be a large Arab bank near Old Street. A porter there in Georgio's pay had confided how to gain access to the vaults where valuables and safe deposit boxes were stored. This obliging gentleman would switch off the alarm before the thieves entered. The bank's locks had all been provided by Security Planning Inc., so duplicate keys could be used. On the night, hired men would break in and raid the place.

Similar raids would be enacted simultaneously at two other City based banks, at a major stockbroker, and at a vast modern office block housing firms ranging from insurance underwriters to futures dealers. All these targets used the locks and alarms of Security Planning Inc.

The victim institutions selected had several vital attributes. They were all either newish or had recently undergone changes in ownership. As they had all been successfully broken into and raided in the past, the current owners had all been persuaded to install Security Planning Inc.'s systems and equipment on a trial basis. Furthermore Georgio had stooges employed in low-grade jobs in every firm involved. These stooges were professional criminals in Lorenzo's pay who by means of phoney ID papers, curricula vitae and references, had obtained their positions some months earlier, specifically to participate in this operation.

Over the next few weeks, Security Planning Inc. would come well into the public eye through nationwide television and newspaper advertising, and people would hopefully flock to buy shares. The proposed victim institutions using Security's locks and alarms would thus develop a false sense of confidence in the firm. The planted stooges knew which buttons to press, which wires to pull, which duplicate keys to turn how many times in which locks.

After the raids were over, it would not take much brains to deduce that all organisations robbed had a common denominator.

Doubtless the police would rush to Security Planning Inc.'s luxurious offices. But what would they find?

Not Georgio Thomassino to be sure. At this point he chuckled heartily. All remaining would be leased offices, office equipment and cars, on which very little money had been paid. Possibly, too, some temp staff, their wages severely in arrears.

Georgio had no doubt that Thompson & Thompson's premises would, upon police investigation, yield a similarly murky state of affairs, but he didn't give it much thought as Lorenzo had told him not to look beyond the sphere of his own responsibility.

Meanwhile Dario was speeding towards Thompson & Thompson in a taxi. He recalled Laura's warning the previous night that Simon and his team were going off the rails. The thought paradoxically made him smile . . .

The morning's work, characteristically unpredictable, had brought Simon a lot of stress. From eight o'clock, the brokers had been bombarded with phone calls from Norman's old clients, insisting on cancelling their purchases of debentures, and retaining their original unit trusts and fixed interest investments. Many letters to the same effect had been faxed.

By mid-morning not one bargain from the debentures sales remained. The brokers had tried to thwart these cancellations, trotting out the tired lines they had been taught at England Securities: 'When you deal with a stockbroker, both you and I must stick by the rule, "Dictum meum Pactum" – "My word is my bond",' they had said.

'If you were making money out of your stock purchases, you wouldn't allow us to cancel. If you don't pay, you will be blacklisted on the London Stock Exchange. You will never deal in shares again . . . ' Another tactic tried was: 'Well we've put through the deals now. It's simply too late to reverse them. Your old unit trusts have been distributed to the institutions. So tough . . . '

None of these lines worked. Arriving in the thick of this turmoil, Simon instructed the switchboard to inform any callers that the brokers were all at a meeting and unable to come to the telephone. Then he turned back to his team. 'Off the phones,' he bellowed. 'Take a rest until I've sorted this out.'

'Norman Thompson has told every single client to cancel,' moaned a broker.

'That's what I thought,' said Simon grimly. 'A client told you that, did he?'

'That's right,' said the broker.

'And me.' 'Me too.' 'Yes . . . ' came from around the room.

'I'll sort that buffoon out,' said Simon.

But Norman Thompson was not to be found on the premises. Retreating into the privacy of the boardroom, Simon rang him at home. Norman's voice on the other end sounded quavering and old, which served only to irritate this ruthless dealing director the more. 'What the fuck did you tell all the clients to cancel for?' he demanded.

There was a long pause, then Norman replied in an indignant tone. 'One of your directors advised it. I was uneasy myself, but he not only confirmed my doubts, he instructed me to arrange for the clients to cancel. He was right, of course. The deals were not in the clients' interests, and well you know it.'

'It was Daniel La Marche, wasn't it?' breathed Simon. It really didn't take much guessing.

'He's the only director here who remotely has his clients' interests at heart,' came the staccato reply. 'Let me tell you, young man, with the direction in which Thompson & Thompson is headed, it won't last the course . . . '

Simon slammed the receiver down on him so hard that it almost cracked. On his way back to the dealing-room, he bumped into Dario. He swiftly explained the situation.

'Is Daniel on the premises?' snarled Dario.

Simon shook his head. 'Only Gerard. Talk of the devil . . . '

The three men want to the boardroom, where Gerard whistled when he heard of Daniel's treachery. 'He means well,' he said, 'but my poor brother has just no idea about business. He fucks up anything he gets involved with.'

'He'll have to resign,' said Dario.

Back in the dealing-room, Simon continued to instruct his team as if nothing has happened. 'You will now be selling shares in Security's satellite companies,' he announced. 'I'll remind you these are Sampsons Inc., Safe Locks Inc., Safe Deposits Inc., Alarm Systems Inc.' He proceeded to distribute sales pitches for them. 'Anybody who isn't going to work can piss off home,' he said.

'Can we push the debentures sales through?' asked a broker.

'They're a write off,' said Simon. 'You win some, you lose some. I don't want the subject raised again.'

Once his team had got into the swing of the new sales campaign, Simon went straight to the boardroom, from where he telephoned England Securities' dealing-room. After a surprisingly short wait, he was put through to a broker.

'Gordon Halcombe, please.' Simon had disguised his voice, making it husky.

'Who's calling?'

'John Wright,' said Simon. This was a pseudonym he had recently concocted with Gordon.

'Gordon,' the broker shouted across the room, without putting Simon on hold.

'I'm busy right now,' came Gordon's voice.

'It's John Wright on the line.'

'Oh him! So long as it's not a client!' Gordon took the receiver. 'Hallo, mate.'

'Have they cottoned on to who I am yet?' inquired Simon.

Gordon laughed. 'My lot wouldn't recognise you if they saw you, should I claim that you were someone else!'

'So what's brewing?' said Simon.

'England Securities are losing a fortune,' said Gordon in a low voice. 'Dominic Gardiner keeps pestering John Falmouth. Client complaint letters about The Merden Group are piling up. The DTI are back nosing about in the building. I'm not sure I can stick it here much longer.'

'Haven't you anything juicier for me? Or am I paying you for nothing?' demanded Simon. Gordon started gabbling, but Simon brusquely interrupted him. 'All right, your time as a spy is up. You can start properly at Thompson & Thompson the day after tomorrow. Bring all the decent brokers, all the leads, all the internal memos you can . . . '

'Here's a nice one, just sent round by John Falmouth,' said Gordon: 'Let me read you a bit. "We taught the brokers at Thompson & Thompson everything they know about securities. We gave them careers. How did they repay us? By stealing our leads. By telling a pack of lies to the clients that Thompson & Thompson have stolen from England Securities. With luck, Simon Hall's team will be prosecuted . . '

'Ha ha ha . . . ' Simon roared. 'Falmouth is obviously taking it personally. Make sure you bring this memo . . . '

'Also, your brokers are listed in this month's edition of England Securities' newsletter,' said Gordon. 'Along with a warning that clients should not deal with them, and with a telephone hotline for obtaining further confidential information . . . '

'No doubt a few more names will soon be added to the list,' remarked Simon drily. 'We'll be suing.'

On his return to the dealing room, Simon saw Daniel who had just arrived, standing at the switchboard showing the receptionist, Susan, an article in the *London Evening Standard*. Susan had relinquished her headphones and was reading over his shoulder.

Upon Simon's approach, Daniel glanced up. 'Dominic Gardiner's trying to close down England Securities again.'

Simon scrutinised the newspaper article, reading that the MP had just brought another motion against England Securities in the House of Commons.

Unable to help smiling, he put down the newspaper. 'Thank you for pointing this out, Daniel,' he said. 'But I'm sorry to have to tell you you're sacked.'

Daniel's features paled. 'What's this for?' he demanded.

'Can't you guess?' said Simon calmly. 'Your best bet is to get off the premises before the others find you here.'

Daniel stared. 'Who do you think you are?'

The sound of their raised voices brought others running. Gerard, who was first to arrive, touched his brother's arm. 'Why on earth did you tell Norman to cancel those debentures sales?'

'If I hadn't, Scotland Yard might be in here today,' said Daniel. 'Can't you see how risky it is to shift a million pounds' worth of funds into the debentures in one fell swoop?'

Dario stepped forward from the background. 'Those debentures are as good as any fixed interest vehicle on the market,' he said.

Daniel eyed him shrewdly. 'You owe me forty grand.'

Dario smiled. Pursing his lips, Daniel punched his mouth. Thompson & Thompson's financier staggered back, clapping a hand to his lips and moaning. Daniel raised his fist again, but Simon grabbed his waist, half lifting, half dragging him back, while Gerard stepped quickly between his brother and Dario. He brought his face close to Daniel's. 'Just get out quickly,' he hissed.

Daniel stood rooted. Stray brokers had gathered around, marvelling at the fracas, hoping to see blood shed. Dario at the other end of the foyer was having a word with the security guard who had been reading *The Sun* in a back office when the violence had started.

The security guard strode forward towards Daniel. He was a one man rescue operation, his mean black eyes gleaming like blackcurrants in his battered red face.

In his element here, he seized Daniel by the collar. 'C'mon, sir,' he said, not unkindly, and dragged him to the lift. Gripping Daniel's arm, he forced him inside it. The deposed director of Thompson & Thompson struggled feebly, like a man in a bad dream against a tide of misfortunes.

Inside the dealing room, Simon pinned four £50 notes to the wall. The brokers stared at the incentives, their mouths watering to have them. Cash in hand was safe not just from the Inland Revenue's clutches, but also from cancellation.

'£200 for the broker who sells the most today, on top of commissions,' shouted Simon. 'Now get on the fucking phones . . .'

The brokers enthusiastically rang their clients, but made few sales.

'They are all waiting to be sold out out of their Security Planning Inc., shares,' said one broker. 'We guaranteed them it would only be a month's hold . . .'

'Tell them to be patient,' said Simon. 'Market conditions aren't looking good. The dollar's skidding. They wouldn't want to come out and lose money, after all.'

'Presumably we're still guaranteeing a minimum 75 cents profit,' said Laura.

Simon nodded. 'That's why we're being careful,' he said glibly. 'We don't want to let our clients down.'

Chapter 15

As work had almost ground to a halt, the brokers went home early that evening. While Laura was strolling down Piccadilly, her mobile beeped. As she had half expected, it was Daniel on the line. She was pleased, not surprised that he should be coming to her in his hour of need.

'Meet me outside the Royal Academy in half an hour,' he said. 'Then follow me discreetly. Don't talk, or show any sign of recognition in case we're spotted.'

She found him outside the gates, hunched in a grey mackintosh which reminded her that it was drizzling and she had no coat. If she didn't find shelter soon, her blue business suit would be ruined.

Aware of this, Daniel walked quickly, leading her through Piccadilly Circus into an old fashioned Italian bar with steamed up windows. They sat at a table for four. Laura wrinkled her nose at the aroma of hot spicy food, blinking in the dim light, while Daniel ordered cappucinos.

'What are you going to do now?' she asked.

'Stockbroking still.' Daniel smiled as he named the firm. 'They may also have room for you . . . '

Laura shook her head. 'I'll be sticking around at Thompson & Thompson for a while,' she said. 'But I'll be your spy in there.'

'Good on you,' said Daniel. He paused. 'I'm meeting Gerry West here shortly, to give *The Examiner* some information on Thompson & Thompson. Would you like to stay and help me?'

Laura shook her head. 'Not while I'm at Thompson & Thompson, or I would lose all credibility there. If you want to destroy the firm, I'll help you, Daniel. But I can be more use to you as a fly on the wall from the inside.'

As she was leaning over, he kissed her on the cheek. 'Take care of Gerard,' he said.

'Of course,' she murmured, and was gone.

Left alone with his own thoughts, Daniel ordered another cappucino. He had fixed up his new job as a "half-commer" or half commission broker, only that morning and was looking forward to starting.

When he thought of Thompson & Thompson, Daniel seethed. In his opinion, not just were the clients being conned, but so were some of the brokers and directors.

He wanted to clear himself before any criminal charges ensued. He would try to rescue Laura. However, Gerard had this time gone too far, had dragged himself in too deep. He would help his brother if he could, but not this time before he had cleared himself. Daniel was looking after number one.

Most annoyingly of all, Thompson & Thompson owed him £40,000. Would he ever see the colour of it? For that reason, too, he would ruin the firm if he could.

The drizzling outside had turned into rain that streaked the bar's front window like a coating of melted glass. Inside, it was snug and warm. Gerry West sure knew how to choose a rendezvous. Daniel resolved to make use of it on another occasion.

Gerry West arrived, dripping wet and full of apologies, half an hour late. It was the first time Daniel had set eyes on him; he was less impressive that he had expected, being a short pudgy man with a shuffling gait, whose grey eyes bulged inquisitively behind large gold rectangular framed glasses. He reminded Daniel of a hamster.

Ordering two cappucinos, Gerry handed over a copy of the contract they had agreed. Daniel scrutinised it in silence. *The Examiner* undertook to pay him £20,000 upon publication of the true and exclusive story of his experience as a broker in the City. Daniel was to make himself available for interviews and photographers as was reasonable. Payment would be rendered a fortnight after publication.

He looked up. 'I resigned as a director today,' he said. As he told his story, Gerry listened hard, prompting him occasionally and scribbling shorthand notes.

Daniel revealed how Security Planning Inc., shares had been sold on the basis of five weeks' hold, with a guaranteed profit. He explained how client leads had been stolen from England Securities. Most of all he railed against the UK stockbroking industry – the deception, the violence, the lust for money and power. He supplied names, names, names . . .

The smooth-tongued fraudster Dario Abella who would hide funds in invisible accounts. Gerard, his own brother, who had been taken advantage of. Norman Thompson, the honest former chairman, who had nonetheless not been able to resist buying shares in Security Planning Inc. The unscrupulous Simon Hall, who had commanded a team of brokers, all small time con men in their own right. What a nasty tangled web it all was!

As Daniel paused to sip his coffee, Gerry put down his pen. 'What brings you to offer *The Examiner* this confession?'

'Confession?' said Daniel. 'You misunderstand. I'm talking about other people, not myself.'

Gerry West frowned. 'But you were there, weren't you?' You made money out of the company?'

'Yes, but . . . '

'You were a director? You had shares in Security Planning Inc. yourself?'

'I didn't know what I was letting myself in for.'

'Shouldn't you have checked?' Gerry spoke in a low whisper.

'You're still getting the wrong end of the stick,' said Daniel. He could feel the sweat forming on his forehead. The interview was not going to plan.

For the first time that evening, Gerry smiled. His teeth were uneven and yellow, contributing to his general demeanour of untrustworthiness. 'Relax,' he insisted. 'I'm not going to be making a scapegoat out of you. It's Thompson & Thompson I'll be tearing to shreds. I know a bit about the company's practices from other sources too . . . '

'John Falmouth, you mean?'

The Fleet Street hack shrugged. 'Why should I deny it? The world knows John is a good friend of mine. We've dined at each other's houses. He keeps me informed about some of the crooks in stockbroking.' He sighed: 'Being an investigative journalist like I am is a risky way of life. I cultivate friends where I can . . . '

He stood up and peered through the window. 'If you will excuse me, I'll brave the rain now.'

'When will your write-up appear?' asked Daniel.

'Perhaps later this week,' said Gerry. 'The photographer will be seeing you tomorrow.'

Daniel met *The Examiner's* photographer at ten o'clock outside the newpaper's main offices in Fleet Street. He was a cheerful lad in his late twenties with a carrier bag in his hand and two cameras strung round his neck. He had a taxi waiting.

They emerged from it outside the Burlington Arcade. The photographer led Daniel down Jermyn Street.

'Slow down,' said Daniel. 'I don't want to bump into anybody I know.'

'Are they all con men too?' asked the photographer.

Daniel stopped dead. 'What on earth has Gerry West been telling you?'

'Look. I'm only the photographer, I don't really have a clue what this is about,' stuttered the boy.

He stopped beside a gleaming red Porsche parked in the road. A grin spread over his cheeky little face. 'Wouldn't a picture of you with this in the background be fabulous. So City! You're the expert, what do you think?'

Daniel noticed a young man in dark glasses and blue pinstripe suit staring at them as he approached. He was obviously the owner of the vehicle.

'You had better ask permission, I think.'

The photographer turned. The young man was getting out his keys.

'May I photograph this gentleman in front of your Porsche?' he asked.

'What for?'

'It's for a fashion magazine,' he lied. 'This gentleman's won an award for his work in the City. We're doing a feature on him . . . '

The Porsche owner hesitated. The photographer took a crisp £20 note out of his pocket.

The Porsche owner pocketed the note. 'OK. But be quick.'

The photographer handed Daniel props he had in his carrier bag. *The Financial Times.* A black folding umbrella. A filofax. 'These will make you look more the part,' he said.

After taking several photographs, he thanked the Porsche owner who had been watching them with a face like a bomb that was about to explode.

As Daniel left, the photographer came panting after him, props under his arm. 'Have you time for one more session? A new location?'

'Get lost,' said Daniel.

That very morning, Gordon Halcombe, dealing manager at England Securities, was restless. He kept sidling up to individual brokers, and exchanging whispers with them. He was priming them for what he called "The Second Great Escape".

He found time, too, to telephone the City recruitment agency that provided him with his trainees. 'I want my next batch to consist entirely of blacks,' he demanded. 'And mind you keep this confidential.'

A broker overhearing him giggled. He was in on "The Second Great Escape", so knew that Gordon must been mischief-making. John Falmouth, who was known to be a racist, would remember this prank forever – it was a pity many of them, including Gordon, would not be around to see his initial anger.

Gordon left for an early lunch, not in company. By half past two, the brokers were back from their lunch, but he was missing. Unease spread amongst the uninitiated like a bug. 'Where's Gordon?' they whispered. Then John Falmouth arrived on the dealing floor, and looked around for him. 'Where the fuck is Gordon?' he demanded.

'I'm here.' Everybody turned and gaped. Gordon stood in the doorway, his hands firm on his hips. His hair was awry, his jacket crumpled, and his tie loose. He stepped forward to face John Falmouth, stroking his beard in a peculiarly menacing manner.

'You've been drinking,' murmured his boss.

'What if I have?' leered Gordon. 'I'm fucking fed up with this place. You're being investigated for fraud, John. Why should we be tarred with the same brush? Unless you give me and my team the right pay rise now, you will be looking for more staff.'

John frowned. 'This isn't the forum for this sort of discussion . . .'

'Sod off.' Gordon turned and as he was walking out, John clutched his arm.

Gordon shook him off as if he was a naughty child. 'Touch me again, and I'll have you charged with assault. Believe me, there will be witnesses,' he said.

Shortly afterwards, the other brokers slipped out one by one, on Gordon's instructions, taking with them all the documentation they could.

They arrived in trickles at Thompson & Thompson, where Gordon greeted them. The only female broker to come, a favourite of Gordon's, kissed him in front of the others. 'Just see how many leads I've smuggled out,' she announced excitedly.

She pulled leads out of her sleeves. England Securities' familiar white client record cards, the mere names and phone numbers on which would be worth tens of thousands of pounds more in commission for herself.

The brokers around her stared, their faces wreathed in smiles. They started giggling as she unbuttoned her blouse, pulling a fan of leads out of her bra.

'Let me help,' shouted Gordon, thrusting his hand in deep. 'Ooh, I just dig the feel of that,' he said, squeezing. She moaned as the leads still lodged there scattered to the floor.

'You'll be pulling your prick out next,' she shouted, darting back nimble as a ballerina. She rummaged under her skirt. In an amazing kind of peep-show, the brokers watched her whip leads out of her knickers. 'Now I'm stimulating the parts your prick won't reach,' she said.

'Bravo,' shouted Gordon, and clapped. The brokers whistled and cheered. The sound could have almost been heard right down Park Lane. Their concealment of leads had been confined to pockets and briefcases. Nonetheless they had made quite a haul, surmising that their level of business at Thompson & Thompson would depend solely on the quality and quantity of leads they had stolen.

Simon came in, smiling at the happy faces. The web was spun again, and more flies had been lured into it. Not so long ago at England Securities, every individual present had been working for him. Now events had come round in full circle.

'It's great to see you all here,' he said. 'I had hoped there would be more of you.'

'John has warned brokers against coming here, as you know,' said Gordon.

The next morning, brokers faced the most incredible shock. Daniel's "story" was plastered over the centre pages of *The Examiner*. Everybody bought copies and spent half the day reading it.

Gerry West had on this occasion surpassed himself in sensationalism. The article was headed: "City Director's Shocking

Confessions". Immediately underneath was a large photograph of Daniel standing smiling in front of a Porsche, by implication his own.

All the brokers at Thompson & Thompson reacted to the article with a mixture of excitement and alarm. Daniel was exposing their practices, even as he appeared to be exposing himself. Thompson & Thompson was represented as a fraudulent broking firm that as good as stole clients' monies. Most of all, the article amounted to a savage self-indictment on the part of Daniel, as ex-director. It portrayed him as a slimy trickster and charlatan who had been running the company almost singlehanded, and who was too ashamed now to keep quiet about it any longer.

As he walked towards The Securities Regulatory Office in the City, Daniel was grinding his teeth. The article had hit him like a thunderbolt, confirming his darkest suspicions as to Gerry West's intentions. The lying bastard had represented him as the villain of the show. Well if it took him all his life, he would get even with him.

In the meantime, the damage had already been done. He had been suspended from his new job, pending investigation by The Securities Regulatory Office. Courageously, he had telephoned them and arranged to visit their investigators to clear up any misunderstandings.

Shown into a comfortable office, he was introduced to the two investigators. They seemed chalk and cheese. Anaemic little Mr. Chadwick, with soft tones, mild manners, and a charming smile. And his colleague, made of sterner stuff, the ironically named Mr. Little, dark haired and snarling. This latter gentleman showed an unadulterated contempt for Daniel. 'You really were a prat to go to *The Examiner*,' he shouted.

Quivering with indignation he stabbed his copy of Gerry West's article with his forefinger, until it seemed he would poke a hole in it.

'Do you think this article represents you as a fit and proper person?'

'It's not what I told the journalist,' protested Daniel quite truthfully. 'He's distorted it beyond recognition.' He glanced sideways at Mr. Chadwick who was watching him as a scientist might a rat in an experiment.

'It's your future you have wrecked, nobody else's,' said Mr. Little.

Daniel ended up commenting on every line of the article, specifying what he had or had not said. 'I wasn't confessing my own practices,' he insisted. 'I was complaining about what went on at Thompson & Thompson.'

'You were a director of the firm, weren't you?' shouted Mr. Little.

'That doesn't mean I condone everything that happened there,' replied Daniel.

'Why too did you allow this ridiculous photo to be taken? How much did *The Examiner* pay you?'

At this point Daniel remained silent and Mr. Little seized the upper hand: 'You're no better than a prostitute,' he screamed. 'Anything they paid you, you should send back, explaining how they have mispresented you.'

When Daniel left, Mr.Little shook hands with him at the door. 'I'm so glad you came up to see us,' he said snidely. 'It's always nice to meet our members face to face.'

Further shocks were in store for Daniel. A policeman delivered him a message at home that he should telephone the Serious Fraud Office. When he did so, he was asked to visit them in relation to Thompson & Thompson. He made an appointment, cursing the day he had ever become involved with the firm.

The only person he told of these events was Laura, who in her turn kept him up to date with what was happening at Thompson & Thompson, where the same repertoire of stocks was being shifted.

Back in the dealing room, Simon paced about. 'Come on you lot, where's your old spunk?' he would shout. But his brokers were avoiding clients, all of whom by this stage only wanted out.

Simon for his own part would avoid seeing Gerard and Dario if he possibly could. All they would say is how they needed more money in.

'My brokers must have new clients,' Simon would retort.

'Pah. Sack 'em if you need to, and get in new brokers,' was Dario's response. 'Gordon's lot are doing fine.'

For recruitment purposes, Thompson & Thompson arranged a lunch at a top West End hotel. Several good brokers still at England Securities were invited, along with the entire staff of Thompson & Thompson.

On the morning of the lunch, Thompson & Thompson brokers assembled in the boardroom, where Simon delivered an inspiring speech. 'If we are to survive, we need more brokers. So make sure you say the right things to our guests. We must recruit them.' He grinned. 'There will be plenty of booze, so get them all drunk. Stress that England Securities is finished, and that they can earn a fortune here at Thompson & Thompson.'

He paused. 'Remember, it's a hard cold world out there. With us, you're warm and safe . . . '

Chapter 16

Everybody was ensconced in a private room for the buffet lunch. Watercolours on the wall depicted imaginary landscapes whilst a glittering chandelier cast a thousand reflected lights around the room.

Like virgins in a brothel, the potential recruits wandered about dazzled by both the magnificence of the surroundings and the sense of occasion. At the end of the meal, all quietened while Dario proceeded to deliver a rousing speech. 'We are top stockbrokers, and our future here in London is assured. Our client base and our staff alike are expanding faster than we dreamed. If John Falmouth causes us any trouble, we will soon sort him out . . . '

At this point, everybody clapped and cheered with drunken enthuasiasm. Simon glanced around the room, proud of his brokers, delighted with Thompson & Thompson. Except, where was Laura? He has seen her arrive with the others. It seemed she had slipped away. He decided to keep this discovery to himself.

But even in the days following the party, Simon never saw Laura. When the others started commenting on her absence, he wouldn't speculate as to her whereabouts.

'Laura's not indispensable,' he would say. 'Nobody is. New brokers are two a penny. Every broker from England Securities invited to the lunch has now joined us.'

One afternoon, with Gerard and Dario to hand, Simon addressed the brokers on their tax commitments. 'What you must all do is set up limited companies which will issue Thompson & Thompson with backdated invoices for all payments you've received to date.'

'That stinks,' said one broker.

'What stinks? Doing things properly?' said Dario.

Most of the brokers complied. Meanwhile, the original buyers of Security Planning shares were still ringing up and endeavouring to sell out. Brokers to a man were refusing to take the calls.

In secret, Dario was increasingly disturbed at Laura's absence. Where had she gone? What was she doing? Mindful of Lorenzo's earlier warnings, he didn't quite trust her.

Meanwhile, he took to spending less and less time in the office, giving Simon and Gerard the excuse that he was negotiating some brilliant deals for Thompson & Thompson. By this stage, the rent on the office, as well as HP instalments on the furniture and equipment were seriously in arrears.

Inside the wardrobe in his bedroom, Dario left a few misleading items of clothing he had secretly purchased for cash, including an oversized scarlet jersey and orange shorts (bright colours were anathema to him) and a tennis outfit (although he didn't play the game).

Like the actor preparing to play Superman in the movie, Dario deliberately started putting on weight. His method was to eat four enormous meals a day. It was hard work at first, then he grew to relish it, living to eat, rather than eating to live. His body started to swell. Soon he would look very different. Only then would he be ready to assume the alter ego of Dale Gatsby.

Other aids to disguise awaited him. Horn-rimmed glasses. A black wig. Smart American casual clothes. He would be transformed into the businessman on an extended vacation, no unusual phenomenon in the United States. At all times he would use the Californian accent he was currently practising.

On the telephone to Lorenzo he said he was considering plastic surgery to change his appearance, but the Franciscan cut him short. 'It's unnecessary,' he said. 'And it can be dangerous. The only such treatment you might need one day is a fingerprint lift, following which you can't use your hands or feet for some weeks. But forget about that right now.'

On Lorenzo's advice, Dario telephoned British Telecom, the London Electricity Board, and British Gas, saying that he was discontinuing using their services and that he wanted neither refunds nor closing bills until he should notify them, as he was moving and wasn't yet sure of the address. In this way, he would be leaving no clues.

Meanwhile, whenever he was in Thompson & Thompson's offices – for two hours a day at the most – he would walk around proclaiming how he had really settled in London, and at Thompson & Thompson. He claimed to be buying a fictitious flat in Knightsbridge to which he would be inviting all the directors and brokers for a house-warming party. Gossip circulated to the effect that he was a man who cared.

Dario Abella, once Roberto Calafato, soon to be Dale Gatsby had never ceased to be amazed at people's gullibility. To any brokers who questioned him, he lied the more. He was abiding by a motto Lorenzo had taught him: Share the spurious with the curious.

Once living in his Los Angeles hotel under the name of Dale Gatsby, he intended to keep a low profile. Lorenzo had warned him that janitors, maids, bell boys, etc., would notice any freakish behaviour, and that tips would make them talk.

But that didn't mean he wouldn't enjoy the high life. Oh no! He would flit when the fancy took him, free as a bird to Las Vegas, New York, or as far as Fiji or Jamaica, perhaps even Tokyo.

Finance would not be a problem. Nor would false passports, ID cards and visas, under different aliases every time ("Dale Gatsby" was exclusively Californian). In perhaps a less honourable way than a boy scout, Dario would be prepared . . .

Which was more than Daniel was! He had visited the Serious Fraud Office, and had answered questions about Thompson & Thompson at some length, in a taped interview, bypassing his right to have a solicitor present on the grounds that he had nothing to hide.

However, to his dismay, the officers interrogating him had seemed interested in nothing more than to what extent he was implicated and as to whether *The Examiner's* article was true.

In the aftermath of that interview, Daniel felt lonely and afraid, in need of support. Dialling the number of Laura's mobile, he could only now get an unobtainable signal. He would, however, keep trying her several times a day.

His only other conceivable source of support was Norman Thompson. In Daniel's opinion, Thompson & Thompson's veteran chairman was a crusty old fool, but there was at least a vestige of honesty in him, as had been proven by his prompt cancellation of the debenture sales.

However, Norman had been well paid for staying around the premises, and had been unable to sell his own shares in Security Planning Inc. He was implicated, as Daniel was, and so might be glad to talk. Daniel dialled Norman. The telephone rang and rang. To Daniel's annoyance, there was no reply . . .

In his living room, Norman Thompson made a movement towards the phone, then felt sick, and staggered back into his armchair. It was probably another call from the blasted Serious Fraud Office.

They had rung a couple of hours earlier, asking him to come and see them. Mumbling a refusal, he had slammed down the receiver on them.

Norman was hazily aware that he had not acted in the wisest possible way, but there again, he had drunk a full large bottle of whisky that morning, and was feeling like the walking dead.

Norman's wife had walked out on him. The note Lisa had left still lay on the coffee table. He could recall what it said word for word:

Norman,

You always were a selfish brute, but now you have gone too far. After Thompson & Thompson is investigated, don't count on my support if you face charges of fraud. Don't expect me to visit you in jail either. Don't you ever try to find out where I've gone or to mend our relationship as it's all over. I'm living with another man. You won't be hearing from me again until I can organise divorce proceedings.

Yours never,
Liz

Retching, he lurched into the bathroom, and reached for the jar of sleeping pills in the mirrored cabinet.

Perhaps he should never have confided in his wife. He had, after all, been taught to be cautious. If he had kept his big mouth shut about goings on at Thompson & Thompson, she might be by his side now. He could have emigrated with her, anything . . .

Pills in hand, he returned to his armchair. He carefully counted them. Then he got up and padding out into the hall, locked the front door . . .

The representative of the Serious Fraud Office rang Norman Thompson's door bell for the third time. A gossipy roadsweeper had tipped him off that Norman was still living there, but hadn't been seen for a couple of weeks. He knew then it was the right flat, at least.

Well it was five o'clock in the morning and if he wasn't in now, when would he be?

The representative sighed. The bugger had probably guessed who it was, and was refusing to answer the door.

He tried the first reserve tactic, stepping back to his car where his girlfriend sat patiently in the front passenger seat.

He nodded to her. She promptly went outside the block of flats herself and shouted, 'Are you in, Norman? Where's Norman?'

She, too, elicited no reply. So he resorted to the second reserve tactic, one that rarely failed.

He returned to Norman Thompson's doorbell and pressed sticky tape over it. The doorbell started ringing loudly and relentlessly. A lingering early morning alarm call to smoke him out! The representative chuckled to himself.

After half an hour, Norman Thompson had still not emerged. Leaving the doorbell taped down, the representative rang the bells of other residents in the block. They answered him through the entry phones, indignant at being roused so early, and making it clear they had no idea where Norman Thompson was. Some mooted that he might have had an accident.

When the police broke into his flat, the representative trailed after them like a bloodhound. They found the old man lying back in his armchair, the jar of sleeping pills empty at his feet. On his face was a smile of peace . . .

News of the suicide spread instantly. Daniel, being isolated from his former colleagues including Laura and Gerard, learned of it not by hearsay but from the national press. His heart sank.

He was not without pity for the old man who he considered had, like himself, been implicated through no fault of his own. However, what concerned him most was the public investigation into the Thompson & Thompson scam that the suicide would undoubtedly engender.

He sensed that the Serious Fraud Office, like the Government, the Stock Exchange, and the masses of punters who had had their fingers burnt in share purchases over the years would seek scapegoats. Would he himself emerge unscathed?

Brokers at Thompson & Thompson were shellshocked to hear of the suicide. They started taking days off, eventually coming in only when Simon told them they would receive long overdue commission cheques. As it turned out, they were invariably disappointed.

On one occasion when all were present, Dario, backed by Simon and Gerard, delivered a speech designed to rekindle lost enthusiasm. 'Forget about old Norman,' he urged. 'He meant well, and his suicide was tragic, but he was nonetheless an interfering old fool. We're better off without him.

'What you should all concentrate on now is making money. 10% commission. Phew,' he whistled. 'None of you was getting that at England Securities.'

The brokers put on a spurt of renewed activity but stopped some days later when investigators from the Department of Trade came into the building. Morale immediately dropped to a new low.

Most brokers were whiling away long hours in the dealing room trading on the account for themselves.

Simon would tip them on what stock to pick up, getting his own inside information from dodgy City contacts who owed him favours.

Usually the price of the stock they had all picked up would soar on the back of takeover rumours. The trick, as brokers soon discovered, was to get out of the shares before Simon and his few close friends did. This coterie had bought so many shares that once it had off-loaded them the price would usually drop purely as a result of their action.

Of course, Simon wanted brokers to stay in the shares until after he and his mates had sold out of them, so he would profit from the swelling of the price engendered by their enormous holdings.

In all cases, brokers pocketed any winnings they made, but refused to pay losses.

Within a short time their brokers were refusing to deal any more, and threatening legal action. Under Simon's guidance, Thompson & Thompson brokers made counterthreats to report them to the Stock Exchange for insider dealing. Simon meanwhile retained the goodwill of his secret City contacts by tipping them a small percentage of his own vast profits.

At this stage Dario, who was both increasingly putting on weight and appearing less on Thompson & Thompson's premises, did his vanishing trick.

He had carefully informed Simon that he was now going abroad on business, that he would stay in touch by telephone, and that he would return, he couldn't say when, but soon.

How excited he was to quit London! He would be starting up a new life, and wouldn't be wanting for money for the rest of his life.

After three months in Los Angeles for the superb Californian climate, he would move to New Zealand for its fishing, next to Hong Kong for its food, then maybe to Thailand for its sexual opportunity.

Later, he might try living in some of the third world countries where sucking up to the politicians and getting into local deals would make him still more money.

In his travels, he would never remain longer than three or four months in one country, so he would never be regarded as a resident there for tax purposes. His passports now included ones from Canada, Brazil, Italy, Australia and USA. His legal address was in Monaco, while his assets were anonymously registered in Liechtenstein and other strategic locations throughout the world.

He would become an international playboy. He would be in a position to skip, free from Government, police or personal pressure, if necessary to the other side of the world.

What would be his new life-style? At last he would find time to indulge his cultural interests, exploring old buildings and museums in ancient capitals of the world, as well as savouring a lavish night life, and meeting new, interesting people who, being on holiday like he was, would have time to cultivate a friendship. He would never work for another day in his life.

Over the next day or two, he would ring Simon Hall back at Thompson & Thompson, making spurious promises that he was fixing ace deals for the company. Then suddenly, pfff . . . Thompson & Thompson would be no more.

There was one thing that bugged him as he started out on his adventures. What was Laura doing now?

If only Dario could see me, thought Laura. After driving across Rome, she had parked the Fiesta on the Via Appia Antica, a short distance from the catacombs. Elaborate make-up and disguise had transformed her appearance.

In large turquoise rimmed spectacles and a long brown wig, she was a new woman. Her deep false tan and pale brown mink coat gave her a monied aura. Her white gloves added a delicate extra touch.

It was Siesta time. The Franciscans, she knew from her mother, would now be snoozing in their cells like landed whales. As a precaution, they always locked their doors from inside. But Laura's mother had the keys.

Laura found the back door open as Anne had promised. She pushed her way into the hall. Her mother was waiting there as scheduled. As she smiled, the incipient wrinkles on her face seemed to disperse.

Anne then ushered her daughter upstairs. She indicated Lorenzo's room.

Pressing her ear against the door, Laura heard him snoring. She nodded.

Anne unlocked the door with a thin grating sound. They tiptoed inside. Laura eased a kitchen knife out of the inside pocket of her coat. Its steel edge gleamed sinisterly in the sunlight filtering between the curtains.

Lorenzo lay on his back, his head facing the two women. As he snored, his body shook rhythmically.

Anne took the knife from Laura then merely stood holding it, trembling and white. Laura sighed, taking it back, and motioning her mother to relock the door from the inside.

Anne was as pale and immobilised as a dead woman while Laura stabbed him. She knifed his heart several times to make sure, and with scarcely a protest, Padre Lorenzo passed into the next world. Clever as he was, he had been no match for the two determined women on their mission of vengeance.

Laura stood back, surveying her handiwork coldly and pocketed her bloodstained gloves. She had learned to kill and to leave no trace of it on the streets.

Upon leaving, it was Laura who had to guide a shellshocked Anne down the stairs and out. When they passed a couple of Franciscans in the courtyard, Anne wanted to run, but Laura placed a restraining hand on her arm. 'Don't be so obvious,' she murmured.

Outside the Fiesta a gang of teenage boys on scooters had gathered. Contemplating a break-in, Laura reckoned. She glanced at them sharply as she and her mother got into the vehicle and they stepped back.

Laura started driving at a furious speed into Rome. Dust swirled under their wheels, rising behind them like a cloak of invisibility. 'We're killers now,' she grimaced.

'In a good cause,' murmured Anne. She was sitting back, her eyes closed and her hands clasped.

They made for a secluded Roman hotel, where Laura had already booked a room. Here, Laura discarded her wig and glasses and put on false eye lashes. Substituting a grey tweed coat for the mink, she applied padding around her hips.

She then cut her mother's hair, fixing her with a grey curly wig, and a new blue dress.

The two women emerged from the hotel within half an hour of entering it. Lorenzo's body might well have already been found, and they had no time to waste getting out of Italy. The sun glared on the streets, as sweating Italians bustled back to work after lunch.

Separating, Anne and Laura mingled amongst the crowds, each as anonymous as she could possibly have wished. Their escape route abroad was thoroughly planned, with a back-up scheme in case anything should go wrong.

Meanwhile, the big day had arrived. Georgio Thomassino sat shivering with excitement in his office.

Every time the telephone rang, he snatched up the receiver. One by one his contacts who would be carrying out the robberies placed orders for security equipment under phoney names. This signified that all was proceeding to plan.

After the deed was done, they would all meet in a disused warehouse in Surrey where his men would dump the proceeds and he would pay them off.

Georgio Thomassino and some trustworthies would stash the haul in various London safe deposit boxes, whose high annual charges reflected the management's discretion.

Georgio left his office punctiliously at his usual 5.30 pm. By 3.00 am he was waiting at the warehouse. His men sat around watching while Georgio's colleagues counted the cash, the gold bars, the share certificates and other valuables plundered. The size of the haul had clearly surpassed all expectations . . .

By 7.00 am, Georgio was in Portsmouth. By 8.00 am he was on the boat to Le Havre, with a few scanty belongings, and his Brazilian passport.

The cash would be transferred discreetly over the next few weeks to various trusts and numbered accounts in Luxembourg, Andorra, Bermuda, Liechtenstein and Monaco, whilst the non-cash remainder of the loot would be fenced, the proceeds following shortly.

As the boat glided out, he glanced nonchalantly over the waters at Nelson's *Victory*.

All that was left for him was to reach Brazil and find a woman who would become pregnant by him. Only then would he be safe from extradition if the law ever caught up with him.

He felt no wrench at parting from British soil, probably for good.

Chapter 17

The story of the audacious robberies was on the front page of all the newspapers. The link was made that all firms raided had Security Planning equipment.

Early in the morning, the police invaded Security's offices. Only a few temps were present and they knew nothing. Suddenly, Georgio Thomassino was wanted for questioning.

A few brokers had come into Thompson & Thompson. Simon was lounging back in his chair, feet up on the desk. He was frowning, and his face was white and weary looking. 'It's all over. No more dealings,' he muttered.

The Official Receiver, a short plump man with a brown beard, introduced himself to the small group present. 'I'm officially closing down this company in the public interest,' he announced.

Brokers prowled the offices like cats, snatching up stray typewriters, dictating and fax machines, stationery items etc., and walking out with them.

The shares of Security Planning Inc., and of its satellite companies were declared worthless, not however before the directors had got rid of their own holdings in them at a massive profit. The newspapers retraced the events of the scam. Gerry West was prolific on the subject, at one point reminding his readers: 'The Examiner gave you fair warning.'

Meanwhile, MPs, captains of industry and City gurus expressed public concern that all this could still happen, after the implementation of the Financial Services Act. The public's eyes were opened. Stockbrokers, it was realised, had become rich through fleecing suckers.

Morale in the City plummeted, along with the FT indices. Sackings were rife. Even Tokyo and New York were adversely affected. One scam seemed to have cast a blight on a privileged group usually able to sweep its digressions under the carpet.

The Official Receiver swapped notes with the Stock Exchange and the DTI. Brokers and directors of Thompson & Thompson were being investigated by the police, even as they were suddenly blacklisted in the City.

Thompson & Thompson clients, trying to ring the now defunct firm and sell their ill fated shares, found the telephone number unobtainable. An action group was quickly formed.

A solicitor acting on the group's behalf wrote to clients requesting a £50 donation, so inquiries could be conducted into the affairs of Thompson & Thompson, with the stated aim of recovering as much as possible of shareholders funds. Most clients complied, although prospects of regaining monies invested seemed bleak. As a journalist put it, the money appeared to have been "spirited away under a cloud".

The action group however, was blessed with the unremitting support of England Securities' boss John Falmouth, who sang like a canary, providing horror stories galore about the Thompson & Thompson brokers.

But some of the clients were strangely quiet. Amongst their number was the well-known MP Dominic Gardiner.

For investing in Security Planning Inc., Gardiner had transferred funds from an Isle of Man account. These funds had even included some party subscriptions. He was in no doubt that the Inland Revenue would be most interested to learn more if he so much as uttered a word. He also dreaded an investigation into his affairs by the Serious Fraud Office.

At first Daniel wasn't worried when the threats came, assuming his caller would give up on him as a hopeless case. The gentleman introduced himself as Geoff Upton, elaborating, 'I'm a private dick acting on behalf of Thompson & Thompson clients. You were paid £60,000 by the firm. The clients have the right to that money. You're going to pay it back . . . '

'Sod off,' Daniel slammed down the telephone receiver.

But the man persisted, ringing up at all hours of the night and day. 'I'm your voice of conscience, Daniel,' he said. 'You cheated the clients. We all know that. You admit it yourself in the national press. Let me quote you . . .

'I have a dossier on you several inches thick. You just don't realise what danger you are in.

'If you try to avoid paying up, you are only delaying the day you do have to. I'll feel it my duty to present my dossier where it counts. How would you like to see your name and photograph splattered over the front page of every newspaper in the country?

'I don't want to make trouble for you. I'd far rather we settled this amicably. But pay me you will . . . '

Daniel changed his telephone number, making it ex-directory. The next thing he knew was the man had turned up on his doorstep and was persistently ringing the bell.

'Fuck off,' shouted Daniel into the speaker.

'No,' replied his visitor.

As Daniel dialled 999, a succession of flashes penetrated the curtains in his living room. Daniel peered through the gap. Geoff Upton, shadowy in the night, was taking photographs.

The CID proved keen to catch the "blackmailer" having identified him as a well known petty con man with a criminal record. A police tape recorder was attached to Daniel's telephone.

In the presence of a clean-shaven detective sergeant, Daniel telephoned Geoff Upton at his contact number. 'I want to arrange a meeting,' he said. 'I'll give you the money, and you must stop bothering me.'

'That's a deal,' said Upton.

'£60,000 is a lot of money,' continued Daniel. 'Can I pay you £50,000? Or £40,000?'

Upton hesitated. 'We'll say £50,000. I can't agree to less than that.'

'OK. Now I'm getting the money out of my building society,' said Daniel. 'I'll meet you next Monday at one o'clock, inside The George in Kensington. The password is Security Planning Inc.'

'Fine,' said Upton. 'Bring friends with you if you want to see fair play.'

'Can I bring my solicitor?'

'No solicitors,' said Upton firmly. 'I don't want any red tape, you know what I mean. We will just settle this thing between ourselves, for once and for all.'

'How do you want the money?' asked Daniel.

'Cash,' said Upton. 'Then I'll give you the dossier, the photographs, everything.'

Daniel arrived in the pub early for the rendezvous, a police tape recorder taped to his chest. He was bearing a carrier bag containing £50,000 in real bank notes provided by the police.

In the background, some ten plain clothes officers were having a drink. The juke box was blaring, and the pub was crowded. Joining the throng at the bar, Daniel proceeded to order a lager.

From the other side of the bar, a man raised his glass to him, and nodded. He was a tough, with a bulldog face, whom Simon Hall, had he been present, would have recognised with a shock. His nose was broken, and a front tooth was missing. His crew cut black hair was greying at the temples. He sipped his whisky, eyeing Daniel. Finally, he approached him.

'What's the password?' murmured Daniel.

'Security Planning Inc.,' croaked Upton. 'You've had a haircut.'

'Since *The Examiner's* photograph was taken, yes.'

'You've got the money?' said Upton.

Daniel nodded, shaking his carrier bag, and opening it briefly so Upton could see the bank notes stashed inside.

Upton glanced around him uneasily. 'Let's do business somewhere else. He glanced around him with pursed lips. I don't like it here. There might be people here you know. There might be people I know. You might even be wired up . . . '

Daniel eyed the black metal briefcase in Upton's grip. 'Is the dossier in there?'

He nodded, snapping the case open, and bringing out a red file.

Daniel glanced through its pages. They were mostly photocopies of clients' letters to the Thompson & Thompson action group. Daniel was cited here and there. He put on an act of shivering with fright. 'This is dynamite,' he said.

'I don't want to keep it,' said Upton hastily. 'Once you have given me the money, that's the last you will hear from me. Of course it works both ways. If you ring my contact number, you'll find I have gone abroad, that it's not known when I will be back, you understand.'

'OK. Now let's meet outside the Public Library in Hornton Street,' said Daniel. 'I'll go there first, so we're not seen together. You follow on ten minutes later.'

Upton nodded.

'Take this money,' said Daniel. 'It's too much to carry about with me.'

Passing the bag over to Upton, he dropped it inside his briefcase.

The police moved in like lightning. Daniel stepped back with a smile as Upton raised his hands defensively. 'All right, I knew this was a set up.'

'You're under arrest, Mr. Upton,' said the detective sergeant.

Another police officer seized on his dossier. Upton clung to it. 'That's private property,' he said. The officer wrenched it from him as his colleagues closed in.

Upton struggled feebly. 'I was having a private drink with this gentleman,' he insisted. 'I've been doing nothing wrong.'

'We'll soon see about that, Mr. Upton,' said the detective sergeant. 'We've got all this afternoon and tomorrow to talk about it, in the police station.'

The blackmailer glared around him like a hunted animal. Ten police officers were surrounding him in a ring. Onlookers were amazed. Never had they seen such a drama in their local.

The detective sergeant visited Daniel shortly afterwards. 'It's a clear-cut case of blackmail,' he said. 'As we thought, his name's not Geoff Upton at all. I'll need a detailed statement from you . . . '

Suddenly, Daniel recalled how his astrologer had predicted disaster. He paid another visit to his dingy Bayswater flat. As always, his familiar dark mentor in a turban shut his eyes and meditated. 'Good shall arise out of the evil in your life. Seize your opportunities. Be bold and be favoured,' he intoned as he politely but definitely pocketed the £150 fee.

The following morning, the telephone started ringing. Daniel answered, half expecting Upton's husky tones again, or if not that, Gerry West following up on the blackmail case.

'Laura,' he said delightedly.

'Listen' she said. 'I want you to fly out to Paris. I'll meet you at the airport there tomorrow afternoon. Bring only necessities with you. Most importantly of all, tell nobody what you're doing.'

'I'll be there,' he said. 'Au revoir.'

Shifting his belongings into a private depository in several taxi loads, Daniel then sent a cheque for his next six months' rent to his landlord, with a short note to say that he was temporarily vacating the premises.

In what seemed like no time at all, he was by Laura's side. Deep tanned, with close cropped hair, in a casual white skirt and blue jumper, she was only superficially changed. He kissed her, savouring her sweet perfume.

She giggled. 'You recognise me, I'm glad to see.' Then she pulled herself back and looked him up and down. 'It's your turn now to change your appearance.'

'You must have missed me,' he said as they climbed into a taxi.

She smiled. 'I don't want you arrested.'

'I've missed you,' he found himself saying. 'But now we can stay together.'

Some weeks later, a thug turned up at John Falmouth's office by appointment. Under the false name of Geoff Upton, he had undertaken assignments for Falmouth, the most recent of which had been photographing and beating up Simon Hall at his home, then attempting to blackmail Daniel La Marche.

Louise closed the door behind him.

'Well?' snapped John.

'I'm on bail for £10,000,' grunted Upton. 'The police have confiscated my passport. Give me £30,000 and I'll not let on that it was you who instructed me to blackmail Daniel La Marche. I'll also never reveal that you instructed me to photograph, then to beat up Simon Hall.'

Falmouth paused. 'You can have £15,000 now. Another £15,000 is yours after the blackmail case has been heard. Wait . . . '

He packed Louise off to the bank to collect the cash from a numbered account.

'What's happened to Daniel now?' asked John.

His visitor shrugged. 'He's not in his flat.'

'If you find out where he is, let me know,' said John.

Louise returned quickly with the cash which John handed to his visitor. Upton counted it and left . . .

Simon Hall met Falmouth in the foyer of the Marlborough Hotel, for a pre-arranged lunch.

'If I go down, you do too,' said the former director of Thompson & Thompson. 'We must work together.'

'Don't ever try to blackmail me,' said John. Without bothering to honour their arrangement, he walked from the hotel – and out of Simon's life forever.

Early that afternoon, Louise took a call for John. 'I'm afraid he's not here at the moment,' she lied. Upon putting down the receiver, she murmured to her boss, 'It's the Serious Fraud Office.'

John glanced up from the SEAQ screen. His face was pallid. 'Look Louise, I've got too many fucking bureaucrats nosing around this company at the moment. I'm taking a break, and going abroad for a few weeks.'

A few days after he had left the country, England Securities, now unable to meet its commitments, folded. The national press cheered the event. The Merden Group's shares plummeted in value. The FT Indices became still more depressed, although some argued this was triggered by other factors. Many UK institutions and private clients predicted only doom and gloom.

Interest rates were still spiralling and estate agents were going bust by the bucketful. City yuppies were proving unable to keep up mortgages on their investment properties and homes . . .

Gerard La Marche, after salting away a cool £200,000 from the Thompson & Thompson scam, was preparing his getaway. Answering an advertisement in *Time Out*, he had found himself a room in Earls Court. Providing references that he himself had forged, Gerard lived there quietly under a phoney name. But not for long . . .

Amongst letters that he picked up from his mailing address at a Central London post office was a note telling him to ring a phone number with a Paris dialling code.

He rang the number from a call box in Bournemouth, so that if the call was traced a misleading impression of his whereabouts would be conveyed. When he said who he was, the sharp voice on the other end of the line said, 'Hold on a sec!'

Johnnie Butler introduced himself. 'You don't know me, but I know you, Monsieur La Marche.' He continued. 'I require you to run one of my stockbroking firms out in Panama that's just been opened by the Ministry of Commerce. My brokers can say what the fuck they like on the telephone there, to clients in Saudi Arabia, Switzerland, even the UK . . . You'll be creaming off so much profit, you will be able to retire after a couple of years.

'You had better start pronto, before the Serious Fraud Office starts making arrests.'

Gerard discussed his remuneration arrangements. They sounded fabulous. As he left the call box, greed flamed up in his heart. Gerard, who had never been anything but a mercenary, was at last starting to realise it.

He caught a plane to Panama almost immediately. As he was flying forth from England's green and pleasant land, he realised that he would probably have no wish to return there.

Simon meanwhile was idling at home all day. He was claiming unemployment benefit, and his wife, Donna, protesting disgust at his laziness, spent many evenings and much of the weekend out socialising with her friends, leaving Simon to look after Mark. Simon would invariably shut the boy in a room by himself, regardless of his crying for attention. Donna found out what he was doing, but curiously enough, didn't interfere.

Simon co-operated all he could with Thompson & Thompson's Official Liquidator, paying the temps' unpaid salaries out of the monies he had personally earned there.

He submitted to being interrogated at the Serious Fraud Office. In the course of his interview, he denounced his fellow directors – the La Marche brothers, and the financier he knew as Dario Abella. He was particularly scathing about Norman Thompson's role. Dead men, after all, told no tales.

Back at home that evening, he discussed the situation with Donna, almost tearfully. 'Perhaps I should leave the country while I still can,' he proposed.

'No, stay,' she said. 'You were conned yourself at Thompson & Thompson, and should blame yourself for none of it. Don't make it seem that you have something to hide.'

Ex-Thompson & Thompson brokers were perpetually ringing him at home. 'The Serious Fraud Office has asked me to visit them, bringing bank statements, evidencing payments by Thompson & Thompson,' each would say.

'See them if you like,' Simon invariably responded. 'We were ourselves all conned by Norman Thompson, Dario Abella and the La Marche brothers. I'm sure I don't need to tell you that any broker who ever says he had known in advance that Security Planning Inc., was a dud, will be paying the price, probably for the rest of his life.'

When the doorbell rang at half past five in the morning, Simon rolled over in bed on top of his wife. She opened her eyes. 'Stop clutching me like a baby,' she said severely. 'Go and see who it is.'

'It might be the police,' muttered Simon. 'I'd better escape out of the back.'

She shrugged. 'If it is, they'll get you. For God's sake, don't compound your problems. Open the door.'

She helped him on with his dressing-gown, slipping on her own too. Taking his arm firmly, she led him downstairs. Simon had a sudden dark inkling that she was betraying him, and out of wishful thinking tried to dismiss this from his mind.

Sure enough, he was under arrest. The police officers' formality didn't scare Simon. He felt merely irritated. What an idiot he had been! If he had only cut his losses and run, the day Thompson & Thompson had collapsed. Why had he ever listened to his wife? He turned to his side, but Donna was nowhere to be seen . . .

At the police station he learned that the brokers with whom he had started up Thompson & Thompson's dealing room, together with Gordon Halcombe, had likewise been arrested that morning. He didn't know whether to be relieved he had company, or to fear how far they might turn on him.

'In court, I'll sing,' he muttered to himself, 'I'll sing a fucking opera, and I'll not go down alone!'

Simon was finally released on £250,000 bail, with a requirement to surrender his passport, and report back to the police station once a week.

He was then served with a court order, banning him from returning to his own home, or even telephoning his old home number.

Immediately, he rang Donna's solicitor, who coolly informed him that she had arranged for another man to move in with her, on the grounds that he, Simon, had neglected herself and Mark.

Unable to stop himself, Simon rushed to the house. Quietly, craftily, he tried the front door. As he had expected, the locks had been changed. How coldly efficient, he thought to himself. He almost had to admire his other half. 'Donna!' he called aloud. As he'd expected, there was no reply.

He crept round the side of the house. Picking up a loose brick from the lawn, he hurled it against a window. The smashing of the glass and the dull thud of the brick on the floor inside set his teeth on edge. He had truly announced his presence now, and there was no going back. Further quietness was superfluous.

He reached inside the window pane, releasing the catch. He climbed inside, cursing as he snitched his trousers, leaving his underpants showing. For brief seconds, his thoughts turned to rape.

As he barged into the living room, he saw Donna. Her back was turned to him. Little Mark, clinging to her skirts, peeped round and chuckled, as if the whole business was one huge joke. Donna was on the telephone, obviously to the police.

'My husband's broken in. Come round immediately . . . ' she was screaming.

Simon strode over and cut her off. Donna turned and glared at him. Contempt puckered her features. What a good actress she was, thought Simon almost incredulously.

'You sodomist. Get the hell out of here!' she shouted.

'Sodomist,' echoed Mark, his little face suddenly screwed up with hate.

Simon wanted to vomit. As he reached out to touch his own family, to get his grip on the racalcitrant pair, he observed the approaching panda car through the window on the road outside. This was no joke; he had to shift his butt!

As the police came into the house, he was gone, having let himself out of the back door. He was running for his own freedom, down a maze of backstreets.

At the earliest opportunity he hailed a taxi. Upon arriving at Victoria station, he telephoned Donna's solicitor again. It transpired that Donna, now living in his house but with another man, was claiming that he'd forced anal intercourse regularly on their son. He slammed down the receiver. What at outrageous lie this was!

Lodging temporarily in Tunbridge Wells, he hired a private detective who discovered that Donna's solicitor was bent, and had in at least fifteen cases worked with the same team of psychologists and social workers to claim child abuse, assembling phoney confidential reports to mislead the judge ordering custody arrangements.

On the recommendation of his detective, Simon had his son picked up mid-morning from school one day. They immediately flew off to Venezuela, where he had enrolled Mark at a private, English-speaking school.

Jumping bail, Simon then fled to join him and arranged for a message to be telegraphed to his wife from Switzerland: 'Don't worry about your son. I'm looking after him. You will see him again in about ten years . . . '

Meanwhile Dale Gatsby was grazing contentedly in his luxurious Los Angeles hotel. He had meals regularly delivered up to his suite, and because he was a good tipper, flowers, champagne, choice fruit, and *The International Herald Tribune* would perpetually appear in his room like magic. His clothes, too, were cleaned and pressed without his asking. He was spoiled, and all for around 150 dollars a day. The disappearance of Dario was now complete.

On impulse, he purchased a quasi title and called himself Sir Dale Gatsby. Although not following his own instincts to keep a low profile, he couldn't resist this, and indeed it paid the desired dividends. His hosts in the best social circles everywhere started falling over themselves to give him the red carpet treatment.

When the self-appointed "Sir" Dale heard that Thompson & Thompson brokers had been sentenced in the UK courts, he smiled to himself. In his view, it was every man for himself. This con man's own conscience was not troubled one jot.

What did haunt him, as he cavorted with classy whores night after night in local bars, was the memory of Laura. It was dawning on him that he had loved the girl. Would he ever now have the chance to make good to her?

Meanwhile, life for Laura, now using her real name again, was no less erratic than it had always been. Maria lived for a while quietly with Daniel in Paris. At his insistence, they had moved into a luxury flat.

Daniel would bully her at night in a way that she would never have thought him capable of.

'Clean up the flat,' he would order her. Or, 'Come out to the casino with me.'

'I'm not your dogsbody!' she snapped on one occasion. 'And I've got a lot on my mind.'

She and her mother were wanted for questioning by the police in Rome, but she would not be returning there. Both women would live abroad, with new identities, for the rest of their lives.

'You won't even confide in me,' he said bitterly.

'I don't trust you, Daniel,' she retorted. 'Look how you're squandering money even now!'

'But we've got nearly a million pounds between us,' said Daniel. 'I can't live just shut in a few square feet, doing nothing all day like you seem to. Besides, money doesn't multiply unless it's used. I'm making all sorts of investments.'

'Gambling you mean,' sneered Maria.

It was a relief for her to get away from him for a week in Berlin, where she met her mother and gave her more money. Anne, who had been travelling around Europe under a new identity, was now planning to settle in Africa as a volunteer teacher. But she would always keep in touch with her beloved daughter.

Upon returning to Paris, Maria felt restless. Daniel was providing her with no emotional support. She now saw him as weak and unstable. One day she would leave him. As it turned out, disaster struck before she had made her move.

Daniel had come back to the flat as usual in the early hours of the morning. This time however, there was the slough of despond in his eyes, the likes of which Maria had never seen. Instead of his usual stomping about raving about the "cunts" who had stitched him up on the roulette table, he rolled onto the bed fully dressed, his head pushing against her breast. He was like a helpless babe. Sensing the depths of his despair, Maria's exasperation melted into concern.

'How much was it this time, Daniel?'

He looked at her, his eyes conveying the terrible truth, and winced as she set her lips.

'You've lost the lot, you bastard,' she snapped, desperately hoping that she was wrong.

He nodded speechlessly.

Blind anger arose in her, unquenchable. Had she not been educating him against gambling? Had she not rescued him from trouble in England, and been his friend? He had squandered a fortune at the drop of a hat and it was no compensation that he had the makings of an honest man.

'So you think I'll be supporting you from now on, I suppose?' she said.

Daniel shook his head. 'I'll get a job.'

'Ha ha,' she cackled. 'That's the best joke I've heard in a long while. You couldn't work any more than a dog could talk.'

The next day, she packed and slipped out of the flat unseen by anybody. She would quietly vanish, leaving Daniel to cope alone. She wanted a man, but Daniel wasn't good enough for her although it had taken her a while to realise it.

She heard news of his suicide on television from the luxury of her Monaco hotel. Daniel had thrown himself out of the window of their flat, and had spewed his brains out on the pavement below, in full view of several horrified passers-by. Even as she mourned, Maria felt a secret feeling of relief.

And with relief came an overpowering loneliness. Never before had Maria felt so abandoned. She was suddenly drained of every iota of wanderlust. She was one of the living dead now, those international travellers without roots, without intimacy, without real purpose. But there were old friends, old colleagues round the world, with whom she would one day meet up, with whom she would work again. She could not change. She was what she was, steeped in corruption. The poison of life had seeped into her veins.

In Panama, Butler's stockbroking firm was flourishing like a hothouse plant. And brokers all over the City of London were packing their bags and gravitating there.

To hell with honesty. To hell with security. To hell with prestige. Nothing on earth would hold these whizzkids back when they smelled money!